THE HEAT (A MENAGE ROMANCE)

A MENAGE IN MANHATTAN NOVEL

TARA CRESCENT

D1713817

My editor Jim takes the comma-filled words that emerge from my keyboard and shapes it into a story worth reading. As always, my undying gratitude.

Cover Design by Eris Adderly, http://erisadderly.com/

Cooking Pot Icon made by Freepik from www.flaticon.com

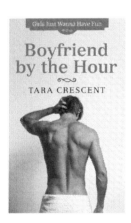

Sadie:

I can't believe I have the hots for an escort.

Cole Mitchell is ripped, bearded, sexy and dominant. When he moves next door to me, I find it impossible to resist sampling the wares.

But Cole's not a one-woman kind of guy, and I won't share.

Cole:

She thinks I'm an escort. I'm not.

I thought I'd do anything to sleep with Sadie. Then I realized I want more. I want Sadie. Forever.

I'm not the escort she thinks I am.

Now, I just have to make sure she never finds out.

THE HEAT

One uptight Southern chef. Two wickedly hot investors who want to teach her to sin a little. A steamy workplace ménage!

My restaurant is failing.

My parents are just waiting to say 'I told you so.'

But I don't want to give up. I'll do anything to save my business. *Anything.*

Then Owen and Wyatt offer me a chance to make my dreams come true.

And I'm tempted. So tempted.

Of course, there is a catch.

Note: The Heat is a standalone ménage romance (mfm) with a HEA ending and no cliffhangers!

The Heat was previously titled Playing with Piper.

1

If you can't stand the heat, get out of the kitchen.

— Harry S. Truman

Piper:

Bad news always comes in threes, my Aunt Vera used to say. Judging from the day I'm having, she was right.

The first blow comes from my restaurant's landlord. "Ms. Jackson," Michael O'Connor wheezes into the phone. "I'm afraid I'm going to have to increase your rent."

My heart sinks to my toes. I've been dreading this moment ever since I took over *Aladdin's Lamp* in early January and discovered the lease was going to expire in five months.

Mr. O'Connor is a nice older man who lives above the restaurant, and he seems to have had a soft spot for my Aunt Vera, from whom I inherited the place. But property developers have been sniffing around, and I know he's been getting offers.

"How much?" I ask, my fingers crossed as I hope for the best.

"Three thousand dollars a month," he responds. His voice softens with sympathy. "I'm sorry, Piper. I know that's a steep increase..."

"But it's still below market rate," I finish. "I understand, Mr. O'Connor."

He promises me the increase won't take effect for another month and he hangs up.

Of course, I can't afford three thousand extra dollars. I'm already struggling to stay afloat. But there's nothing I can do, so I get dressed and trudge toward the restaurant. If I'm lucky, we'll have a larger lunch crowd than normal.

I'M NOT LUCKY — the place is almost empty. I don my chef's hat and apron and take over from Josef, the surly Lebanese man who loosely functions as my sous-chef. The reason I say loosely? Josef has a pretty serious alcohol problem, and doesn't show up to work on any kind of regular basis.

Not for the first time, I wish I could fire him, but Aunt Vera's will forbids me from doing so. I'm not allowed to fire any of the existing staff unless I can give them a year's salary as a severance bonus. I'm stuck with Josef, who fails to show up to work every third day, and Kimmie, who chews gum in front of the customers. My only useful employee is the waitress I hired a month after I took over. Petra is a gem.

"I've made the lentil soup," Josef says, wobbling a little as he speaks. Great, he's drunk already. I make a mental note to taste the soup before I send it out, when my cell phone vibrates in my pocket.

I look at the display and grimace. It's my mother. Cue the second disaster of the day.

"Darling," she exclaims when I answer. "Are you sitting down?"

This is Lillian Jackson's standard greeting when she has some piece of gossip to give me. "No mother," I reply. "I'm working."

She huffs dismissively. My mother thinks *Aladdin's Lamp* is a hobby of mine, and one day, I'll get tired of playing chef, go back home to New Orleans, and marry some suitable young man from the right family. Trying to get her to take what I do seriously is a waste of time, and I don't even try. "What's the matter?" I ask, hoping she'll get to the point quickly.

"Your cousin Angelina is getting married," she responds. "Piper dear, this is going to be hard for you to hear, so I thought I should be the first person to tell you. She's getting married to Anthony. You remember Anthony, don't you? Your fiancé?" Her breath catches. "Piper, I'm so sorry, honey."

"Ma, I'm fine." *So much drama.* Anthony and I went on five dates before he proposed in front of the entire family on Christmas Eve, knowing I'd be pressured into saying *yes.* My break up with him was the topic of gossip for my mother's friends for months.

Kimmie's come in with a ticket, and she gives me an impatient look. I need to get working on it. I can't afford to chase away the small handful of customers I have. "Anthony and I are old history," I tell her. "I'm very excited for Angelina. Listen, I have to go, okay? Some diners just walked in."

"Your father and I are very worried about you, Piper," she pronounces, ignoring my feeble attempt at ending our conversation. "We're coming up to see you."

My heart sinks. Oh God, more family interference. "You are?"

"Yes dear." Her tone is firm. "We've already bought our airline tickets. We're coming this weekend."

"Ma." I exhale in annoyance. "I work in a restaurant. I can't take the weekend off, you already know that." I've said this to my mother a million times. She never listens.

"Don't be ridiculous, dear." She dismisses my concern with an airy laugh. "Of course you can. You're in charge, aren't you? You can do whatever you want."

I bite my tongue and count to ten. *Just tell them you can't entertain them,* a voice inside me urges. *Tell them your rent was increased by three thousand dollars. Tell them you're on the verge of failure, and you can't afford to take a weekend off. Tell them that Sebastian Ardalan, a two-star Michelin chef, didn't think your restaurant would survive another six months in business, and you're feeling bruised and damaged as a result.*

But I've never been able to effectively stand up to my mother. My moments of rebellion are few and far between. Most of the time, I just do as I'm told. It seems easier that way.

Kimmie's tapping her feet in annoyance. I need to get off the phone. "Fine," I sigh. "I'll see you in a few days. I have to go now."

I hang up and fight the urge to bang my head repeatedly against the ancient walk-in freezer. The damn thing is temperamental and will probably just stop working.

It's just after noon, and already, my day is a wreck.

Troubles always come in threes, Aunt Vera used to say.

I wonder what lies ahead.

2

The past is strapped to our backs. We do not have to see it; we can always feel it.

— MIGNON MCLAUGHLIN

Owen:

I meet Eduardo Mendez at a busy McDonald's, where a constant stream of people enter and leave, and no one gives two men seated in a corner a second glance.

"Lamb." The detective greets me, his voice a raspy growl, as always, rendered hoarse by the two packs of cigarettes he smokes each day.

I nod in reply, feeling the familiar excitement rush up and grip me. Mendez has a job for me. He never makes contact otherwise.

I take a sip of my steaming hot coffee and wait for him to speak. In the seventeen years I've known him, I've learned Mendez can't be rushed. Whatever he wants, he'll tell me when he's ready.

"Hell's Kitchen," he says at last. "What do you know about it?"

I know enough to avoid it. The Manhattan neighborhood of Hell's Kitchen has rapidly gentrified in the last couple of decades, but before its revitalization, it was home to poor and working class Irish Americans. Given my past, it's not the safest neighborhood for me to spend time in. The death sentence on me has never been lifted, and if someone wanted to curry favor with those in charge back in Dublin, they might think that killing me is the best way. "Not a lot."

He coughs. "Word on the street is that the Westies are moving back in."

"In Hell's Kitchen?" I raise an eyebrow. "The neighborhood's been clean for decades."

"I'm telling you what I know," he snaps. "The opium trade is flourishing, and these guys aren't dealing on street corners anymore. They're using local restaurants to distribute." He fixes me with a piercing look. "You know what that's like, don't you, Lamb?"

Just like that, the memories come rushing back. My mother's voice, raised in argument with my father. He wants to testify against the mob; my mom urges caution. *What if they come for us?* Even now, even after seventeen years, I hear the fear she's trying to conceal. *What about me? Aileen? Owen?*

And my dad replies, his voice always clear in my mind. *Someone needs to fight for what's right.*

They'd both been right and they'd both been wrong. Someone did need to fight for what was right, and the Gilligan's crime syndicate had come for my parents and baby sister. The only reason I'd survived was because I'd snuck out for a very illegal cigarette.

I shake my head to clear it. The past always threatens to

overwhelm me. Mendez knows exactly what he's doing. My *da* died fighting the mob. I won't let them win.

"What do you need me to do?"

He pushes a list toward me. "I need intel," he says. "You're in the restaurant business. These are our list of suspects right now. Get close to them, see what you can find out about their finances."

I run my gaze down the names, and I recognize a few of them. Two in particular jump out, *Emerson's* and *Aladdin's Lamp*.

Max Emerson came to us, looking for half a million dollars, but we turned him down last week. However, *Aladdin's Lamp* is still in play. My partner Wyatt and I have eaten there every day for the last two weeks, on the recommendation of our friend Sebastian Ardalan, but we haven't yet decided if we're interested in the place.

It's time to kick it up a notch. If Mendez needs to find out what's going on at *Aladdin's Lamp*, the easiest way is to invest in it.

"Let me see what I can do." I drain my coffee and rise to my feet. "I'll be in touch."

3

All happy families are alike; each unhappy family is unhappy in its own way.

— Leo Tolstoy

Wyatt:

When I walk into my office Thursday morning, my assistant Celia looks up. "Wyatt," she says, "I need to talk to you."

I gesture for her to follow me. "What's up?"

"Sandra from Reception called me this morning. She said there was a man in the lobby who insisted on seeing you." She pauses. "He told her he was your father."

I'm about to take a sip of my coffee, but hearing those words, I freeze. Twenty years ago, my father had ducked out to grab a drink at the local pub, and had never returned. He sent my mother a letter telling her he couldn't cope anymore, and he disappeared from my life. I was thirteen. I haven't seen him since that day.

"My father." My voice is even. Nothing betrays the sense of shock that explodes through me.

"That's what he said. I've never heard you mention your father, so I went downstairs to see what was going on, but he'd left by the time I got there." She gives me a worried look. "I didn't know what to do."

I clench my hands into fists. A vein pulses at my forehead. *Deep breaths, Wyatt. Calm down.* I force myself to bury all the emotion that rises to the surface. The feeling of abandonment when he left, the secret, shameful envy that my father was able to escape, leaving me stuck with my mother.

Celia shifts in her seat and I realize I've been silent for too long. I smile at her. "My father is dead," I lie easily. "I don't know who this man is, but he's an imposter. If he shows up again, have security deal with him, please."

She frowns in puzzlement, but doesn't contradict me. "Of course, Wyatt," she says. "Oh, and Owen called to say he'll meet you at the usual place for lunch."

Right. *Aladdin's Lamp.* "What time?"

Celia checks her notepad. "He'll meet you there at one."

"Perfect. Thanks, Celia."

My heart still pounds in my chest. Not even the prospect of finding a new restaurant to rescue is enough to distract me from my shock. *My father's back.*

I wonder what he wants.

MY INSTINCTS WARN me to stay away from *Aladdin's Lamp.* The place is a dump. Signs of benign neglect are everywhere. The red curtains have been faded pink by the sun. There's a large crack in the front window, with a strip of duct tape across it. At each table, a dusty vase with plastic flowers serve as decoration, along with a kitschy lamp. The table-cloth is stained, the menu is laminated and the waitress in her pink-frilled apron cannot stop chewing gum long enough to take our order.

I want nothing to do with it, but I will hand it to Sebastian Ardalan. He's right about the chef; the food shows flashes of brilliance.

"This is really good." Owen digs into his chili with gusto. "There's potential here."

"The place is called *Aladdin's Lamp*," I complain, not for the first time. "Why does it have chili on the menu, Owen? The tabbouleh is garlicky. The hummus doesn't have enough tahini in it. And this lentil soup has way too much salt."

"We've eaten here for two weeks," he points out. "The Middle Eastern food is terrible, and everything else is great. You should know that by now."

"Why are you so gung-ho about this disaster?"

"Come on, Wyatt." Owen gives me an amused look. "Since when did you get so boring? Think of this place as a challenge."

"I'm thinking of this place as one health-inspection away from being shut down."

Owen rolls his eyes. "Oh for fuck's sake," he says. "It isn't even close to failing and you know it. You just have an exaggerated need for cleanliness." He lifts his hand to catch the waitress' attention. "If the chef has a moment," he says, giving her a charming smile, "could you tell her we'd love to chat with her?"

She nods and departs. I look at him with exasperation when she's out of earshot. "We haven't investigated the place. Who knows what kind of deal we could be walking into?"

"Look around, Wyatt." Owen's eyes sweep the near-empty dining room. "This isn't a large restaurant. Worst case scenario, we put in two hundred and fifty grand in this place and it fails. So what?"

I don't like going investing in a restaurant before investigating it, but Owen seems committed. "You're doing this then?" I ask, already resigned to doing the deal.

"You don't have to," he replies. "But yes, I'm definitely investing in this place."

"Asshole." There's no rancor in my voice. "Fine, I'm in. But the chef had better toe the fucking line."

Owen leans back in his seat. "Your bark is worse than your bite," he says with a grin. Then his eyes widen and his smirk broadens. "There's the chef. Why don't you tell her what you told me?"

I look up to see a slender blonde woman thread her way toward us. She's got pale skin and red lips, and her hair is the color of the sun's rays at first light. Her hips sway slightly as she walks, and I find it suddenly difficult to breathe.

When she reaches our table, she glares at us, her hand on her hip. "You've eaten at my restaurant for two weeks," she says, her voice hard. "What are you playing at? Who sent you?"

Help me. When she speaks, her voice has a pretty Southern lilt that goes straight to my cock. Across me, Owen is struggling to hold back his laughter. He knows I can't resist a Southern accent. I've never been able to.

"My name," Owen says, "is Owen Lamb. My partner here," he gestures toward me, "is Wyatt Lawless. Sebastian Ardalan suggested we stop by."

She goes still. That wasn't the answer she was expecting to hear. "Lawless and Lamb?" she whispers in shock. "Sebastian Ardalan sent you?"

Then our words register fully. Her back stiffens. "I'm not interested in anyone's pity," she snaps. "Not Sebastian Ardalan's, not yours."

My cock goes from being somewhat interested to rock hard in a second. Pretty, Southern, and feisty? *This woman is kryptonite.* "I don't invest in restaurants because I feel sorry for them," I reply calmly. "I invest in restaurants with potential." I look around the empty front room. "You clearly aren't setting the world on fire. The question is, do you want to?"

I sigh as I realize I've verbally offered this woman a deal. *Damn Owen.* The only thing I take comfort in is that someone in the kitchen can cook. The chili really *is* fantastic.

4

The bargain that yields mutual satisfaction is the only one that is apt to be repeated.

— B. C. Forbes

Piper:

Trouble always comes in threes.

When Kimmie tells me that the two men who have eaten at my restaurant every day for the last two weeks are back again, my first instinct is to suspect my mother of sending them to spy on my restaurant. I wouldn't put it past her at all.

Then I come out and they introduce themselves, and my heart nearly stops. The names Owen Lamb and Wyatt Lawless are legendary in the New York restaurant scene. Five of their restaurants have Michelin stars. They own the top 10 list on Yelp. They run the best restaurants in the city. A Lawless and Lamb restaurant doesn't break even — it succeeds wildly.

Under different circumstances, I might also notice that they are very good looking men. When Wyatt Lawless' gaze bores into me, I wonder how his stubble will feel against my skin. Owen Lamb's blond hair glistens in the sunlight, and I want to lick the dimples on his cheeks.

But as soon as they open their mouths, I forget their good looks and their accomplishments go flying out of the window. Instead, I fight the urge to smack the silly smirk off Owen Lamb's face and punch Wyatt Lawless in the mouth. *You clearly aren't setting the world on fire.* I'm already reeling from Sebastian Ardalan's casual dismissal of my restaurant. Wyatt Lawless can take his callous words and shove them up his ass.

My mother's voice sounds in my ear. *Well-behaved Southern women don't punch strange men, dear.*

I grit my teeth and shove her out of my head. "What are you talking about, gentlemen?"

Wyatt Lawless surveys me with dark, expressionless eyes. "How long have you run this restaurant?"

People who answer a question with a question infuriate me. I pull up a chair next to them and sit down. "I inherited *Aladdin's Lamp* six months ago," I bite out.

Owen Lamb's blue eyes shine with curiosity. "And you want to run it?" he asks. "Why don't you sell it?"

Because cooking in a small cafe like this has been a dream of mine since I was a little girl. Because if I fail, I'm convinced my parents will make me move back to Louisiana. Because I'm running away from a lifetime of pleasing other people and all I want to do is live my own life.

I'm not going to tell these men that; I'm not going to tell them anything. Besides, I've been taught not to air my dirty laundry in public. *Well-behaved Southern women don't bitch about their family.* "I'm not ready to fail."

That seems to be enough. "Fair enough," Owen Lamb says. "Let me get to the point. Are you interested in a deal? If you are, we'll buy a stake in your business. We'll invest some money, but largely, what we bring to the table is our expertise. I've been in the restaurant business all my life. I'll help you in the back of the house. Wyatt," he gestures to his partner, "is the marketing genius. He'll get your name out there, bring the customers to your door."

God knows I could use help. I'm not stupid; I'm in over my head. *Aladdin's Lamp* has been losing money steadily ever since my family dragged Aunt Vera back to Louisiana. Aunt Vera was rich enough to afford to cover the losses, but I'm not. The restaurant needs a makeover desperately, but makeovers cost money and I have none. Even though I plow every dollar I make back into the business, progress has been glacially slow.

Yet I'm not delusional. This doesn't make any sense. A thousand chefs in the city would sell their firstborns for a chance to work with Lamb and Lawless. I'm not special. "Why are you here?" I ask bluntly. "Why me?"

"Like I said," Owen says, his gaze on the bowl of chili in front of him, "Sebastian Ardalan suggested we check this place out."

Sebastian Ardalan dotes on my roommate Bailey. If she asked him to help me, he would move heaven and earth to fulfill her request. My heart sinks as I realize that this isn't about me, my abilities, my talents or my dreams.

But I can't afford to turn them down. My rent's been increased by three thousand dollars, and my bank account is close to empty. I've run out of options.

"Yes." It feels like I'm stepping on a new path, and there's no turning back. "I'm interested. Tell me more."

5

My yesterdays walk with me. They keep step, they are gray faces that peer over my shoulder.

— WILLIAM GOLDING

Owen:

"Are you going to tell me what's going on?" Wyatt asks as we head back to the office after lunch. "Or are you going to keep me in the dark?"

"What do you mean?" I stall. Wyatt's going to lose his mind when I tell him about meeting Mendez this morning.

My partner rolls his eyes. "Come on, Owen," he says. "I've known you a very long time. You didn't jump to invest in *Aladdin's Lamp* on Sebastian's recommendation. Something else is up."

"Fine." It isn't as if I can keep the truth from Wyatt anyway. "I met Eduardo Mendez this morning."

A hiss of disapproval escapes Wyatt. "Please tell me," he

says, his voice exaggeratedly patient, "that that asshole hasn't recruited you in one of his schemes again."

"You don't have much of an opinion of New York's finest."

"I do. Mendez isn't one of them," he retorts as we walk into our downtown Manhattan office. "The last time he involved you, you got shot, remember? You spent three weeks in the hospital."

"It was only a flesh wound." It had hurt like a mother-fucker, but I'll just be making Wyatt's point for him if I admit that.

"How many times does it need to happen before you walk away? Mendez is manipulating you; he's been manipu-lating you since you were sixteen. He's using your anger about what happened in the past as fuel, and you are reck-less enough to fall for it." His voice is both disapproving and weary. The years Mendez has been absent from our lives have been good years. Wyatt and I have bought stakes in fifteen restaurants and tripled our net worth. More than that, we've helped fifteen chefs live their dream.

But the lure of revenge is always too great.

We enter Wyatt's office. Wyatt settles into his chair and straightens a piece of paper on his desk so that it's perfectly aligned with the surface. "It's been what, five years? I was hoping he was finally going to leave you alone."

"He's reaching out for help. It would be irresponsible for me to ignore his request."

"Irresponsible?" He raises an eyebrow. "After what happened to your parents, wouldn't staying alive be the best possible revenge? Walk away, Owen. You've been lucky so far. Don't push it."

"No." My voice is cold. We agree on many things, Wyatt and I, but this is the one divide so great that we will never be able to cross it. "The Westies killed my father. I will do what-ever it takes to see them behind bars. My parents deserve justice."

"Fine." He gives up, his tone clipped. "Do what you will. Where does *Aladdin's Lamp* figure in this?"

"Mendez has a list of restaurants that he wants me to check out. Piper Jackson's restaurant is on top of that list. Even if she isn't involved, it gives me an excuse to hang out in Hell's Kitchen and investigate what's going on."

Wyatt looks exasperated. "So now I'm investing in restaurants because of Mendez's schemes?"

"Oh come on," I mock. "It's not that much hardship to help Piper, is it? I noticed the way you looked at her. You want her."

Wyatt shrugs. "That's true, but irrelevant. I don't get involved with people I'm in business with."

"You don't get involved at all."

We both glare at each other, fists clenched. Then I shake my head. Wyatt and I are the best of friends. We normally get along very well. Today's meeting with Mendez has me on edge more than I'm prepared to admit.

And something's bothering Wyatt as well. I look around his office for clues. It's spotless, not even a paperclip out of place. "What happened?"

"What do you mean?" He sounds wary.

"Wyatt, this office is a fucking barometer of your mood. If it's this tidy, then something's upset you."

He sighs. "My father tried to contact me today. Celia said he showed up at Reception and asked for me."

"What?" My head snaps up. "Are you sure?"

He pushes to his feet and strides to the window. "I reviewed the security tapes before lunch. It's him alright."

He stares absently at the view of the city streets. "Time hasn't been kind to him."

"What does he want?"

Wyatt looks bleak. "Money, I assume. What else do people want?"

I wish I could protest and suggest that his father just wants to reconnect, but I know better. The man has been absent from his son's life for twenty years. Last month, a reporter did a fawning feature of Lamb & Lawless' incredible success in the Wall Street Journal. The timing can't be coincidental.

"You could always talk to him and find out."

"No." Wyatt's lips tighten. "My father walked out on me when I was thirteen. He left me in a house that wasn't fit to be inhabited, with a mother who was mentally ill. A woman who insisted on saving every newspaper, every plastic bag, every empty tin can. I couldn't reach the refrigerator without worrying that I'd knock something over. I lived in fear that somebody would find out." His hands clench into fists at his side. "The time for talking has passed."

"What are you going to do?"

"I told Celia to call security the next time he shows up."

When Wyatt was eighteen, he left home, and he hasn't stepped inside his mother's house since then. He's obsessively tidy as a response to the chaos he grew up in. His control never wavers. He never relaxes. It's not a healthy way to live.

I shake my head. Avoiding his father isn't going to help, and involving security is just going to escalate the situation. Wyatt needs to confront his demons and face the man.

Still, should I really be giving advice on facing the demons of the past? I'm not doing very well with mine.

6

In trying to please all, he had pleased none.

— Aesop, Aesop's Fables

Piper:

Two days after I shake on a deal with Owen Lamb and Wyatt Lawless, my parents fly into town.

"Let me look at you," my mother orders as soon as she catches sight of me. She surveys me critically for a few seconds, then she sniffs. "You've put on some weight."

I haven't, but there's no point arguing with her. "Hello dad," I greet my father. "How's the oil business?"

"Volatile." He doesn't sound too concerned. My parents are more than rich enough to survive a few temporary downturns.

My mother homes in on my hands. "Piper, your nails," she cries out. "Honey, surely they have manicurists in New York."

"I'm a chef," I respond tersely, feeling the beginnings of a stress headache. In two minutes, my mother's managed to criticize two things about me. It's exhausting dealing with her. "I can't have long nails."

She ignores me. "We'll get that dealt with when I'm here," she promises. "Now, honey, be honest with me. Are you upset about Anthony and Angelina?"

Oh for crying out loud. "Mom," I say, my voice heavy with patience, "Anthony and I went out on five dates. I don't even know why he proposed, and we were engaged for less than twenty-four hours. I'm not upset. I'm very happy for Angelina."

"The guy's an idiot," my dad interjects. "Piper's better off without him. How's the restaurant coming along, Piper?"

"I'm surviving," I say evasively.

"I talked to Janice," my mother interrupts before I have to get into detail about *Aladdin's Lamp* and my new partners. "She said Angelina is going to ask you to be a bridesmaid."

"I can't do it." My reply is immediate. Knowing Angelina, her wedding is going to be a production. I don't have time for it, and besides, we aren't close. We haven't even spoken in two years. I suspect the only reason she's asking me to be a bridesmaid is to prove to everyone that she didn't steal my boyfriend from me.

"But honey," my mother frowns, "you know everyone will gossip if you aren't part of the wedding."

"I don't care." I'm not used to defying my mother, but I need to hold firm on this issue. I can't keep flying to New Orleans for wedding events every weekend. Fridays, Saturdays and Sundays are my three busiest days. There's no way I can leave Josef in charge of *Aladdin's Lamp* while I'm off on bridesmaid duties. He drinks too much to be trusted. "I'm sure Angelina will understand."

"Leave it, Lillian," my father advises, surprising me. My

mother's the more vocal of the two, but my dad doesn't approve of me living so far away from home either. Still, I'll take advantage of the respite. "Tell you what, why don't I take my favorite two ladies shopping, then we'll have a nice dinner somewhere? Piper, I'm sure you can steer us somewhere good."

Oh dear. I talked to Owen Lamb on the phone this morning. The two of them wanted to meet me to discuss changes to the restaurant, and the only time they were available was seven this evening. "I'm sorry, I can't stay for dinner." I don't know why I'm apologizing. It isn't as if they asked me if this weekend was a convenient time to visit before they showed up. "I have a meeting with my partners that I can't miss."

"Partners? Partners in what?"

Of course she'd catch that. "*Aladdin's Lamp* has two new investors."

My mother's eyes narrow. "I thought that was against the terms of the will?" She looks at my dad for clarification. "It was, wasn't it, Matthew?"

I grit my teeth and count to ten. *What are you going to do, rat me out to Aunt Vera's trustees, mother?* I want to yell. But well-behaved Southern women don't raise their voices. "It's allowed as long as I retain majority control," I bite out. "I plan to."

"Oh for crying out loud, Piper. At what point are you going to give up this charade and move back home?" My mother's eyes brim with the ready tears that she can summon at will. "Every day, you're getting older. Angelina is three years younger than you, and she's already engaged. You don't even have a boyfriend. At your age, I was married for seven years. Isn't it time you stopped this rebellion, and got on with your life?"

"I am getting on with my life." Ten minutes in her company, and I sound like a surly teenager. "I'm doing something I care about very much. You should be happy for me."

"That's enough." My father's voice is firm. "Piper, you've upset your mother. Apologize."

For what? "I'm sorry, mother," I say, just to keep the peace. "Look, let's not argue. Why don't I show you around the city before I go?"

"Can't you cancel the meeting, dear?" The tears miraculously vanish. "After all, we see you so rarely."

Oh God. Cancel a meeting with Lamb and Lawless. They've already hinted I'm not serious about *Aladdin's Lamp.* If I blow them off, they might just walk away from the deal. Nothing's signed yet. I can't let that happen. I can't believe my mother would suggest such a thing.

Of course, it's not the first time. Three years ago, I'd got a job as a waitress at a high-end French bistro called *Le Papillon.* I was working my second weekend shift when my mother called me in a panic because my father was having a heart attack. Of course, I flew home immediately, only to find out it had been nothing more severe than acute indigestion. Worse, my mother had known it wasn't serious before I boarded the flight, but didn't tell me because she thought it was nice that I was coming home.

I know what I should do. I should put my foot down, tell my parents that I can't have dinner with them, and get to that meeting. But I'm really, *really* bad at direct confrontation, and when my mother starts to cry, I just want to capitulate.

"What if we do an early dinner?" I bargain instead.

I can eat a quick meal and still be on time, right?

I'M NOT ON TIME. It's almost eight by the time I make it to *Aladdin's Lamp*. Part of me desperately hopes that Owen Lamb and Wyatt Lawless have given up on me and gone home. I'm not in any shape to confront them, not after enduring several hours with my parents.

No such luck. They're seated in a corner booth, identical disapproving expressions on their faces.

I am in such trouble.

"I'm so sorry." The last time we met, we didn't get off on the right foot. I resented their implication that I wasn't taking the restaurant seriously. Today, my tone is contrite. I'm fifty-five minutes late to a business meeting, and they have every right to question my commitment.

Wyatt looks up. "Glad you could join us." His tone drips sarcasm.

Owen is blunter. "Piper," he says, "I don't know where to start. This is bullshit on so many levels." He draws a breath and proceeds to lecture me as if I were five. "First," he says, "what kind of head chef has plans on a Saturday evening? You're supposed to be here at dinner service, Piper. Chefs don't get weekends off."

I guess he does know where to start after all, I think snidely. Inwardly, I curse my mother. I told her I had to leave. I warned her I had an important meeting. Did she listen? No, she disappeared into the Saks Fifth Avenue dressing room with a pile of clothes to try on right when I had to leave, and all I could do was fume silently and wait for her to finish.

Not true, Piper. You could have left.

Wyatt cuts in, his voice still icy. "If you are laboring under the misconception that this is a nine-to-five job, you need to rethink your career choices."

Ninety seconds. It's taken ninety seconds for me to go from apologetic to full-on-fury. They're giving me grief about my hours? Kevin only works Fridays and Saturdays since I can't afford to pay him for more than that. Josef is massively unreliable. For the last six months, I've started work at ten in the morning, and I've left at midnight, every single day of the week except Mondays.

I swallow a lump in my throat. *No excuses, Piper. Just keep quiet.*

"Then, there's this food." Owen gestures to the plates in front of him with an expression of distaste. He hands me a fork. "Taste the lamb."

Shit. Josef must have improvised a special, but I know for a fact that we don't have any fresh lamb in the refrigerator. Did he really use frozen meat for a special?

I chew into the lamb and grimace as soon as I taste the over-seasoned dish. It's frozen alright. What on earth was Josef thinking?

I'm in my personal episode of Kitchen Nightmares. "The mussels haven't been cleaned," Owen continues grimly, gesturing to a fish stew. "The lentil soup tastes like the cook dumped a cupful of salt in it. The lettuce in the salad is wilted and the dressing tastes like it came out of a bottle."

Every single thing he's saying is true, but his words sting.

"I'm not going to lie to you, Piper." Wyatt takes over the task of chewing me out. "I'm quite perturbed by this."

Seriously, who talks like this guy? *Quite perturbed?* He sounds like a stiff, uptight Colin Firth. Except Colin Firth is yummy, and Wyatt Lawless is a jerk.

"I'm looking for passion and commitment from you, a burning desire to make this restaurant succeed." His eyes flicker in the direction of my Saks Fifth Avenue bag. "I can't have you skip out on work to go *shopping*. Two thirds of all restaurants in New York fail in the first year. The clock's ticking."

I sit there in silence, fighting the urge to defend myself.

They think I don't want this, but they're wrong. *I want this more than anything in the world.*

7

It does not matter how slowly you go so long as you do not stop.

— Confucius

Owen:

"I can't believe how late she was." Wyatt still sounds pissed when he storms into my office Monday.

"She showed up eventually," I argue from behind my desk, though I'm more than a little irritated with Piper myself. "She was late, that's all."

"That's all?" Wyatt's voice rises in outrage. "That's all? She showed up at eight to a seven o'clock meeting."

I cock my head to one side, and watch Wyatt pacing restlessly in front of me. "She's getting under your skin, isn't she?" I've seen Wyatt around Piper. He can hide it from other people, but I know him too well. He's fighting his attraction to her. Half of his grouchiness is just an acute case of blue balls.

"Fuck off."

My lips twitch. "Are you free tomorrow night? Saturday was a bust, but Piper really needs some help. I thought we could start with the menu."

He comes to a dead halt in front of me. "Had we not agreed to invest, I'd be tempted to walk away, Owen," he says bluntly. "There are a thousand restaurants in the city that we could work with. Instead, we've managed to pick a rich Southern princess who thinks this is a game. I don't like wasting my time."

"Why do you think she's rich?"

"Her handbag is Prada and it costs three thousand dollars. I should know - I bought one for Maisie last year."

"Really?"

He nods. "How does a chef whose restaurant is empty more often than it's full have enough money to buy a Prada bag? And if she has money, why doesn't she use it to fix the restaurant? Three thousand dollars would go a long way in that place."

"If she spends it on the restaurant, she attracts attention." Mendez might be on the right track with his suspicions, after all. I wonder what Piper Jackson is mixed up in.

Wyatt sighs. "I shouldn't have told you that. You're determined to investigate this, aren't you?"

"I am."

"Fine. Let's meet Piper tomorrow night. Might as well get it over with."

"That's the spirit," I say dryly. "Talking about Maisie, did you see her blog post today?" I turn my screen toward him. "She's managed to talk Yelp and the Hell's Kitchen business association into sponsoring a reality TV-style contest for local restaurants."

Maisie Hayes, Wyatt's ex-girlfriend, runs a very popular

food blog in New York. I haven't seen her in a while, but I read her blog regularly, as does everyone in the industry. She's entertaining and very insightful.

"What?" Wyatt looks surprised, and he's silent as he reads the announcement. "Good for her," he says when he's done. "She's wanted to expand into television for a while. She must have been working on this for months."

I nod. Say what you want about Maisie, but she doesn't shy away from work. "Incidentally, did Celia tell you that Carl wants to meet? The restaurant next to him just shut its doors. He's going to pitch an expansion to us."

Wyatt glances at his phone. "Yes, it's on my calendar at two tomorrow."

I frown. "I thought she was going to book it for today. Carl said the competition for this lease is going to be fierce."

Wyatt looks uncomfortable. "She probably tried, but I'm busy this afternoon. I'm meeting Stone Bradley in an hour."

His admission surprises me. Last week, Wyatt's plan had been to bury his head in the sand and pretend his father didn't exist. "To try to find your dad?"

He nods reluctantly. "I decided to get Bradley involved over the weekend. I don't like feeling out of control. I don't know where my father is or what he wants. It's time to fix that."

I snort. Wyatt likes being in control? Talk about stating the obvious. "You don't know anything about Piper either," I quip, rising to my feet. "How come that's not bothering you?"

A stupefied expression crosses his face. I laugh and leave him to it. I'm prepared to bet that we'll have a dossier on our new partner by the end of the week.

～

Wyatt:

Stone Bradley is exactly on time. "How's it going, Mr. Lawless?" He shakes my hand and pulls up a chair. "How can I help you?"

Bradley's a consummate professional. I don't have to warn him to be discreet or caution him that what I'm saying is private. I pay him an exorbitant sum of money for two things. He's entirely trustworthy, and he gets results. "My father attempted to contact me a few days ago." I take a deep breath. "Prior to that, I haven't heard from him in twenty years."

"Ah." He pulls out a notebook from his briefcase and leans forward, his pen poised to take notes. "His name?"

"Jack Lawless."

"Age?"

"Sixty-six."

"You have a recent picture of him?"

"Footage from the security cameras in the reception area. I'll arrange a copy for you."

"Good." He looks up. "You said you hadn't seen your father in twenty years."

"He left my mother," I answer tightly. My hands clench into fists under the table. *Bradley's relentless questions are a necessary evil,* I tell myself. "My mother is a hoarder. I guess he got tired of living in a pigsty."

His gaze bores into me. "How old were you when he left?"

"Thirteen. Is that really relevant to your investigation?"

"You have to let me do my job, Mr. Lawless," he says mildly. "You never tried looking for your father? Never tracked him down?"

"No."

"And you want me to find him now?"

I don't really know what I want. "For the moment," I reply, "just figure out where he is. Don't make contact."

"Will do." He rises to his feet. "I'll be in touch."

When he's gone, I lean back in my seat and loosen my tie, trying to choke back my frustration. My father wants something from me, and I don't know what it is. I can't get a solid read on Piper Jackson. I don't know anything about her — her background, her previous restaurant experience, her hopes and dreams. I've never gone into a partnership with someone feeling this unprepared.

I feel like I'm losing my grasp on what's going on, and I hate that feeling.

8

The best way out is always through.

— ROBERT FROST

Piper:

My girlfriends and I get together every week on Monday evenings to drink, eat and dish about what's going on with our lives. We even have a name for ourselves — we're the inaccurately named Thursday Night Drinking Pack.

So far this Monday, we've had a lot of rum. We've talked about Bailey's two men, and we've nagged Gabby about her trust issues. When there's a lull in the conversation, I lean forward, glaring at Bailey. Though I know it was my fault, I'm still resentful at the way Wyatt Lawless and Owen Lamb scolded me on Saturday, as if I were an irresponsible child.

Had Bailey not interfered, the two of them wouldn't even know I exist. Yes, the money they're investing is a blessing, but if the two of them persist in treating me as patronizingly as they have so far, I'm not going to be able to work with them. Already, my reservoirs of patience have been seriously exhausted. "Talking about good looking men," I pick up from the previous conversation, "Tell me about Wyatt Lawless and Owen Lamb."

Bailey looks puzzled. "Who are they?"

"Two guys who've eaten at my restaurant every single day for the last two weeks," I reply. "Every single day. I'm not in the front of the house all the time, so it took me a while to realize it. Then on Thursday, they offered to become my partners."

A look of guilt spreads on her face. "Okay," she confesses. "Don't be mad. I yelled at Sebastian for upsetting you, and he felt so bad that he promised to talk to a couple of his friends about your restaurant."

A couple of his friends? I keep forgetting that Bailey doesn't know the restaurant world. She has no idea who Wyatt Lawless and Owen Lamb are. She doesn't know how intimidated I am that they're going to be working with me. "Bailey, do you even know who these guys are?"

"Not a clue," she says, with a shrug of her shoulders. "Should I know?"

I shake my head. "I guess not, you don't work in the industry. Lawless and Lamb are legendary. They have something of a Midas touch. Their restaurants are very popular." And if Bailey hadn't interfered, they wouldn't have given me a second look. Somehow, that's the bit that upsets me the most. I haven't earned this partnership. It's been given to me on a whim, and it can be taken away just as quickly.

"That's good then, right?" Bailey sounds nervous. "You aren't irritated with me for telling Sebastian?"

A hot surge of shame washes over me. I'm letting my resentment of Wyatt and Owen spill over to Bailey, and that's not fair. She's just trying to help. "No, of course not. You did what you thought was a good thing."

"So what's the problem?" Katie leans forward. "They are good at what they do and you need help. Do they want too much money? Or equity?"

"It isn't that." I don't like talking about my difficulties. Even though these women are my best friends, and would never take advantage of my vulnerability to hurt me, I prefer to keep my emotions bottled up. "They just rubbed me the wrong way, that's all."

Wendy's playing with her phone. "Is this them?" She hands me the device, shaking her head in bemusement. "Seriously, what am I doing wrong with my life? The only guys I meet are smarmy lawyers. Bailey finds two studs, Gabby decides to hook up and voila — she finds a couple of hotties, and now you as well?" She gulps down her drink. "Life is *so* unfair."

"Pictures can't reveal personality," I snap. My cat Jasper, looks up at my tone, decides nothing is wrong and puts his head down again. "These two are smug, self-satisfied, and annoying as all fuck. You can have them."

They exchange glances. I almost *never* swear. "You don't have to work with them if you don't want to," Bailey says cautiously to me. "Do you want me to ask Sebastian if he knows anyone else who can help?"

Mr. O'Connor needs an extra three thousand dollars for rent. Yesterday, only ten people came into the restaurant for lunch. All day, I tried to find another way out of the situation, but there isn't one. If I don't want to fail, I need to figure out how to work with Wyatt Lawless and Owen Lamb. "No," I reply, suppressing my sigh. "I'll suck it up. These guys are really good."

"And really hot," Wendy adds, her eyes still on her phone.

They might be hot, but they are jerks. And I've never, ever been attracted to assholes.

~

WENDY FINDS me in the kitchen before she leaves. "Are you okay, Piper?"

"I'm fine." I force a note of cheer into my voice, but she's not convinced. Wendy is a divorce attorney. Reading emotions is second-nature to her. Only a therapist would be more dangerous.

She takes a deep breath. "Your parents were in town this weekend, weren't they? I might be out of line, but their visits always seem to upset you."

I know why I have such difficulty opening up to people. As a teenager, my mother scoffed at my dreams and used my hopes as a weapon against me. When I told her I wanted to be a chef, she'd sneered. "That's what we hire people for, Piper," she'd said, her words dripping condescension.

I used to sneak away in secret to the kitchen, begging Maria, our Latina cook, to show me what she was doing, until my mother caught me one day. "Next time I see you in the kitchen, Piper," she'd said to me, her voice icy, "Maria loses her job. I'm not raising my daughter to toil away behind a hot stove."

"You think?" I ask bitterly. "They took me shopping at Saks Fifth Avenue, bought me a pointlessly expensive purse that I didn't want, then insisted I join them for dinner. I was an hour late to a meeting with Owen Lamb and Wyatt Lawless."

She whistles softly. "Were they still there?"

I nod gloomily. "Oh yes, they were there and they were furious with me. I don't blame them. I'm pretty mad at myself. I'm a grown woman, but when it comes to my parents, I have no backbone."

Wendy looks puzzled. "Couldn't you just have told your parents it was urgent? You have a job, you can't just take off whenever you like."

"I did. Repeatedly. They just don't listen to me." I groan in frustration. "They bought me a three-thousand dollar purse. I don't have money to pay rent at the restaurant, and I'm carrying around a Prada bag. My life's a joke."

"A Prada bag?" Her eyes gleam with interest. "Can I see it?"

"Sure." I lead the way to my bedroom and pick up the red-orange leather bag. Don't get me wrong; it is beautiful. I just didn't want it.

"Oh, pretty." Wendy looks at me. "You don't like it?"

"I'd much rather pay rent." Right now, if I can't figure out some other way around it, I'm going to have to go to Wyatt Lawless and Owen Lamb and grovel for enough money to cover Mr. O'Connor's increase.

"I'll buy it from you, if you'd like," Wendy offers.

I look up, startled at her generosity. "I was just complaining," I stammer. "Not hinting that I needed money."

She rolls her eyes. "I know, Piper. We've been friends for six years, you don't think I know that? My thirtieth birthday is coming up, and I want to buy myself something nice to mark the occasion." She grins. "I'll even loan it to you when your parents come to town."

I hug her tight. "Thank you. I was dreading having to ask Owen and Wyatt for money."

Her face scrunches in sympathy. "I'm sorry," she says. "I'm partnering with an absolute jerk of a lawyer right now on a case, so I can understand how hard it is to work with someone when you just want to punch them. Hang in there." She chuckles. "And if they get too insufferable, call me for backup. I'm very good at kicking ass."

She pulls out her checkbook and writes me a check for the purse. She hugs the bag close to her chest, her eyes sparkling. "See you next Monday?"

"Not unless I kill Lamb and Lawless first," I tell her gloomily. "Be prepared to come bail me out of jail."

If *Aladdin's Lamp* fails, my parents will have me on a plane to New Orleans faster than I can blink, back to a life in which I felt stifled and out-of-place. If biting my tongue in front of Wyatt and Owen is the price I have to pay, so be it. *The restaurant isn't going to fail,* I promise myself. *Not if I have anything to do with it.*

9

The eyes are useless when the mind is blind.

— Unknown

Owen:

"Thanks for meeting me, you guys." Carl Marcotti shakes our hands vigorously, and escorts us to our table, gesturing to it with an expansive wave. "Sit, sit. You're eating lunch, aren't you?"

"Wouldn't pass it up for anything," Wyatt replies. "The entire way here, I've been having visions of your lasagna."

He laughs and signals over a waiter, who hurries up to take our orders. Once we've decided on food, we get down to the real reason we're here. "You want to expand?" I ask him.

He nods eagerly. "We're busy every night," he says. "There's an hour wait for a table on the weekends. We don't take reservations, but if we did, we'd be booked every single night."

I look around. Carl's right, *Paesano's* is hopping. Three

waitresses weave in and out, carrying steaming plates of pasta, fish, and meat. One of them detours to deposit a plate of bruschetta at our table with a smile. "Compliments of the kitchen."

We dig in as Carl flips open his laptop. "If you look at the numbers..." he starts.

"Already looked at them," Wyatt interrupts. "I agree with you, Carl. You're in great shape, and you're definitely ready to take *Paesano's* to the next level. What's it going to cost to lease the place next door?"

He exhales in relief. "Thirty grand."

"A month? Fuck me." I've lived in Manhattan for seventeen years, and I'm still shocked at the price of real estate in this city.

He laughs. "Insane, right? But I'm confident we can do enough business to cover it."

Wyatt doesn't look surprised at the price tag. "We're in. You'll need another couple hundred grand to renovate the space, right?"

Carl shakes his head. "The place is in good shape," he says. "There shouldn't be too much remodeling necessary. One fifty should cut it, and we'll be ready to open in four months."

Carl's chomping at the bit. He's done his homework, and he's made sure he's prepared for this meeting. It's a stark contrast to Piper.

"I was afraid you guys would say no," he confesses as our food shows up.

"Why?" Wyatt raises an eyebrow.

"Well, you turned down Emerson recently, and word is that you guys bought a stake in Piper Jackson's restaurant." He sounds sheepish. "I thought you might not want to take on too many projects at once."

Everyone knows everyone in the restaurant industry. No doubt Max Emerson's bitching about how we didn't invest, and Piper's probably the target of everyone's envy. I feel a brief moment of regret about that. I don't want to throw Piper to the gossiping wolves.

Wyatt leans forward. "You know Piper?"

Carl nods. "We started culinary school together. She was the most talented chef in our class." He shakes his head. "Great girl, Piper. She's had a tough time of it."

"In what way?" Wyatt asks. He takes a bite of the lasagna and closes his eyes in appreciation. "This is fantastic, Carl."

"You haven't investigated Piper's background?" Carl gives us a curious look. "That's weird. You guys knew my underwear size when we did our deal."

I chuckle. Carl's exaggerating, but only just. The background check was painfully thorough. We skipped a lot of steps because of Mendez.

Wyatt clears his throat. "It's a long story," he says, giving me a dry look.

Carl elaborates. "Piper's parents cut her off when she joined culinary school," he says, chewing on his veal. "She worked her way through the program. It took her almost five years to finish. Then, after graduation, when she was about to start working for *Le Bernardin*, her aunt died and left her *Aladdin's Lamp*."

"She inherited the place?"

"Six months ago," Carl confirms.

"Well, that sounds like a lucky break," Wyatt says, echoing what I'm thinking.

Carl snorts. "The place was badly run down when Piper took it over. You think it's a dump now? You should have seen it at the start of the year. Half the chairs were broken.

The walk-in freezer hadn't been emptied and cleaned in seven years. And that's not even the worst of it."

"What's the worst of it?" I ask.

"You know her staff? The waitress who smells of cigarette smoke, and the sous-chef with an alcohol problem? The waitress makes sixty grand in salary and the sous-chef makes a hundred. A hundred thousand fucking dollars." Carl shakes his head. "She's going broke paying for them, but she can't fire them. The trustees of her aunt's estate won't let her."

"You're joking."

"I wish," he says soberly. "The poor kid. Her family is determined to see her fail."

"How do you know all this?" Wyatt asks curiously. His brows are drawn together in a frown.

He shrugs. "Everyone talks, you know how it is. But mostly it's because people like Piper. She got a raw deal, and she never once whined. You won't hear her complain. She just gets quiet, and then she gets to work."

She'd done that on Saturday. The two of us had yelled at her and accused her of wasting our time, and she hadn't said one thing to defend herself. Now, to find out she's been dealt an impossible hand, and she's doing the best she can to play the game, even if defeat stares her in the face?

Perhaps I should have yelled less and listened more.

Judging from Wyatt's expression, he's feeling the same way. "Thanks for telling us this, Carl," he says quietly. "I really appreciate it." He takes a sip of water, but his lasagna stays untouched. Like me, he's lost his appetite.

10

Failure is only the opportunity to begin again, this time more intelligently.

— HENRY FORD

Piper:

I'm determined not to blow my second chance.

Yes, you don't like them, I mutter to myself as I do kitchen prep by myself on Tuesday evening. Josef is, unsurprisingly, late. He doesn't know the precise terms of Aunt Vera's will, but he has learned in six months that no amount of bad behavior can get him fired. By any rights, he should have been let go a dozen times over, so he's reached the conclusion that I'm a pushover.

I'm only a pushover where my parents are concerned. I just can't afford to fire Josef.

My knife moves rhythmically as my mind wanders. Wendy thought Wyatt and Owen were attractive. She'd practically been drooling at her phone. Are they? I'm trying to picture them, but all my mind brings up is the image of them yelling at me on Saturday night, their lips twisted with disapproval.

Objectively, I guess they are attractive, if you like your men with a side of asshole. I don't, I never have. Yes, that dark beard of Wyatt's is all kinds of sexy, and Owen's shoulder-length blond hair makes me want to run my hands through its thickness.

And then rip it out, because he's a jerk.

My lips twitch at that thought. Maybe he'll stop lecturing me then. Maybe Wyatt will stop looking at me with those dark, measuring eyes.

"I'm here, I'm here." Josef bustles in. "Ah, I see you've got the lentils cooking. And you've made the hummus too. Excellent."

I straighten my shoulders. This situation with Josef is deteriorating rapidly. "You're almost an hour late," I say coolly. "Do I need to remind you that you're supposed to be here at three thirty?"

"The subway wasn't running," he says sullenly.

If I'm to believe Josef, the subway fails on a weekly basis, and the MTA is made of a bunch of incompetent idiots. I wonder how much of a fool he thinks I am. "Make the salad dressing," I snap. "Lawless and Lamb are going to be here for dinner, and they've asked for us to prepare three dishes that represent *Aladdin's Lamp*. On Saturday, you served them frozen lamb and dressing out of a bottle. Let's do better today."

I brace myself for a resentful silence, but Josef nods eagerly. "Of course. I know the perfect three dishes."

"You do?" This is a rare display of enthusiasm from Josef. Call me selfish, but I don't want to squash it. It would be really nice if my sous-chef would actually do the job I pay him for.

"Yes. I've a great recipe for a vine-wrapped grilled salmon, served with a basmati pilau," he says. "I can braise a lamb shank, serve it with couscous. Also, a grilled chicken with pomegranate sauce." He rubs his hands together. He's almost bouncing on the balls of his feet; he's so eager to get going.

I gaze at him doubtfully. The truth of the matter is, my specialty isn't Middle Eastern food. I'm competent and I can follow a recipe, but I don't know enough about the cuisine to be able to improvise. I've cooked Southern food all my life, and I learned to cook classical French cuisine in school, but ask me to cook anything else and I'm well outside my comfort zone.

Until I took over at the start of the year, Josef was the head chef at *Aladdin's Lamp.* Maybe this is the challenge he needs to take an interest in cooking again.

A voice at the back of my head warns me I'm making a mistake. *Sebastian Ardalan didn't want to hire Josef,* it says to me. *He wanted to hire you.*

It's been a long, hard struggle, and that voice isn't as confident as it once was. It's been smothered into silence by crushing bills, ground down by an unending stream of obstacles. It's been stifled by the cool contempt I saw in in Wyatt Lawless' eyes on Saturday, by the open disgust I heard in Owen Lamb's voice. "That sounds good," I hear myself say. "What can I do to help?"

I WALK out to the restaurant floor to greet them when they arrive. It's eight on a Tuesday evening. The restaurant is almost empty — only one other table is occupied, by a young couple holding hands and sighing in pleasure over my macaroni and cheese. Seeing them, my heart fills with emotion. This is the reason I became a chef, for the simple joy of watching someone enjoy my food.

I'm still smiling when I spot Lamb and Lawless, though my smile dims as I approach them. When I see their faces, all my ire from Saturday night comes back. *Well-behaved Southern women don't show emotion,* I remind myself. "Thank you for coming," I say politely. My mother will be proud of my even tone. Years of etiquette lessons are finally paying off.

Wyatt looks up, his expression troubled. "Hello Piper."

"Mr. Lawless," I nod tightly. I don't care what's bothering him. He's just here to eat a meal. Today, Owen Lamb, who is the expert at kitchen operations, is the person I need to impress, and he's probably smirking like a fool, the way he usually does.

He isn't. He doesn't meet my gaze. A cold fear trickles through me. They can't be pulling out of the contract, can they? We haven't signed anything yet. All I have is a verbal agreement. In the state of New York, a verbal agreement is binding, but I know that won't make any difference. If they walk away, I don't have money to sue them.

Don't be silly, Piper. That's the worst case scenario. That's not going to happen.

"You wanted to taste three signature dishes today," I blurt out, a distinct tremble in my voice. "Right?"

Wyatt's troubled look intensifies. "Yes please."

Please, I beg. *Please let the salmon dish be okay.* I'm about to excuse myself to check on Josef's fish before it leaves the kitchen, when Kimmie flounces out carrying two plates.

"Vine-wrapped grilled salmon, served with a basmati pilau," she says, her lips bared into a smile.

I only swear when I'm really, *really* angry. The instant I spot Kimmie with the plates, I reach that point. What the fuck is Josef thinking, sending the dishes out without my approval? I'm the head chef. Nothing leaves the kitchen without my say-so.

"You're not joining us, Piper?" Owen asks politely, failing to notice that my blood is boiling with rage.

My fingers clench into fists. I don't care that well-behaved Southern women don't punch people. Right now, I want to kick, scream, and lash out at everyone. At Owen and Wyatt for bailing on a deal. At Josef for exploiting a moment's weakness, and at Kimmie, for that smug smirk on her face, and for the rhythmic movement of her jaw as she chews her ever-present gum.

All I can do is wait silently for them to taste the dish.

Owen Lamb gives the grape-leaf wrapper a dubious look. "In the Middle East," he mutters, poking at the covering with his fork, "these are typically fresh."

In the Middle East, perhaps. At *Aladdin's Lamp*, they come out of a jar.

He doesn't say anything else; he doesn't need to. He peels the grape leaf back, and cuts a small piece off the edge. When he tastes it, he pauses. For a moment, there's complete silence in the air, then he shakes his head. "Food," he says quietly, "shouldn't taste of preservatives."

A fist wraps around my heart, squeezing it tight. Wyatt spears a piece of salmon on his fork, and lifts it to his mouth. He chews experimentally, then his eyebrows rise. "You made this dish, Piper?"

I should throw Josef under the bus. He sent out the

salmon without waiting for me. He knew I'd want to taste everything first, and he sent out the food anyway.

You okayed his dish, my conscience reminds me. *This is your restaurant. No excuses. No whining.* "I'm the head chef," I answer quietly.

"That wasn't what Wyatt asked," Owen says mildly. He pushes his plate away and delivers his verdict. "Too heavy on the pomegranate molasses, drowning out the delicate taste of the fish. The pilaf on the other hand, is distinctly under seasoned." He lifts his head up and surveys me with his clear blue gaze. "What's next?"

More pomegranate molasses, unfortunately. "Grilled chicken," I tell them. "I need to head to the kitchen to see to it."

Wyatt nods. "Come back out when you're done. We'd like to talk to you."

They're going to back out of this deal. I can sense the words hanging in the air, unsaid for the moment, and my heart aches with grief. My options have narrowed to nothing. Thanks to Wendy's help, I'll make rent this month, but what about next month and the month after? By the fall, I'll be back in New Orleans, and everything I've struggled for in the last five years would have been for nothing. "Sure," I reply tonelessly. "I'll do that."

"WHAT DID they think of the salmon?" Josef's eager voice assaults me as soon as I walk into the kitchen.

I have no energy left to soften the blow. "The sauce for the salmon had too much pomegranate molasses. The pilaf was under seasoned."

I swipe my finger through the pan where the sauce was made, and sure enough, Owen Lamb is right. Used sparingly the molasses adds depth and richness. In the sauce Josef made, it is cloyingly sweet. It would have drowned the taste of the fish.

His face flushes. "It did not," he snaps. "What do they know about food anyway?"

"Everything." That's the reason it hurts so much; that's the reason Sebastian Ardalan's prediction that *Aladdin's Lamp* would close in six months cut to the bone. Lawless and Lamb are the best at what they do. Their approval matters to me.

"Is the chicken ready?" I taste the sauce and poke at the meat, and I can hear their voices in my head already. "Passable," Wyatt Lawless would pronounce. "Generic," Owen Lamb would say. They'd both be right, but it's too late to do anything about it.

Sure enough, in about five minutes, Kimmie returns to the kitchen, the barely touched plates in her hands. "What did they say?" I ask, dreading the answer.

Kimmie looks a little dazed. "Mr. Lamb said that it was unworthy of you," she says, "And Mr. Lawless told you to fight." Her message delivered, she goes back to chewing gum. "They're strange."

That was unworthy of me.

Fight.

I contemplate their words, despair threatening to press in from all sides, then suddenly, a light shines on the truth.

I'm a fool. I'm a stupid, blind fool. I've been too busy moaning and moping about money and my parents and all the things I lack, and I've failed to realize what I do have.

I have friends who believe in me.

I have talent. Sebastian Ardalan, a two-Michelin star

chef ate at my restaurant, and he *liked* my food. The couple at the table earlier had practically licked their plates clean.

Le Bernardin offered me a job when I graduated. Sebastian Ardalan would have offered me a job. I've let the steady dripping corrosiveness of my parents' words eat away at me. I let Josef suggest the signature dishes? Shame on me. I'm the head chef. Until the doors close, this is *my* restaurant. And I'm going to make Owen Lamb and Wyatt Lawless a dish that represents my cooking.

"We're not serving the lamb," I tell Josef. "Get me two skillets. I'm going to serve Owen Lamb and Wyatt Lawless my macaroni and cheese."

If they're going to back away from the deal, they're not going to do it after tasting a dish Josef made. They're going to do it after tasting one of mine.

11

Three things cannot long stay hidden: the sun, the moon and the truth.

— BUDDHA

Wyatt:

The macaroni and cheese is a revelation.

Creamy and cheesy, with a tang from jalapenos, black olives and tomatoes that Piper's added to her sauce. The top of it is crusted with a mixture of panko and parmesan, seasoned with salt, pepper and herbs. It is absolutely fantastic.

I've had forgettable meals at *Aladdin's Lamp*, but this isn't one of them. This is... transcendent.

And yes, I'm using the word transcendent to describe macaroni and cheese.

"So we've learned once more," Owen says at my side, "that the Middle Eastern food here is forgettable, and everything else is amazing. Why do we keep ordering Middle Eastern food?"

"Because I like Middle Eastern food, and because the place is called *Aladdin's Lamp*?" I reply through a mouthful of food. My mother would frown at me if she could see me. For all her faults, and there were no shortage of them, she taught me good table manners and always made sure my clothes were cleanly laundered.

If you were in rags, somebody might have come to check on you, and she couldn't have that.

That thought from my past is sour, and the food is good, and I would rather focus on the food.

It isn't just my past that I want to forget today. It's also Carl's words. From the moment he told us about Piper's circumstances, I've found it difficult to breathe. I've always thought of myself as tough, but fair. I've never been an asshole.

Yet we've both been dicks to her.

I can't blame Owen. The work he's doing for Mendez blinds him, it always has. His father, mother, and baby sister were murdered by the mob. After that, he's entitled to a blind spot the size of the state of Texas, if that's what he wants.

But me? I should have done a background check on her last week. Distracted by my father's sudden reappearance, I didn't.

That's not a reason, Wyatt. That's an excuse.

She comes out of the kitchen, her head held high, her eyes fixed on us. Earlier this evening, she'd seemed diffident, tentative. Now, she looks the way she did the first time we met her, when she told us she didn't want our pity. She blazes. She is steel and determination; she is fire that will either warm me or burn me.

I don't care which, really.

"Gentlemen," she comes up to us. "I hope the last dish was..." She hesitates, then finds the perfect word. "*Worthy.*"

But the blood that had pounded through my veins when I saw her approach freezes to ice as soon as she opens her mouth. Because though her words are defiant, the accent is still pretty, still Southern.

We have secrets, Owen and I. Dark secrets, kinky secrets. Secrets we've never apologized for, secrets we've barely bothered to hide.

But secrets can be chasms.

My world is filled with chasms. Between me and my mother is a gulf that has widened with each passing year. Between my father and I lies an insurmountable rift. Owen and I will never see eye to eye on Mendez's schemes.

All of those divides narrow compared to this one. She's a debutante from the South. Her parents expected her to find a husband in college and marry on graduation.

And Owen and I share women, and we like it that way.

Maisie and I broke up because of my sexual preferences, and I've learned an important lesson from it. No matter how my cock might stir at the sound of Piper's voice, this is not a chasm that can ever be crossed.

12

Alone we can do so little, together we can do so much.

— HELEN KELLER

Piper:

I sit down at their table. For a few minutes, there's silence and neither of them will look at me. My fear solidifies in my throat. They're going to bail.

Then Owen looks up. "You realize we're going to rename the restaurant, right?"

My heart starts beating again. He said *we.* "You aren't backing out?" I exhale in a long shuddering breath, trying my hardest to hold it together and not break down in sheer relief. "I thought you were going to pull out of the deal and walk away."

"No." Wyatt's voice is curt. There's a peculiar sort of clenched anger on his face. He's acting like I've accused him of torturing puppies. "I don't walk away."

Owen shakes his head at me in warning. *Leave this be.* "Before we talk about the menu," he says quietly, "both Wyatt and I owe you an apology." He looks down at the yellowed tablecloth. "We've made a lot of snap judgments about you."

Wyatt looks up and meets my gaze squarely. "And we were wrong about almost everything."

"What?" My voice comes out as a surprised squeak.

Wyatt's expression is genuinely contrite. "I misjudged you," he says openly. "You were late to our meeting, and you showed up with a three-thousand dollar purse when your restaurant is in trouble. I put two and two together, and reached eight."

"I talked to Carl Marcotti today," he continues. "He cleared up a lot of my misconceptions. You worked your way through school, didn't you? Your family didn't help."

"No, they didn't help." My voice is a whisper of sound in the quiet room, the normal noise of the city seemingly muted in this moment.

"Instead," Owen says gruffly, "they saddled you with a rundown restaurant, overpaid employees, and a set of conditions that almost guaranteed you would fail."

"I thought I was doing something wrong." I'm close to tears.

Wyatt shakes his head. "You're being hard on yourself, Piper. You were thrown into an impossible position. Given the circumstances, you've done a great job to keep the place going."

I swallow. This is the first time someone in the restaurant business has ever told me I'm doing a good job. For the first time in five months, I don't feel alone.

Wyatt places his hand over mine, and awareness jolts through me at his touch. My senses instantly go on high alert. "I was wrong to judge," he mutters, his voice gentle. "But I promise to make it up to you. We're here now. We're your partners, and we're going to make things easier."

So many images dance through my head. A restaurant crowded with guests. The constant worry about money lifted from me. Being able to tug free of the invisible strings that tie me to my parents. Images of Wyatt pulling me close to him as Owen watches...

Whoa. What was that? Focus on the restaurant, Piper.

"Thank you." I'm still in shock. "What do you mean, you're going to rename the place?"

Owen's lips twitch. "Piper," he says, his eyes dancing with amusement, "the place is called *Aladdin's Lamp*, and there's macaroni and cheese on your menu. That's demented."

I give him a withering glare, but it rolls off his back. He's laughing at me again, but strangely, it doesn't bother me as much as it did a few days ago. Maybe it's because for the first time in our brief partnership, they're actually on my side. "I don't know if I can rename it," I confess. "The trustees have set up some very strict rules about what I can and can't do."

"At every turn," Wyatt remarks with a frown, "the terms of your aunt's will keep coming up." He gives Owen an annoyed look. "I hate how unprepared I am. Piper, do you have a copy of the terms and conditions?"

I nod ruefully. "I do."

"Good. Let's see what we're facing."

∽

Owen:

When Carl told us about Piper's struggles, I wasn't sure what to think.

There's a part of me that desperately wants to believe Piper's involved in something nefarious, so I can act. My burning desire to avenge the death of my family hasn't gone away in seventeen years.

But the more rational voice in my head points out that she's probably innocent. Restaurants mixed up with the mob lose money year after year, but somehow manage to stay in business. Piper's situation is very different. I can smell her desperation. Without help, she's not going to survive the rest of the year.

Mendez called me this morning. "Well?" he'd barked into the phone. "I haven't heard from you, Lamb."

"We just met last week," I'd pointed out. "I can't drop everything and do your bidding."

He'd huffed in displeasure and hung up.

Now, as I watch Wyatt flip through the terms and conditions, I wonder why I'm dragging my heels on investigating the restaurants Mendez asked me to. My mother's face swims in front of me. I remember my sister's toothy grin and my father's hearty laugh.

They're dead. I'm alive. I should have been with them when the gunman came. I might have been able to do something.

Or I might have shared their fate.

I make up my mind. Tomorrow morning, I'll give Max Emerson a call and propose a meeting. Maybe I'll tell him I'm reconsidering my decision to pass on his restaurant. Whatever it takes to get access to his books.

And Piper? I don't know. I don't know what to do about Piper Jackson.

∼

"THIS IS INSANE." Wyatt says flatly.

We've just spent the last two hours going through all one hundred and thirty one pages of the terms and conditions, and it's left me with fresh respect for Piper. Despite a thousand restrictions and constraints, despite a set of trustees who scrutinize every move she makes, she's kept this place running for five months.

"Why did you take this on?" I ask her, leaning back in my chair. "Carl said you had an offer at *Le Bernardin*."

"Hubris." Her tone is wry. "I went home for Aunt Vera's funeral. I didn't think I was going to inherit anything; I didn't even know Aunt Vera owned a restaurant in New York. Then the executor of the will told me I needed to make a decision right away." She looks sad. "Running my own restaurant has been my dream my whole life, and it was being offered to me. I accepted without finding out what I was getting into, and I've been paying for it ever since."

"Yes, well, you're not the only one who jumped in without doing any due diligence." Wyatt rolls his eyes in my direction. "This is a problem," he says, tapping the book in front of us.

Piper stiffens, and he frowns at her. "Will you relax?" he says exasperatedly. "We told you, we're not going anywhere. This is a problem to be solved, not an insurmountable obstacle."

She exhales. "I'm sorry."

A lightning flash of inspiration strikes me. I need an excuse to investigate the kitchen, and the three of us need to stop tiptoeing around each other. I'm Irish; I've made my best friends in a pub, over several pints of Guinness. We aren't in Dublin and the Guinness in New York is undrinkable, but that doesn't have to stop us.

I get to my feet. "We got off on the wrong foot. Why don't we toast to our partnership, and then we can make our battle plans. Knowing Wyatt, he already has a dozen ideas. Piper, where's your booze?"

I hold my breath. Is she going to let me in the kitchen without supervision? I only need a few minutes. Though I don't know exactly what I'm looking for, I trust my instincts. If something's amiss, I'm confident I can find it fairly quickly.

It's ten at night. The restaurant is closed. The sous-chef and the gum-chewing waitress are gone for the day. The exterior lights are turned off. The three of us are alone in the front, our papers spread out all over the table. "There's wine and beer in the refrigerator in the kitchen," she says. "There's also a bottle of vodka in the freezer, if you want to get good and wasted."

"Do you get good and wasted? You don't seem the sort."

"Another snap judgement?" she mocks gently, her smile softening her words of their sting. "Yes, Mr. Lamb, I've been known to have a drink or two from time to time."

"You've got to stop calling us that, you know." Wyatt grins lazily at her. "Especially if we're going to get good and wasted together. Mr. Lamb. Mr. Lawless. You're very formal."

"Fair enough. Owen, you want help finding it?"

"I'll manage," I say, keeping my voice casual. I head to the back. I have only minutes to search the place. Trying to be quiet, I do a quick scan of the room, opening drawers and cupboards, checking out the pantry, bending down to search the shelves underneath the counters.

Nothing seems out of place. Even Wyatt would approve of how clean the kitchen is. The dishes have been done. The skillets have been cleaned and neatly stacked for the next day's work. The garbage has been emptied. Piper's sous-chef Josef must have seen to this.

Shaking my head, I return to the front with the bottle and three glasses. Piper shoots me a curious look. "Couldn't resist checking out the kitchen?" she asks me. "Did I pass the Owen Lamb inspection?"

I have to chuckle; she doesn't miss much. I'm very rapidly reaching the conclusion that she's clean. Opening the bottle, I pour three generous shots. We each grab one and lift our glasses. "A toast," I say, "to our new partnership. To new beginnings."

We clink glasses and I take a sip. "This is good stuff." I say, looking at the label. Piper Jackson is full of surprises. "You're a vodka drinker?"

"No," she replies. "My roommate Bailey gave it to me at the start of the year. By that time, I'd realized I'd made a mistake. I needed consolation."

"This bottle was unopened."

Her lips twitch. "I work around knives and fire," she points out. "Vodka seems stupid." She returns to the earlier conversation. "You said something was a problem?" she asks Wyatt.

"You're allowed to take on partners," he answers, "but you'll have to stay the majority owner." He sips at the vodka. "That's not a problem. Owen and I almost never take a majority stake in a restaurant. But," he frowns, "*Aladdin's Lamp* is valued at two hundred thousand dollars."

"I know," Piper says, looking confused. She sits up as understanding dawns. "Crap. They won't let you invest more than a hundred grand."

Ah. Wyatt's right. This is a problem. *Aladdin's Lamp* could be very successful, but for that to happen, it's going to take quite an infusion of capital. A hundred grand isn't enough, not in a city where routine renovations cost half a million dollars.

Wyatt nods. "Exactly. We're going to have to get creative."

"We can't cook the books." Piper looks unhappy as she speaks. "Aunt Vera's son Colton was pretty angry I was left the restaurant. He's waiting for me to mess up. The trustees can demand to see my accounts anytime, and I have to comply." Her lips twist into a grimace. "It's in the fine print on page sixty-five."

Wyatt opens to the indicated page and reads the relevant section. "What a pain in the ass," he mutters. "I'm not suggesting we cheat the system," he clarifies. "Any ideas, Owen?"

Is it the shared act of drinking together that makes us allies? Is it my search in her kitchen, which has revealed nothing out of place? Is it Piper's willingness to be open and honest about her business? Is it the muted fear in her eyes that we're going to back out, a fear I want to soothe away? Is it the raw talent I tasted when I ate the macaroni and cheese?

I don't know. What I do know is that I want to help. When we agreed to our deal at the start, I didn't give a shit about Piper Jackson. I was here because of Mendez's suspicions.

Not anymore. I'm invested now. Piper deserves to be successful, and I'm going to help her. We're going to fill this place every night. *Whatever it takes.*

I look around the place. "Getting this place fixed up won't be cheap," I warn. "The tables can be salvaged, but that's about it. The equipment in the back needs to be replaced as well. We can do a lot of the work ourselves to keep the cost down, and we can buy stuff in auction lots, but even with that, we're still looking at sixty grand, minimum."

Piper winces. "Right now, I'm breaking even, but not for long. Mr. O'Connor raised my rent by three thousand dollars."

"O'Connor?" My voice sharpens. "Is that your landlord?"

She looks faintly puzzled by my interest. "He lives upstairs," she explains. "I think he liked Aunt Vera. Even with the rent increase, I'm still paying less than market rate."

O'Connor is an Irish name. Is he mixed up with the mob? My spine stiffens. "How long has he been your landlord?"

"Since the place opened," Piper answers. "The last twelve years."

I sigh inwardly. Mendez might be right after all. If her landlord is involved, *Aladdin's Lamp* could be the site of mob activity without Piper's knowledge. This has the potential of being very bad.

Wyatt gives me an irritated look. He knows I'm thinking about Mendez, and he's not interested in my suspicions. He's got a determined light in his eyes. I've seen Wyatt Lawless like this before. He's in problem-solving mode. "Our marketing budget is razor-thin," he says. "*Aladdin's Lamp* is getting some buzz with restaurant industry insiders, but you aren't doing anything to attract the public. We'll need to get you some exposure."

Help her first, Owen, I rebuke myself. *Investigate the landlord later.* We fall silent, trying to think of a solution to our problems. "Wait a minute," I say slowly, as the seed of an idea forms in my mind. "What about Maisie's contest?"

Wyatt straightens. "That could work." He turns to Piper,

his lips curving into a smile. "How do you feel about being on TV?"

Piper:

"TV?" I stare at them, my mouth agape. "What are you talking about?"

Wyatt explains. "You've heard of Maisie Hayes, the food blogger?"

"Of course." Maisie's New York restaurant blog is very entertaining. She's witty and funny and she knows her food. I'm not the only one in the business who reads her blog every day.

"Well, Maisie is organizing a reality-TV-style contest for restaurants in Hell's Kitchen called *Can You Take the Heat?*. I can probably get you in, but the contest starts in a month, and we have a thousand things to do before then. It won't be easy."

No, it won't be easy. But Wyatt is right — we have no marketing budget. Given the constraints, this is probably our best option. I sit up, my spine tingling with excitement. I want to win, damn it. I want to show my parents that despite their best efforts to thwart me, I can succeed. "Yes." My voice comes out loud and enthusiastic, and I flush. *Well-behaved Southern women don't raise their voices.*

"I'm in," I say in a quieter tone. "Whatever you want to do, I'm in."

"Excellent," Wyatt says. "Let's get to work. Here's what we need to do."

An hour later, we have a plan. Several plans, actually.

First, we've decided to rename the restaurant. It's now

going to be called *Piper's*. "A bit vain, don't you think?" I ask Wyatt and Owen doubtfully. "Naming the place after myself?"

"People are going to flock here for your food, Piper," Owen says grandly. "Of course it has to be named after you."

I giggle, charmed by Owen's statement. We've made significant inroads into the bottle of vodka, and we're all feeling the effects. I'm tipsy. The alcohol plays a role in my light-headedness, but so does the relief of knowing I don't have to face this alone.

I've misjudged Owen and Wyatt, the same way they've misjudged me. Today feels like a renewal of sorts. *New beginnings.*

"Okay," I agree. "What kind of food should *Piper's* serve?"

"Not Middle Eastern," Wyatt says at once. "I love Middle Eastern food, but that's not your strength. Why on earth did your aunt decide to open *Aladdin's Lamp* anyway?"

"It's a family secret." I lean forward, lowering my voice to a whisper. I can't seem to stop smiling. "When she was in her twenties, she had an affair with a man from Egypt, but her parents found out and dragged her back home in horror. Years later, she opened the restaurant as a way to remember him."

I reach for the bottle to pour myself another shot, but Wyatt puts his hand over my wrist. "Pace yourself, Piper," he advises. He gets me a glass of water. "Drink up."

I frown at him. "Are you my mother?" I demand, my words slurring. "I'm not a child, you know."

"Trust me, Piper. I'm well aware of that fact." Wyatt's eyes gleam with an emotion I can't quite identify. His hand still remains on mine, and my body prickles with an unexpected heat. He's got nice eyes, Wyatt. The color of dark chocolate. A girl could gaze into them all night.

Oh. *Oh.*

I can feel myself sway toward him. For a moment, he watches me, sharp interest in his gaze, then he stiffens and pulls his hand away. My entire face flushes at his rejection. "So what should I cook, then?" I ask, my voice cool.

"Southern food," Owen replies promptly. "Fried chicken. Macaroni and cheese. Ribs. Soul food. That's your sweet spot and you know it. Why else do you have mac and cheese on your menu?"

"It's my most profitable dish." I stop to consider his words. *Oh my God.* They're totally right. I've been drowning in the weeds, and I've never stopped to think there might be clearer water ahead. "I am an idiot," I exclaim, shaking my head. "How did I not see that?"

Owen reaches out and ruffles my hair. "That's what we're here for," he grins. "To give you the benefit of our wisdom and experience."

God, they can be conceited. "Of course." I flutter my eyelashes at him. "Please, Owen," I mock. "Please tell me what to do. I'll do anything you say."

"Will you?" His blue eyes hold mine for just an instant, just long enough for me to feel a spark of heat. My imagination is throwing up one carnal image after another. Me on my knees in front of Owen as Wyatt watches. Owen's hand tangling in my hair, pulling me toward his crotch. Wyatt unbuttoning my shirt, his expression knowing.

You're not attracted to assholes, I remind myself. But that's precisely the problem. They aren't being assholes anymore, and because of that, I'm seeing what Wendy noticed right away. They're two very attractive men, and I haven't been on a date, let alone anything else, in a really long time.

Don't be an idiot, Piper, I scold myself. *They're your partners, nothing else.*

My pulse beats in my neck and I force words out through my dry throat. "You know what I mean."

Everything's frozen for an instant. It feels like anything can happen. The night is alive with possibility. My blood is racing, and my body feels heavy with desire. Do I dare act on it?

My mother's voice rings in my ear. Well-behaved Southern women *definitely* don't get into threesomes.

I pull back. "We'll also need to do something about this space."

There's a brief flicker of disappointment in Owen's eyes, gone before I even really register it. "I'll start keeping an eye on the auction lots," he says. "Let's see what we can get for cheap. First though, we'll need a new sign. I'll arrange for one tomorrow."

"I'll draw up a contract," Wyatt adds. "And though I'm not looking forward to it, I'll talk to Maisie."

"Why not?" The vodka's making me bold and curious. "Why don't you want to talk to her?"

"We used to date," he replies, his tone making it clear that I should change the topic. "It's not a big deal."

I don't know why that bothers me. Guys like Wyatt and Owen are hardly likely to be single. They're good looking and wealthy. In New York, where women outnumber men by a significant margin, they can pick and choose whoever they want. For all I know, they could be in relationships right now.

That thought depresses me even further. *Time to call it a night, Piper,* I tell myself, before I can allow myself to wallow further. Imaging a threesome with them is a pleasant fantasy, but allowing myself to think that it could happen is the most foolish thing I can do. We live in different worlds, and in any case, I have a restaurant to save.

"I have to go." I rise to my feet. "Let me know when the contract is ready."

They get up as well. Once again, they give me troubled looks. Stupid vodka. It's making me think of things that I've ignored for so many years now. It's making me realize how long it's been since I felt the weight of a man's body against mine, and it's making me yearn for their touch.

This is insane. I need to get out of here.

13

If you would be a real seeker after truth, it is necessary that at least once in your life you doubt, as far as possible, all things.

— RENE DESCARTES

Owen:

The next morning, my head's throbbing and my mouth is dry. The room sways and tilts around me.

And that's not even the worst of it.

Nothing happened, I console myself, though it wasn't for lack of trying. Last night, Piper was vulnerable and tipsy. Thankfully, no one had crossed the line, because it would've been a huge mistake. We don't take advantage of drunk women, and we don't sleep with people we're in business with. The lines get too tangled.

I make myself a cup of coffee and call Max Emerson. He

picks up on the second ring. "Owen Lamb," he says, an edge in his voice. "What a surprise."

I'm not a fan of Max Emerson. The kindest word I could use to describe him is sleazy. Though he wanted Wyatt and I to invest in his gastropub, he was extremely secretive about his operations, and a couple of times, he flat-out lied to us. "Max." It takes effort to sound neutral. "How've you been?"

"I can't complain, Owen." He still sounds pissed. "Great things are happening for *Emerson's* every day."

I very much doubt that. *Emerson's* is, at best, run of the mill. Max's chef is mediocre, and the menu is generic. About the only thing the place has in its favor is its location. I rub at my forehead and wish I had the good sense to formulate a plan before I called Emerson. "That's great to hear, Max."

"Yeah," he continues. "We're participating in *Can You Take the Heat?* and we're going to win. I'm sure you've heard of the contest. Yelp is going to put the winner on the front page of its website for three months. You guys are going to regret picking Piper Jackson instead of me."

My hackles rise. *Don't mention Piper's name,* I want to growl.

I have to say I'm surprised *Emerson's* is participating in Maisie's show. Wyatt's going to want to know that.

I make a snap judgement. I don't want to talk to this guy anymore. I'll find the information I'm looking for in other ways. "I heard the news," I lie. "I was calling to congratulate you on being selected." My tone hardens. "Unfortunately, you aren't going to win, Max. Piper Jackson's taking part in the contest as well. And we all know that when it comes to a contest between her and you, you're going to lose."

I hang up before he can respond, then I shake my head at my impulsiveness. Wyatt better be able to sweet talk Maisie into letting Piper into the show.

AFTER LAST NIGHT, I'm convinced Piper is clean, but I'm not sure about her landlord. Once I've showered, I head out toward *Aladdin's Lamp*. It's a little after nine in the morning, and I expect the place to be empty.

Sure enough, there's no one about.

There are things I learned in Dublin that I haven't let myself forget. I could pick the lock and let myself in, but there's nothing to see there. Instead, I slip into the narrow alleyway between Piper's restaurant and the building next door, and head to the back.

There are three possible ways a restaurant can be mixed up with the mob — money-laundering, drugs, and an illegal gambling ring. I have access to Piper's books, so I can rule out money laundering. My goal today is to search for any evidence of drugs or a gambling ring.

The alleyway smells of stale urine and rotting garbage. Though it's bright outside, this pathway is dim, the tall buildings on either side obstructing all sunlight. I walk slowly, looking for signs of drug activity, but nothing seems out of place.

Which leaves a gambling ring. I curse under my breath as I reach the dumpsters in the back of the building. Gamblers like the trappings of the good life — fancy Scotch and smuggled cigars from Cuba. If an illegal gambling ring is being run from Piper's restaurant, there'll be empty bottles in the trash.

Fucking Mendez, I think sourly. I hate rooting through garbage.

Five minutes later, I've rummaged through the waste and the recycle bins, and I've found nothing. I'm ready to give up when a voice speaks. "What do you think you're doing?"

I freeze, because the grey-haired man who asks the question is also holding a sawed-off shotgun, and it's pointed right at me.

Shit. This must be Piper's landlord.

I raise my hands up in the air, very slowly. "Hello," I say cautiously. "I'm Owen."

"Are you now?" His voice remains hard. "What are you doing in my dumpster?"

"Your dumpster?" I act as if I've just realized who he is. "Ah, you must be Piper's landlord."

He relaxes slightly, but the barrel of the gun stays fixed on me. "And who are you?"

"My name is Owen Lamb. I'm one of Piper's new partners."

He finally lowers the weapon. "Sorry about that," he says gruffly. "But you can never tell in this neighborhood. I'm Michael O'Connor."

What does he mean, you can never tell in the neighborhood? The crime rates in Hell's Kitchen aren't high. There's nothing that warrants pointing a gun at me. What is Michael O'Connor worried about?

Damn it. Each lead I follow seems to produce more questions than answers.

"No worries." I reach forward to shake his hand. "I appreciate you watching out for the place."

He nods curtly. "What were you doing back here anyway?" he asks. "This is a strange place to be hanging around in."

I search about for an excuse, cursing the vodka for the fuzziness in my brain. My head feels like a construction crew has taken a jackhammer to it. "Food wastage," I improvise. "I'm trying to get a handle of how much food we throw away."

He raises an eyebrow at my explanation. "By poking around the garbage? Odd way to go about it."

"Well," I shrug, not knowing what else to say. "I'm a very hands-on partner."

Michael O'Connor is staring at me. "You're an Irishman, aren't you, lad? I've lived here for forty years and I've never lost my accent. You neither, from the sound of it." His face scrunches into a puzzled frown. "Do I know you from somewhere? Your face looks really familiar."

Shit. *This time, I'm really in trouble.* Hell's Kitchen is filled with Irish immigrants, and Michael O'Connor could be working for the Westies. I'm the spitting image of my father. If he figures out who I am, I'm in danger.

Not just me. Everyone I care about could be hurt. The Westies demonstrated their ruthlessness seventeen years ago when they killed my mother and my sister as revenge for my father's betrayal.

I've done something really stupid by coming to Hell's Kitchen. I've put Piper and Wyatt in danger.

14

Better to get hurt by the truth than comforted with a lie.

— KHALED HOSSEINI

Wyatt:

When the sun streams into the bedroom, I wake up, my dick uncomfortably hard. My head is filled with images of Piper sandwiched between Owen and I, her head thrown back in abandon as we both touch her, tease her, pleasure her.

She's not that sort of girl, Lawless.

I throw off the covers and rise to my feet, anxious to banish the fantasies from my mind.

I've been attracted to Piper since the moment I met her, but until yesterday, I'd been able to dismiss her as a spoiled rich girl who was used to having everything handed to her.

Now, things are different. She's had to fight for her dreams, and I respect her for it.

It makes the attraction that much harder to resist.

Last night, her eyes were soft and shining. When she thanked us, there had been such a fervent note of gratitude in her voice that I found myself angry at all the people that have made her doubt herself. Piper's an excellent chef. Sebastian Ardalan would hire her in a heartbeat, and he's the pickiest fucking employer in the city. She should be ready to kick ass and take names.

Owen and I had walked her to her apartment. "Are you going to be okay?" I asked her when we got to her front door. "Is your roommate going to be home tonight?"

She had giggled at that. "If she does come back here, I'd question her sanity," she'd said with an impish grin. "She's got two hot men at her beck and call. Lucky Bailey."

Her roommate was in a threesome, and Piper wasn't freaking out? My cock had gone rock hard at that, and Owen and I had exchanged startled looks. Then Piper had swayed slightly, her eyes closing, and that had dashed my hopes of anything happening. "Thank you for believing in me," she'd whispered. "I won't let you down."

I'd felt like I'd been doused in cold water. I'd been trying to think of ways to get her naked, and she was just grateful she had allies. I felt like a louse. Owen and I had disengaged ourselves as quickly as we could.

It was probably for the best.

She needs us to save her restaurant. We can't make a pass at her under those circumstances. It wouldn't be right.

Speaking of saving her restaurant, I need to man up in a hurry. It's time to call Maisie.

"Maisie, how's it going? It's Wyatt."

We've exchanged a couple of polite emails since our

break-up nine months ago, but this is the first time we've talked. Maisie sounds surprised to hear from me. "What's up?"

I massage my temples as I consider my words. Our relationship ended on cordial terms, so I don't really need to tiptoe around her contest, but her rejection had wounded me. I should have never got involved with Maisie Hayes. She was too much of a good girl for someone like me.

"I need a favor."

"Sure," she says agreeably. "What is it?"

"I saw your blog post about the contest in Hell's Kitchen. I'd like to enter a restaurant."

"Oh." Her voice is curious. "One of your ventures?"

"Yes, it's a small restaurant called *Piper's*." Or will be as soon as we get the new sign ordered. "Owen and I just invested in the place."

"All restaurants that want to be on the show need to submit an application," she tells me. "The deadline has passed, but I'll make an exception for an old friend. Get me the details today, and I'll see what I can do."

"Thank you."

"No problem, Wyatt."

Maisie broke our relationship off because of my desire for kinky sex. I should have known things wouldn't work out. She was too concerned about her image, and a threesome would have been bad publicity.

After the break-up, I made myself a promise. I'm not going to look for anything serious anymore. I've tried to keep things casual. My needs are incompatible with anything real.

An image of Piper flashes in front of me, her blue eyes hazy with desire. Ruthlessly, I dismiss it. She's my partner. Nothing else.

15

Your only obligation in any lifetime is to be true to yourself.

— RICHARD BACH

Piper:

The next morning, my head still hurting from the vodka, my heart still stinging from last night's rejection, I call Wendy. "I need you," I tell her. "You're the most sensible person I know. Help me."

"If you really killed them, you need to give me a retainer," she quips, her voice amused. "What'd you do, Piper?"

"Not over the phone." I bang my head against the wall, once, twice, three times for luck. I'm such an idiot. I can't believe the way I threw myself at Owen and Wyatt last night. I need Wendy to slap some good sense into me.

"Do you have time to come by my office before you open?" she asks. "You can buy me a cup of coffee."

"Sounds good. See you in an hour."

"I ALMOST KISSED THEM."

Wendy's perfectly manicured eyebrow rises. "You did?" She sounds more curious than scandalized. "I thought you didn't like them."

"They were nice to me yesterday." Hearing those words spoken out loud, I wince. God, I sound pathetic.

Wendy looks intrigued. "Tell me everything, Piper," she orders. "Start at the beginning."

"Owen and Wyatt came into the restaurant last night to taste my signature dishes." I tell Wendy the entire story. How afraid I'd been that they would back away from their deal, the way they'd apologized for assuming the worst of me, our plans for the reality TV show, and finally, the moment where I almost kissed them. "Damn that vodka," I mutter. "Tell me something. I'm crazy, right?"

"In what way?"

I flush. "It's been a long time since I've been with a guy," I reply, looking down at the table. "And then there's Bailey with Daniel and Sebastian, and Gabby had that threesome, and all of a sudden, there was a little voice in my head that whispered, '*Why not me?*'"

To tell the truth, I can't even remember the last time I went on a date. Life has become all about work. Working three low-wage jobs to make enough money for culinary school, then slaving away in front of the stoves at *Aladdin's Lamp*. The idea of getting dressed to go out seems foreign to me.

You love what you do, I remind myself. *You love the process of creation, of seeing people enjoy your food.* Except the words feel like false comfort after the almost-possibility of last night.

"How long has it been?"

Trust Wendy to hone in on that little detail. "Five years," I whisper, my cheeks flaming.

She sits up straight. "Five years?" she repeats, her voice aghast. "You've been celibate for five years?"

"Will you keep your voice down?" I demand, annoyed. "I'm well aware of how much my life sucks. You think I want this? I work every evening of the week except Mondays. I start work at ten in the morning, and finish at midnight. What guy would want to date me?"

"Owen Lamb and Wyatt Lawless," she replies. "How did they react?"

I think back to last night. "There were a couple of moments where I thought they wanted me too," I admit. "But they didn't make a move."

"Still," she points out, "they're right there. All you have to do is reach out..."

Reach out and touch them. Kiss them. Feel their hands all over me, the press of their bodies against mine...

I set my coffee cup on the table and give Wendy a serious look. "Two guys? Can you imagine my mother's reaction?"

She shrugs dismissively. "Pardon my French, but your mother has a fucking kitten no matter what you do. You're an adult. You're allowed to do the things that make you happy. Running *Aladdin's Lamp*, kissing Owen and Wyatt, whatever you want."

I shake my head. "I don't think so," I say bleakly. "I know my weakness, Wendy. I'm terrible at standing up to my parents. I've always been terrible at it. I made one brave move in my life when I turned down Anthony and moved to New York for culinary school. I can't risk messing up with Wyatt and Owen. They are my partners, and they are investors in my restaurant. I'd be a complete idiot if I let anything happen."

"Maybe you're right," she says reluctantly. "You shouldn't sleep with your partners. Things can get ugly if it doesn't work out. Your focus should be on the restaurant." She smiles at me cheerfully. "There's a silver lining. When you win the contest and you're beating away customers at the door, you can always hire a proper sous-chef and start taking some time off. And then, you can date whoever you want."

Wendy's right.

I can't stop thinking about the look in Owen's eyes last night when he asked me if I would do anything he said. I can still feel Wyatt's palm over my wrist when he told me to pace myself.

Then, like a bucket of cold water, my mother's voice sounds in my head. *Well-behaved Southern women do not have threesomes.* Except she'd never say the word *threesome*, because even in her wildest dreams, I wouldn't do something so self-indulgent and wicked.

16

Coming together is a beginning. Keeping together is progress. Working together is success.

— Henry Ford

Piper:

The next month is hectic.

Wednesday, after talking to Wendy and resolving to keep things between Owen, Wyatt, and myself professional, I go to Wyatt's office and sign the contract. "Read the small print," he says, leaning back in his chair and giving me a dry look. "I don't want you to regret anything."

"I don't make the same mistakes twice," I reply, pouring over the contract carefully. "I make new ones."

He laughs. Once I've signed the documents, Owen joins us and the three of us look at restaurant signs. "Simple yet classy," Wyatt decrees. "That's going to be our brand."

We pick a design that fits our needs beautifully. The sign

itself arrives on Friday. The word *Piper's* is in italicized cream lettering on a dark grey background. It takes my breath away. It is *gorgeous*.

I watch a worker on a ladder take down the old faded *Aladdin's Lamp* sign, and put up the new one. I'm not embarrassed to admit there are tears in my eyes.

The day after that, someone arrives to replace the cracked glass in the front window, and a woman with curly brown hair shows up with planters filled with flowers. My restaurant transforms in front of me, going from looking faded and tired to warm and inviting.

It's difficult not to hug Wyatt and Owen, but I remind myself of my resolution.

New menus are printed on thick cream paper, tucked inside dark brown leather binders. I can't stop stroking them; I can't believe this is actually happening. It is with a huge smile on my face that I feed the worn *Aladdin's Lamp* menus into a shredder.

There is a metaphor here. I hope I'm destroying my old life in favor of a brighter future.

On Sunday night, after we've closed for the evening, Owen shows up with a drop cloth, brushes, painter's tape and three gallons of charcoal grey paint. "We can't afford painters," he says with a grimace. He's wearing faded khaki shorts and an old grey t-shirt. "So, we paint."

"Is Wyatt joining us?" I ask curiously. So far, whenever something needs to get done, the three of us have done it together. It feels strange that he isn't here.

Owen shakes his head. "Wyatt," he says, "does not deal well with chaos. I don't think he could cope with the mess we're going to make." He moves the tables together in one heap in the middle, away from the walls, then piles the chairs on top of them. "I lucked out and found some chairs in an auction. Good quality dark wood, and they were just seventy bucks each. They'll arrive sometime during the week."

I do some math in my head. "Three thousand five hundred dollars," I conclude.

"Add another two grand for cushions," Owen advises. "It's still a steal."

He's right, but I can't stop worrying about money. I give the paint a dubious look. "Will the room become too dark with this grey?"

"We'll update the lighting as well." He gives the cheap fluorescent lights a disgusted look. "Wyatt's taking care of that. He knows a guy."

"Wyatt knows a guy," I repeat. Every day they hand me multiple invoices so I can track our spending. It's nerve-wracking to watch them spend thousands of dollars without blinking an eye.

Owen gives me a reassuring look. "You have to spend money to make money," he says. "And let's be honest. A dump like *Aladdin's Lamp* isn't going to win *Can You Take the Heat?* But *Piper's?*" He winks at me. "I have it on good authority that the chef is magnificent. She's going to blow everyone away."

I'm warmed by his praise. Picking up a roll of painter's tape, I smile at him. "Let's do this."

There's a sharp knock at the door, and the handle turns. "We're closed," I start to shout out, then stop in surprise as Wyatt walks in. He's dressed casually as well, and he's holding two pizza boxes in his hand. "What are you doing here?"

"As tempting as it would be to leave the two of you to deal with this," Wyatt replies, gesturing to the pile of tables and chairs in the middle of the floor, "I decided that wouldn't be right. Piper, I assume you haven't eaten."

The aroma of the pizza makes my stomach rumble. Wyatt's right. The new sign and menu have been attracting more walk-in traffic. Over half our tables were full tonight, a first for me. I've been on my feet for hours, and I've had no time to grab a bite. "You are my hero," I tell Wyatt fervently, reaching for a slice. "Owen, give me a few minutes to inhale some pizza, then I'll help."

Owen sinks to the floor next to me. "There's no hurry," he says lazily. "We have all night and all day tomorrow to get this done. Wyatt, you didn't bring any beer, did you?"

Wyatt laughs. "What kind of friend would I be if I forgot the beer?"

He goes outside, then returns with his arms laden with shopping bags. Owen gets up to help him. "How much beer did you bring?"

"Tile," Wyatt explains succinctly. "I was worried that the grey paint would make the room look too dark, then I remembered the wallpaper and mirrored tiles and we had left over from *Alessandro's*."

My curiosity aroused, I peep in the bags Wyatt has brought. The wallpaper is a bright abstract red and yellow print. "We can tile the back wall," Wyatt explains. "And frame the wallpaper so it looks like art." He helps himself to a slice of pizza, and opens a can of beer. "It isn't fancy, but I think it'll work."

"It'll more than work." I laugh out loud in glee. "Wyatt, this is perfect. Thank you."

His gaze lingers on me. In a rush, all my desire comes hurtling back. *Stay away from them,* a sensible, practical voice warns me. *You're making too much progress to risk it all for one night of pleasure.*

But what a night it would be...

He clears his throat and breaks the spell. "You're welcome, Piper."

THE LAST FOUR weeks have been almost too good to be true. In thirty days, the restaurant has been completely transformed. It's gone from a faded dump to a jewel that shines and sparkles. The food's changed from hit-or-miss Middle Eastern to a contemporary Southern cuisine. Even Josef and Kimmie seem on board with the transition. Josef has shown up to work on time three days in a row, and yesterday, Kimmie didn't chew gum once.

It all changes on Thursday.

I should have known there'd be trouble when I mentioned to my parents that I had two new partners. But I'd been focused on saving the restaurant, and I'd failed to notice their reaction.

When I get into work Thursday morning, I find a notice waiting for me. It's from Grant & Thornton, the law firm that are the executors of Aunt Vera's will.

I read their letter with nerveless fingers. It states that they have reason to believe the terms of the will aren't being complied with. They're going to send an accountant to do a full audit of my books on Tuesday. And, if that's not enough, until the three year probationary period is over, I'll be expected to open my books for a monthly audit.

Damn it. This is nothing other than thinly disguised harassment. When we signed the paperwork to make Wyatt and Owen partners in my restaurant, I'd dotted my i's and crossed my t's, and I'd sent Grant & Thornton a copy of all the paperwork.

The timing couldn't be worse. Owen, Wyatt, and I have been spending every waking moment at *Aladdin's Lamp*, getting it ready for the contest. I've been cooking the new dishes we've concocted, again and again, until I can make them in my sleep. We've found a new meat supplier, we're auditioning two vegetable suppliers and we're getting new appliances in the kitchen. Next week is also the first round of the contest.

Already I'm stretched to the max. Now I have to deal with my parent's latest passive-aggressive move? I slump into a chair and rest my head on the table, and I struggle not to burst into tears.

17

Supreme excellence consists of breaking the enemy's resistance without fighting.

— Sun Tzu, The Art of War

Wyatt:

Owen and I have just walked into *Aladdin's Lamp* when my cellphone rings. I glance down at the display, but the caller id is blocked. Shrugging, I pick up. "This is Wyatt Lawless," I say, as Owen heads to the back to look for Piper.

"Hello, son."

I haven't heard my father's voice in twenty years.

Everything stops. I can't hear the honks of the cabs, or the rumbling from the subway under my feet. The bustle of Manhattan recedes into the background.

My palms are damp and my fingers white where I grip the phone. My pulse races. One thought dominates. *I can't have this conversation here. I can't be overheard.*

Pushing the door open, I go outside. Leaning against the brick wall, shaded by the newly installed blue and white awning, I take a deep breath. "What do you want?"

He responds to my question with one of his own. "Why don't you want to meet me, Wyatt?"

Why don't I want to meet him? *Is he fucking kidding me with this shit?* "Why would I want to meet you?" My voice is hard as steel, but my hands are shaking. "It's been twenty years. You think you can just waltz back into my life and pretend everything's fine?"

"I'm your father. You're my son."

"You forfeited the right to call me that when you walked out on mom and me."

"When was the last time you stepped foot into that house, Wyatt?" At my silence, he laughs grimly. "Can you really blame me for leaving? Your mother would rummage through the trash and take out every empty can I discarded. She wouldn't let me throw away anything. You remember the stacks of old newspapers in the living room, Wyatt? You remember the milk crates of old tin cans that lived on the couch? There was nowhere to cook a meal. No space to sit and drink a pint." His voice is heavy with self-pity. "One day, I reached breaking point. I couldn't take it anymore."

I want to hang up, but I can't. My fingers refuse to press the disconnect button. I keep listening, the words hammering into my brain, bringing back images of a past I've done my best to forget. Finally, when he stops talking to draw breath, I interrupt. "You abandoned a thirteen year old child when you left." The sun's beating down, but I'm chilled to the bone. "There's nothing you can say that will excuse that. I have nothing to say to you."

I end the call. For a very long time, I stare into the street, seeing but not registering the cars, the pedestrians, the rhythm of the city.

Finally, I rouse myself out of my stupor. My father is meaningless. I have a restaurant to fix.

But when I walk into the restaurant, I see Owen sitting at a table, gazing helplessly at the tears streaming down Piper's cheeks.

18

The best thing to hold onto in life is each other.

— AUDREY HEPBURN

Wyatt:

My heart twists painfully in my chest when I see Piper crying. I cross the room in long strides and pull up a chair next to her. "What's the matter, honey?"

Her shoulders shake with her sobs, but she doesn't reply. *What happened,* I mouth to Owen, who shakes his head. He doesn't know either.

It kills me to see her so upset. A wave of wrath for whoever caused this surges over me. I put my arms around her and pat her on her back, while Owen laces his fingers in hers. "Piper," I repeat. "Tell us what the problem is, and we'll fix it."

She feels so soft in my arms. Her hair smells like lavender and oranges, and it takes all the willpower I possess to keep from touching it, touching her. I'm bewildered by my emotions — I want to protect her and take care of her. I never want to see a tear in her eyes again.

She takes a deep breath, and shifts in my grip. I release her, jolted by the sense of loss I feel. "What happened?" I ask for the third time.

Owen wipes the tears away from her cheeks with his fingertips. "Please tell us, Piper." His expression reflects the helplessness I'm feeling. "We're here for you."

She attempts a watery smile and holds out an envelope. "This happened," she says, her voice catching in a hitch. "My parents have been at work."

I scan the letter quickly, and my lips tighten. Owen reads it when I'm done, and his face turns grim. "We can handle this," I soothe her. "We're not trying to hide anything."

"I know," she says quietly. "They're just looking for an excuse to control me."

She sounds as if she's given up. She's been strong for so long, fighting to forge her own destiny. Her parents don't want her to be happy — they just want to run her life.

"Parents should love and support their children," I say quietly, placing my hand over hers. "But sometimes they don't. I should know. My mother is a hoarder."

Owen looks up, startled. I never talk about my childhood.

Only a few minutes ago, I walked outside so Piper and Owen wouldn't overhear my conversation with my father, but it feels strangely liberating to reveal the truth. I've been living under the crushing weight of a secret for a very long time.

"My father left us when I was thirteen," I continue. "When I was growing up, I learned quickly that my house wasn't like the homes of my schoolmates, but I couldn't risk asking anyone for help."

"Wyatt." She squeezes my hand tightly. "I'm so sorry."

"I'm not looking for your pity."

She flinches, and I'm filled with shame. That came out harsher than I intended. "I'm sorry," I apologize. "I didn't mean to snap at you." My lips turn up in a small smile. "You feel betrayed by your parents. I can understand that feeling."

Owen rests his hand on her thigh. "Don't worry about your books. We'll handle your accountant. You just worry about cooking."

She draws a shuddering breath. "I'm sorry," she says.

"For leaning on your friends?" I brush a strand of hair back from her face. "You should never be sorry about that."

She gives us a tremulous smile. "I have to stop letting my parents get to me," she admits. "What about you, Owen? What are your parents like?"

Owen:

What are your parents like, Owen?

How do I even begin to answer that question? Wyatt has bad memories of his childhood; I have only happy memories of mine. My mother laughed a lot. My father bought my mother flowers every Sunday because he loved her and wanted to make sure he always showed it.

"They're dead."

Piper draws a deep breath, probably to say something like '*I'm so sorry*'. Before she does, I continue, almost blurting out the words. "They were killed."

Her expression turns shocked. It's Wyatt's turn to look at me strangely.

"What happened?" she asks, then she flushes. "I'm sorry. That was nosy of me. If you'd rather not talk about it, I understand."

I shake my head. "No, it's fine. It was seventeen years ago."

I can feel the calluses on Piper's hand, the cuts and burns that a chef earns, almost a badge of honor in the profession. The rest of her is soft. There's a gentleness about Piper and a kindness that is so much a part of who she is. Sitting here, holding her hand, with Wyatt on the other side is almost enough to fill the void that was left when my parents and sister were killed. *Almost.*

"My parents ran a restaurant in Dublin. In those days, the gangs were a lot more powerful than they are today. The Westies decided they wanted to use our restaurant as a base for their various dealings."

I pause to draw a breath. When I first came to America, Mendez had arranged therapists for me, but my grief had been too close to the surface, and I hadn't been ready to heal. I hadn't wanted to find peace when my entire family lay dead. My happiness would have been a betrayal.

"My da didn't like it, but he didn't have a choice." They'd distributed heroin from the back and they ran an illegal gambling ring after hours. That was why I knew exactly what to look for in Piper's back yard. "One day, someone got shot outside our restaurant. My father saw it happen, and he agreed to testify in court."

"My ma was afraid of the mob. Her father and brother were low-level members; she'd seen the brutality up close. But my father wanted to do the right thing." I swallow. "The night before he was to take the stand, a gunman walked into the hotel where the police had hidden them, and he shot them. My mother, my father, and my baby sister."

"Owen," she whispers. She pulls me into a hug and envelops me in her warmth. "I'm so sorry." In her embrace, the pain lifts, and I feel something I haven't felt in seventeen years. Peace.

I could stay there forever. It is such a tempting vision. I could tell Mendez to fuck off. I could help Piper win the contest. I could...

Yeah, Lamb, what? You think Piper wants to get involved with Wyatt and you? You think she's interested in your kinky shit?

Her breasts press against my chest. I fight the urge to run my hand along her curves, to cup those firm globes, to bend my mouth against her lips. "We should get moving," I mutter. "We need to open for lunch in thirty minutes."

Wyatt makes a strained sound of assent. Piper's hand is still laced in his, and he's made no move to free himself.

This is a very bad idea.

This is a worst idea in the world.

My fingers move of their own volition. I cup her chin in my hands and I lean in, so close to her face. I brush my lips against hers in a soft, fleeting kiss.

Her eyes meet mine. There's confusion in her expression, but there's also desire, and it's that desire that has my heart hammering in my chest. I move my hand over the back of her neck and draw her in again, and this time, when I kiss her, she kisses me back with a passion that takes my breath away.

She tugs at Wyatt's hand, drawing him closer. Wyatt makes an indistinct sound of need, before leaning in. He presses a kiss against her cheek, and she turns toward him, her expression tentative. "Piper," he mutters. "You are like a drug in my veins."

Their lips meet in a slow, soft kiss. I watch, my dick hardening. I want to drag her out of here, take her to the nearest horizontal surface, pull off her pants and dive into her.

Wyatt's eyes are glazed with heat. His hands move up to cup her breasts over her shirt.

Just then, the front door opens with a squeak. "I'm sorry I'm late," Josef says loudly as he walks in. "The stupid train was so fucking slow."

The three of us pull apart. Piper jumps to her feet and rushes to the kitchen. Her face is flushed and her lips are swollen. Josef looks at Wyatt and me with curiosity. "How's it going?" he asks, his voice belligerent.

Wyatt nods curtly. "You're late."

That shuts him up. "I'll go help Chef Jackson," he says, slipping away.

Wyatt exchanges a look with me. "What just happened?" he asks, his voice dazed.

I don't know. *I have absolutely no idea.*

19

If you are not too long, I will wait here for you all my life.

— Oscar Wilde

Piper:

I work through the lunch service, my brain a seething mass of confusion.

This wasn't the same as the night with the vodka. Then I could have blamed the alcohol. Today? It's early in the morning. The only person responsible for my behavior is me.

I want them.

I sauté, fry, and bake on auto-pilot, powering through one ticket after another. After about an hour, I hear someone come into the kitchen. I lift my head up to tell Kimmie that her order isn't ready, but it isn't Kimmie. It's Owen.

"Hey Piper," he says, his expression wary. "The vegetable vendor is here. Do you want to talk to him?"

The look on his face makes my insides twist. I don't want things to be weird with the three of us because of my impulsiveness. Their friendship has become really important to me. "I do," I tell him, wiping my hands on my apron and untying it. "I'll be right out. Josef, can you and Kevin manage in here for about twenty minutes?"

We've been much busier at the restaurant. As the money flows in, I've increased Kevin's hours. Today, he's working both the lunch and dinner shifts. He looks up now as he hears his name mentioned, and grins cheerfully. "We've got it, Chef."

Josef nods as well. "Nothing we can't handle," he agrees.

I follow Owen out. "Josef's work ethic seems to have improved," he remarks quietly as we walk to the front.

"Yeah, I've noticed that too." I seize on the topic as a way to avoid the awkwardness between us. "The changes around here have been good for him. Just as well," I quip dryly, "since I can't afford to buy him out."

"Yet." He squeezes my shoulder. "It won't be long, Piper Jackson, before you take the city by storm."

There's a lump in my throat as I hear the confidence in his voice. *What are you doing, Piper? Are you willing to lose this friendship for a night of pleasure?*

Wyatt's still sitting at the same table we kissed at, talking to a grey-haired guy in a checked shirt. "Ah, here's Chef Jackson," he says, as we walk up. "Piper, this is Duncan Bright. He runs a cooperative that works with several farms in the state."

"Mr. Lawless tells me you're looking for locally sourced food," Duncan says. "We supply with several restaurants in Manhattan, including some of Lawless and Lamb's other properties."

Duncan Bright's prices are reasonable, and he comes

highly recommended by Wyatt and Owen. We quickly hammer out a deal. When Duncan leaves, I rise as well. "I should get back to the kitchen." I avoid looking at Owen and Wyatt. It's too awkward.

"Sure," Wyatt starts to say, then I hear a familiar voice exclaim. "Oh my God, Piper, look what you've done to the place!"

It's Wendy. She comes up to us, a big smile on her face. "Bailey's been raving about how amazing the place looks," she says. "I had to come check it out." She notices Wyatt and Owen for the first time. "Hi," she introduces herself, "I'm Piper's friend Wendy. You must be Wyatt Lawless and Owen Lamb."

They get to their feet politely. "Good to meet you." Owen flashes her a grin. "Are you part of the mysterious Monday night drinking club?"

She laughs. "It's officially called the Thursday Night Drinking Club. We just meet on Mondays because that's when Piper can make it." She's looking around. "Look what you've done," she says, her voice admiring. "Piper, this is brilliant."

"I couldn't have done it without Owen and Wyatt." It isn't just Josef's passion that's been rekindled as a result of the changes here. It's mine as well.

I show Wendy around. Then a group of eight people walk through the door and I groan. "I better get back to the kitchen to make sure things are under control. Give me about fifteen minutes?"

"Sure," Wendy says. "I can chat with Owen and Wyatt in the meanwhile."

Wyatt:

Wendy's smile switches off the instant Piper heads back to the kitchen, and she glares at us. "So," she says, her voice heavy with insinuation, "the two of you and Piper."

I'm not going to pretend I don't know what she's talking about. Thoughts of the three of us have been on my mind ever since I met Piper. "You don't approve of us."

"I don't know what I think of you yet," she corrects, her voice steely. "Here's what I do know. Piper's the nicest person in the world. She's good-natured, she's kind, and she's hard-working. She's practically perfect, but she has one flaw. She's hopeless at advocating for herself. Her parents treat her like crap, and she lets them walk all over her. And I'm not sure you guys are much better. You treated her like dirt."

"Treated. Past tense. We were wrong."

She continues as if I haven't spoken. "She's vulnerable. Then you guys show up and wave a magic money wand, and all her problems are solved. Tell me how it's right that you get involved with her."

"You're misjudging us," Owen says quietly. His fingers are balled into fists at his side. "We would never hurt Piper."

Wendy is relentless. "She hasn't been on a date in five years." Her dark eyes pierce us. "She should be treated like a princess. She slaves away in front of a hot stove all day. She deserves flowers and wine and chocolate, and she needs someone who will stick around. She is entitled to more than a quickie."

"Why are you telling us this?" I keep my voice even, though I'm reeling with shock on the inside. *Piper hasn't been on a date in five years?*

"Because she's my friend and I love her. If you're going to stick around, then make your move. But if you're just looking for easy pussy, think again. You hurt my friend and I will hunt you down and make you regret the day you were born."

I like Wendy. She's like a protective mama bear. "You have nothing to worry about." I meet her gaze squarely. "Whatever happens, we have no intention of hurting Piper."

She gets to her feet. "Tell Piper I had a work emergency."

As she turns away, I notice her handbag is the same color as the one Piper was carrying. "Nice bag," I tell her.

Her voice is as dry as kindling. "Isn't it? I bought it from her a month back, when she wasn't sure if she could make rent, and she couldn't come to the two of you for help."

When Owen and me had looked at her and assumed the worst.

"She has us now," I reply. "We aren't going anywhere."

She makes a noise that's half-snort, half-scoff, and leaves. Once she's gone, I turn to Owen. "Piper hasn't been on a date in five years?"

"So I heard." His expression is unsettled.

"I think we should ask her out properly, not grope her in her restaurant."

Owen gives me a searching look. "You heard what Wendy said. You can read between the lines. Piper doesn't do casual sex."

"I'm not looking for casual sex." That's always been my problem. I have a void in me that I ache to fill. The problem isn't that I want too little. It's that I want too much.

"Okay." Owen takes a deep breath. "Me neither. But in case you haven't noticed, there's three of us. A ménage is a one-time thing for most people. You, more than anyone else, should know that."

"One step at a time." I lift my head up in greeting as Piper walks back to us. "Hello again."

"What happened to Wendy?" Piper asks, sitting down. Her hand massages her neck. "God, what a day. It almost makes me long for the days when the only people eating here were the two of you."

I chuckle. "Here, let me." I knead at the tight knots of stress in her neck. "You're working too hard. We should hire a couple of line cooks to help you out. We can afford it."

"Once the auditor comes and goes." Her voice is anxious. "I don't want to give them any openings."

"Shh. Relax." My fingers keep working to ease her tension.

"Wyatt, what are you doing?" she whispers.

"Don't overthink this, Piper."

"I kissed *both* of you," she blurts out. She's holding herself erect, her body language betraying her agitation.

I'm a little surprised. Part of me was prepared for her to pretend that it didn't happen. "Do you want us to forget about it?" My heart beats faster in my chest as I wait for her answer.

A long moment of silence passes. "No," she says finally. Her cheeks go pink as she looks at both of us. "You weren't weirded out by what I did. Why?"

Owen is more direct than I am. "Should we have been?" he asks her.

"Piper," I say, taking her hand in mine. "We're not going to pressure you, and we're not going to judge you. Tell us what you want."

She hesitates, biting her lower lip. Finally she takes a deep breath and appears to reach a conclusion. "I want you. Both. Does that make me a pervert?"

"*Pervert* is such a strong word," Owen replies calmly. "The two of us want you as well. But not now, and not like this." He reaches forward and laces his fingers in hers. "Have dinner with us Sunday night."

"I work Sunday nights."

"I know. Come over once you're done."

"Why not today?" Her expression is curious, careful.

"We don't want to rush you into anything," I reply. "Right now, our hormones are raging, and we aren't thinking coherently."

"Oh." Her face falls. "I understand. You want time to change your mind."

"No," Owen cuts in. "We've wanted you from the first day we saw you. We aren't going to change our minds."

"Oh," she says again, this time in a different note, on a sharp intake of breath. "Sunday night?"

"It's a date."

Though my voice sounds confident, I can't help remembering the sadness I'd felt when my relationship with Maisie had ended. I hope I can keep from repeating the same mistake with Piper.

20

Ponder and deliberate before you make a move.

— Sun Tzu, The Art of War

Owen:

"Here's the list." I push the piece of paper toward Mendez. "Three of them are clean, including Piper Jackson's place."

We're at the same McDonald's we met at last time. Mendez eats a breakfast sandwich while I sip my coffee. I'm in a peculiar mood this morning. Wyatt and I had meetings all afternoon yesterday, so we couldn't linger at the restaurant.

In any case, Wyatt's right. We work with Piper. We need to give her plenty of space. The last thing I want her to think is that our investment in her restaurant is dependent on whether she sleeps with us.

"This is great." Mendez stares at the list of names. "What about *Emerson's*? And *The Pear Tree?*"

"I don't know." I take a deep breath. For the first time, I want out. I need to keep a low profile in Hell's Kitchen; I can't afford to snoop around for Mendez. At any time, Michael O'Connor might figure out who I am, and if he's connected to the Westies, shit will hit the fan.

My priorities have changed. I've promised to help Piper win *Can You Take The Heat?*. I've told her I'll make her restaurant profitable. This is not the time for me to be distracted by Mendez's dirty work. "I can't sort it out. You're on your own."

He stops eating and looks up. "Why's that, Lamb?" he asks, his voice hard.

I bristle at his tone. "I didn't realize I needed to offer you an explanation."

He notices the steel in my expression. "Suit yourself," he shrugs. "You're not obligated to help me. I can find someone else to help me track Cassidy."

I freeze. Seamus Cassidy was the man who ordered the hit on my family. What's he doing in New York? He's supposed to be doing life in an Irish prison. "Cassidy is out of jail?"

Mendez smiles mockingly. "I thought you didn't want to get involved. Didn't you just tell me that?"

"Fuck you," I growl. "You know things are different if Seamus Cassidy is back, and that's exactly why you brought him up. Don't think I don't know how you operate, Mendez."

He doesn't deny it. Instead he pushes the list back to me. "I'll be in touch."

∿

Wyatt:

In the shock of kissing Piper, I'd almost forgotten my father's phone call, but the next morning, he's the first person I think of. I dial Stone Bradley. "My father made contact yesterday," I say bluntly as soon as he answers.

"Hello to you too, Mr. Lawless. Did he show up at work again?"

"No, he called me."

"Hmm. Did you have a phone number for him?"

"No." I run my hand through my hair in frustration. A week after I hired him, Bradley produced an address for my father, but I haven't acted because I don't know what to do. I want him gone, but this isn't the movies. I can't break his kneecaps because I don't want to talk to him.

"The studio apartment in Brooklyn he's staying at," I think out loud. "Whose name is on the lease? Can we evict him?"

Bradley answers immediately. "I'm going to recommend against it." He clears his throat. "Let me be honest. Your dad is a washed-up drunk. Your best option is to meet him and pay him off. If you go on the offensive, who knows what he might do?"

"No." My tone brooks no opposition. "There will be no pay off. There will be no meeting. I will give my father nothing."

"The past still haunts you." Bradley's voice is sympathetic. "I can relate to the desire to forget your childhood."

I rise to my feet. I'm done with this conversation, done with Bradley, done with being analyzed. "Get him evicted," I snarl into the phone.

I should tell Bradley to put a tail on my father and have

someone keep an eye on his movements. But I'm too angry, and I'm not thinking straight.

21

Never above you. Never below you. Always beside you.

— WALTER WINCHELL

Piper:

I go through the rest of the week on auto-pilot. Though I exchange emails and texts with Owen and Wyatt about a million little details, I don't see them. It doesn't take a genius to figure out what they're doing. They're giving me space.

I don't want space, and I don't want to be logical. I want passion.

Saturday night, when I get home after a long shift at the restaurant, Bailey's sitting on the couch, reading something. Jasper's at her side, half-asleep as usual. "Hey," I say, surprised to find my roommate at home. "How come you aren't with your guys?"

"Because I need to work," she replies with a grimace.

"I've got an inch-thick stack of papers to read, and I'm too easily distracted when I'm with Daniel and Sebastian.

I grin, taking in the huge arrangement of pink flowers on the coffee table. Roses, lilies, and daisies spill out of a clear glass vase. "They sent you flowers because they couldn't bear you being away for one night? That's both sweet and excessive."

Her eyes dance with amusement. "They aren't for me."

"What?"

"The flowers. They aren't for me." Her smile widens to a grin. "Anything you want to tell me, Piper?" she teases. "Who's sending you flowers? My money's on those hot partners of yours."

I cross over to the bouquet, and search for a card. There's a small white envelope tucked among the blossoms. My heart beats in my chest as I rip it open. It's been a very long time since someone's sent me flowers.

You're special to us.

"What does it say?" Bailey's voice is curious. "Come on. Spill."

I hand her the note silently. I don't know what I thought it would say. Some flirty reference to tomorrow night. Not this. Tears well up in my eyes.

"Are you going to cry?" Bailey sits up, alarmed. "Shit. Piper, sweetie. Come here. I'll find vodka."

That makes me laugh. "No vodka," I say, holding up my hand. "Vodka is what started this." I plop myself on the couch, and scratch Jasper behind the ears.

"So Wyatt and Owen think you're special. Special in a *Piper's A Very Talented Chef* kind of way?"

"Special in an *I Have A Date Tomorrow Night With Them* kind of way."

"Oh." She digests that silently. "Both of them?"

I nod.

"Oh," she repeats. "Are you going on this date?"

I exhale. "I think so." Bailey's in a threesome herself. I thought she'd be more enthusiastic. "You aren't judging me, are you?"

She shakes her head immediately. "Of course not," she says, biting her lip. "Okay, this is going to come out wrong no matter how I word it, so I'm just going to blurt it out. Are you sure you're up to this?"

"What exactly are we talking about?" I ask cautiously. "Because if you are going to talk sex positions, I'm going to need that vodka first."

Her lips twitch. "No sex positions, I promise. I'm talking about people's reactions when they find out." She makes a face. "Did I tell you Daniel's sister and her fiancé broke up because Daniel, Sebastian, and I are in a threesome?"

"Really?" I look up, shocked by her revelation. "When did this happen?"

"A week ago." She waves aside my concern. "It's a good thing. Graham was a douchebag. But Piper, be honest with me. Can you see yourself introducing Wyatt and Owen to your parents?"

God no.

She interprets my expression correctly. "I thought so," she says. "It all seems like fun and games, but people can get hurt. The world is not used to three people in a relationship."

"I think you're getting way ahead of yourself here." Jasper's fur feels warm and soft under my fingers, and he purrs as I pet him. "I'm not getting into a relationship with them. I'm just going to dinner."

Bailey gives me a knowing look. "Just be careful. There's

no shortage of guys in New York. You don't have to pick something so complicated."

I'd like to be angry at Bailey, but she's absolutely right. I can't see myself introducing Wyatt and Owen to my parents. Even imagining their reaction makes me shudder. *Well-behaved Southern women definitely do not date two men at the same time.*

Then I look once again at the card in my hand. *You're special to us.*

"You know something, Bails?" My voice is soft, but I'm more certain than I've ever been. "I'm not good at standing up to my parents, and I admit that the idea of telling them makes me want to throw up. But you know what I'm sure of? I'm going on that date tomorrow night."

Bailey grins widely. "In that case, in the immortal words of my roommate, go forth and fornicate."

It's pouring rain Sunday evening. It's a good thing the restaurant is almost empty because I'm so nervous that my hands shake as I cook. A couple of times, I almost send out a dish without seasoning it. Finally, Josef's had enough. "Chef Jackson," he says exasperatedly, "You should leave early and get some rest."

Rest is not what I'm planning on getting, my friend.

"Do you mind?"

He shakes his head. "There's just three tables here," he says. "We're less than an hour from closing. We're done for the night."

I don't protest. I don't want to show up at Owen's condo smelling like fried chicken. If I leave now, I'll have time to go home, shower and change into something sexy.

I can't believe I'm actually going on a date.

With two guys, a voice inside me whispers. *Slut.*

A wonderfully hot shower later, I'm calmer. I know Owen and Wyatt well enough to know that nothing will happen if I don't want it to. For the moment, I've even silenced the condemning voice in my head. I dress in a purple sundress that's been pushed all the way to the back of my wardrobe, and I head out.

Even though it's stopped raining, I opt to take a cab to Owen's building. I've been on my feet all day, and I'm fighting exhaustion. *This is why you don't date,* I remind myself. But I can't stop the prickle of excitement skittering up my spine.

Owen's building is a five-story brick mid-rise in the Upper West Side, with a bakery at street level. I look around for an entrance to the residences upstairs, but can't find it. Fishing out my phone, I call him.

He answers on the first ring. "Don't tell me you've changed your mind, Piper."

"I'm downstairs," I tell him. "I just can't figure out how to get in."

"I'll be right there." In two minutes, a door next to the bakery entrance opens, and Owen comes out. "There you are," he says in greeting, his eyes heating up as he takes me in. "You look great."

My insides tighten. "You're just saying that because I'm not wearing chef's whites," I quip, trying to ease the butter-flies in my stomach.

Perhaps he senses I'm nervous, because he smirks in a very familiar way. "You're probably right," he agrees. "Come on in."

There's an elevator, thank heavens. Owen punches in the

button for the top floor, and we're whisked up. "Penthouse?" I tease. "That's fancy."

He chuckles. "I like my peace and quiet. There's just two apartments on the top floor."

"Your neighbor isn't a drummer then?" That's not the brightest thing to say. In my defense, I haven't been on a date in years.

He gives me a surprised look. "My neighbor's Wyatt. I thought you knew that."

I shake my head as the elevator doors open into a small hallway with two doors on either end. Owen turns right and pushes a door open. "Here we are."

"Wow." I stop in my tracks as soon as I walk in, and look around. Owen's apartment is spacious and colorful. There are windows everywhere. The walls are covered with contemporary art. A grey sectional dominates the living space, accented by red and cream cushions. "This is not what I expected."

"What did you expect?" he asks, quirking an eyebrow at me.

"I thought it would be more monochromatic."

He laughs. "That's Wyatt's place you're describing. I'm sure he'll give you the tour at some point. Since the rain's stopped, I thought we'd eat outside."

"Outside?"

"Wyatt and I have exclusive access to the roof. Come on." He leads the way to a balcony, and we climb up a metal staircase to the rooftop patio.

The scene that greets me takes my breath away. There are candles everywhere. A vase on the coffee table overflows with flowers. Music is playing through hidden speakers, something soft and melodious, and Wyatt's sitting on the L-shaped couch, holding a bottle of beer in his hand. He rises to his feet as I approach. "I'm glad you could make it." His dark eyes hold me captive.

I shift my weight from one foot to another. I'm nervous all over again. "This is very lovely," I stammer.

Wyatt's lips twitch. "You're being formal again, Piper. I thought we were past that. Would you like a drink? Champagne?"

Flowers, candles, music, and champagne. I'm a little overwhelmed. "Yes please." I sit on the sectional with a sigh of relief, kicking off my shoes.

"Long day?" Owen hands me a flute of champagne, and sets down a tray of cheese, crackers and olives on the table.

I snag a piece of Cheddar and munch on it as I reply, focusing on work as a way to avoid thinking about the night ahead. "Lunch was busy. Dinner, not so much. The weather kept people at home."

He sits down on the other side of me. "I'm not surprised, it rained cats and dogs."

I take a sip of the excellent champagne, sighing in pleasure. Today was a scorcher, hot and humid, but the thunderstorm has cooled the air. As I drink the champagne, I sink back in my seat, finally allowing myself to relax. Wyatt pats his lap. "Put your feet here," he orders.

"Why?"

He rolls his eyes. "Obviously, I want to torture you by tickling your feet," he says dryly. "I'm going to give you a foot massage, Piper."

"Foot massages lead to sex." Those words escape my lips before I can stop them. I clasp my hand to my mouth in horror, but it's too late. "Damn it, I wasn't supposed to say that out loud."

Owen chuckles. Wyatt is struggling not to laugh. "I promise you," he says solemnly, "that my intentions are pure as snow. You've had a long day on your feet. I'm trying to ease the ache."

The ache that demands to be eased isn't in the balls of my feet.

"Piper." Wyatt's gaze is steady. "I'm not going to deny that I'm hoping you'll spend the night." He glances at Owen. "We both are."

"But," Owen says, picking up where Wyatt left off, "if you don't want that, then we'll just eat dinner. You've been working far too hard. Take some time off. Relax. Eat a meal someone else made for you."

As Owen speaks, Wyatt's fingers knead away at my feet. His hands are firm, his touch sure. He works on me until I'm limp and relaxed. "Thank you," I murmur.

"You're welcome." His eyes linger on my face. "Shall we eat?"

OWEN HAS MADE a shepherd's pie and salad. Both dishes are delicious. "Classic Irish comfort food," he says, with a grin. "It's a little intimidating cooking for you, Piper."

"Are you kidding?" I pause, my fork poised in mid-air. "I wish someone would cook for me every day. This is delicious. You made this?"

He nods. "My parents owned a pub in Dublin," he says, his expression nostalgic. "As soon as I was old enough to reach the counter, my ma put me to work."

"My mother hated when I entered the kitchen," I confess. "Cooking was for staff. Wyatt, do you cook?"

He shakes his head. "I survive on microwave meals."

There's obviously more to that story. Wyatt works in the restaurant industry. I've never met someone in the business who didn't cook to some degree or the other. "How come?"

He doesn't meet my gaze. "I don't do well with messes."

Of course. I've put my foot in my mouth. I've seen Wyatt's office, neat to a fault. He's always impeccably dressed. If I go to his apartment, I'm willing to bet that there won't be one item out of place. All in response to the way he grew up.

Time to change the topic. I shift the conversation to *Can You Taste The Heat?*. The first round is next week. Yelp has already featured each participating restaurant on their website, and has invited customers to check us out. Like most reality TV contests, the winning restaurant will be chosen based both on popularity and the judges' opinion. "Do you know when the judges are coming to eat?" I ask Wyatt.

"Thursday," he replies. "But the public can vote until noon on Saturday."

I nod in understanding. I have to be on my A-game all three days. I'm ready for the challenge.

We wrap up dinner and Wyatt refills my glass of champagne. The night air is cool. Up here, I can still hear the sounds of the city, but I feel removed from the hustle and bustle. A breeze blows, and goosebumps break out on my skin. "Are you cold?" Wyatt asks, his voice low and warm. He moves closer to me, while Owen gets up to turn on the electric fireplace. "Would you like us to warm you, Piper?"

This is the moment of truth.

My hands tremble. "I've never done something like this before."

They stay silent, waiting for me to continue. Owen's thigh brushes against mine, the contact making me shiver. Underneath my dress, my nipples harden.

"I don't have a lot of experience with men. I'm not very adventurous about sex."

"What do you want, Piper?" Owen's voice caresses my soul. "Do you want to be adventurous tonight?" His fingers trail up my bare arm.

It seems safer to confess my desires at night. Thoughts tumble out in the dark, things I wouldn't dare say in the brightness of daylight. I can't look at their faces. "I'm not here because I want a threesome."

Owen's fingers stop their wandering. Both of them go very still. Their eyes are wary, watchful.

"I never wanted a threesome," I correct myself. "I never wanted two guys to take me at the same time. But..." I swallow the lump in my throat and force myself to continue. "I'm here because I want you. Wyatt and Owen. I have fantasies about the two of you." I place my hand on Wyatt's thigh. "I imagine the two of you touching me, and I can't stop wondering what it would feel like."

Wyatt's worried expression vanishes, and an understanding look fills his face. "You're still nervous."

I bite my lower lip. "I haven't had anal sex before," I admit, grateful that they can't see me blush in the dark. "I don't want things to tear."

Owen snorts. "Give us some credit, Piper."

Wyatt exchanges a glance with Owen. "Piper," he says soothingly. "Relax. Take a sip of your drink."

That's a good idea. I do as he says. "I'm sorry," I mutter, embarrassed by how naive I sound. "I should probably go."

"If you'd like," Wyatt says calmly. "Or you can stay, and we can explore. Will you play a game with us?"

"A game?" My voice comes out in a squeak.

"A game." Owen smiles at me, a gleam in his eyes "I'll ask you a question, and you answer. Yes or No."

"I don't understand."

"Let me demonstrate." He takes the glass from my hand, and sets it down on the coffee table. "Piper, may I kiss you?"

"Here?" I look around. The buildings that surround us are the same height, and it's extremely unlikely that we can be seen by anyone.

"Here," Owen says. "Yes or no, Piper?"

"Yes." I raise my eyes to meet his. "Yes, I want you to kiss me."

Owen's hand wraps around the back of my head and tugs me nearer. His lips are warm and soft against mine. He threads his fingers through my hair, and his tongue teases at the seam of my lips until I soften and part my mouth. His touch is light and teasing, but I can sense the depth of his need, and it's every bit as raw and powerful as my own. I lose myself in his kiss.

Through the haze in my brain, I feel Wyatt's touch at my back. "May I unzip your dress, Piper?" he asks.

We're *outside.* I've never done something this daring before. "Can anyone see us?"

"No." Wyatt is quick to reassure me. "We can't be seen up here. But," he says, with a trace of amusement in his tone, "You'll have to keep your voice down if you don't want to be heard."

There's no point pretending that this isn't what I came here for. I don't want to be coy. Tonight, I want to *feel.*

"Yes," I say clearly. "Please unzip my dress, Wyatt."

Wyatt makes quick work of it. The dress falls to my waist, and my pink lace bra comes into view. Owen growls in pleasure. His eyes are heated as he looks at me. "So beautiful."

Wyatt presses kisses down the curve of my spine, his hands caressing the sides of my breasts. I hold my breath as his thumbs near my erect nipples, but he refuses to touch them. Owen watches my reaction, his nostrils flared. "You like this, don't you, Piper? Knowing that you have the two of us in the palm of your hand?"

They can have anyone they want. *It's surreal that they want me.*

Owen gives me one final kiss, then he pushes my shoulders back against the couch. "She's lovely, isn't she, Wyatt?"

Oh God. They're *discussing* me as if I'm not even here, and it's turning me on. I squirm in my seat. I can't believe how aroused I'm getting.

Wyatt trails a finger over my nipple. His touch is light and teasing. I whimper in frustration. *Harder,* I want to scream. *Please touch me properly.* But it's taken all the courage I possess to come here tonight, and I'm not bold enough to ask for what I need.

"I want to taste you," Owen rasps. "Yes or no, Piper?"

"Oh God yes," I almost sob out. "I thought you'd never ask."

They lower their mouths to my nipples. They lick each erect nub and suck it between their lips, and their teeth nibble at my flesh. Seeing their heads bent over my breasts sends a shiver of desire shooting through my core.

I'm a paper boat on a stormy sea. I'm hurtling, out of control, on an ocean of scalding hot lust.

I throw my head back on the couch and close my eyes, almost overwhelmed with how good their touch feels. Wyatt's beard prickles against me. Owen's stubble chafes at my tender skin. I press my fingers against my mouth to muffle the moans that I can't hold back.

When they stop, I almost shriek in protest.

"Piper." Wyatt's voice is hoarse with need. His hand strokes my calves, inching upward to my thigh. "Stand up."

If I stand up, my dress will fall to the ground, and I will be almost naked in front of Wyatt and Owen, wearing my lace underwear and nothing else.

"Yes or no, honey?" Owen asks calmly. "No pressure."

My insides clench and twist. I like this game. Each time they ask me to do something, I'm turned on. When I comply with their requests and see the open appreciation in their eyes, I feel like a goddess. And I've never felt like a goddess before.

You're special to us, they'd said in their note. These aren't just empty words. They're making me feel special now.

"Yes," I whisper. I get to my feet, standing in the narrow gap between the couch and the coffee table. My dress falls to the floor. I'm illuminated by the ever-present lights of Manhattan and the silvery gleam of moonlight, almost naked, shivering slightly as the cool breeze caresses my body, exposed to their gazes.

"Take off your bra," Owen orders.

"What happened to Yes or No?" I ask, my hands reaching for the clasp behind my back.

"You always have the right to say no," Wyatt says quietly. "At any stage, at any point, at any minute, you can always change your mind." He gives me a direct look. "But if you aren't saying no, then take it off."

I unclasp my bra and toss it on Owen's lap. He chuckles at my gesture. Wyatt's staring at me. "God you're beautiful," he says quietly.

Owen nods in agreement. "Now the panties, baby," he says implacably.

In for a penny, in for a pound. I strip them off and toss them on the couch. Owen catches them in mid-air. "Are you wet, Piper?" he asks me with a wicked look. He brings my panties to his nose and inhales deeply. I go beet-red with embarrassment. I can't believe what he's doing.

Wyatt rises to his feet. He moves behind me, clearing our glasses and the candles away from the coffee table. "Lie back," he instructs, once he's done. "Spread your legs, Piper."

Oh God, oh God, oh God, I can't believe this is actually happening.

I'm a little slow to comply. Wyatt's hands wrap around my ankles, pushing my legs apart. "If you want me to stop," he says, "all you have to do is say no."

I hold his gaze. "I don't want you to stop."

A smile illuminates his face. "Then why am I prying your legs open?" he asks pointedly.

I flush and cover my face with my hands. "Because," I groan, "I've never done this before."

"Hang on." Wyatt draws back and looks at me with complete astonishment. "You've never had oral sex before?"

This is really embarrassing. "I've done it. I've never had it done to me."

"Fuck me." He runs his hands through his hair. I risk a glance at Owen, who's looking as shocked as Wyatt. "The guys you've been with are fools, Piper. Spread your legs. Let's fix this gap in your education."

Owen kneels at my side and kisses me. His fingers play with my nipples, pinching them and pulling them. My breasts go heavy with desire, and I gasp with pleasure at his touch.

I've had sex before, but it's never felt this way. My first time was in the back seat of a car, a rushed and painful experience I have no desire to repeat. I had a boyfriend for the few months I went to college in New Orleans. Our sex life was good enough. Sure, he never went down on me, but that seemed like a minor flaw.

Now, as Wyatt part my folds, I realize how wrong I was. He breathes on my pussy, and goosebumps rise on my skin. "So pretty," he mutters. He pushes a finger into me. "God, you're so tight."

It's been a very long time, Wyatt.

He removes his finger. His hands hold my thighs open, and he bends his head toward me. His tongue licks at my slit, and when he reaches my clitoris, he sucks it in between his lips.

I almost jump off the coffee table as pleasure shoots through me.

"You like that, Piper?" Wyatt asks. "Owen, you've got to taste her."

"Move over and I will," Owen retorts.

Again, I blush at the way I'm being discussed, and again, wetness gushes from my pussy.

"Not yet." Wyatt resumes licking me, his strokes long and steady. I'm lost in a delirious haze. I ache everywhere. My nipples throb as Owen teases them. I tremble as they feast on me, as if I were a rare delicacy to be savored.

My muscles start to clench. Wyatt senses that I'm close to the edge, because he pushes two fingers inside me. "I want to feel you, Piper." His tongue dances over my clit, harder, faster. I gasp and my fingers grip at the nearest object, which happens to be Owen's blond hair. "Please," I cry out.

Wyatt thrusts his fingers in and out of me. His tongue swirls tight circles around my bud. I whimper and try to flail out of his grip, but he doesn't let go. I'm so close. Every muscle in my body tightens.

Then Wyatt sucks my clit gently between his teeth. The

dam bursts and I explode, shaking as a tsunami of pleasure washes over my body.

When thought returns, I'm mortified. *Well-behaved Southern women do not spread their legs so wantonly and they certainly don't scream their orgasms.*

Owen grins at me. "I think it's my turn," he says with relish. "It doesn't seem fair that Wyatt gets to be the only one to taste your sweetness."

I sit up in mild alarm. "I need a break first." My body is sated, and my pussy is swollen and sensitive. If Owen goes down on me, I will fall apart. *Can one die from coming too much?*

Owen helps me to my feet and I collapse on the couch. Wyatt hands me a blanket. "I don't want you to get cold," he says.

I chuckle. "Either you're being very chivalrous, or you just don't want your chef to get sick four days before the first round of the contest." I give Wyatt a dry gaze. "Which is it?"

"I don't like to lose," he says blandly, though he winks at me as he says it.

I lean against Owen's shoulder while I sip my champagne. "You made me come," I say, blushing as I remember the way I fell apart. "I should return the favor."

"What's your hurry?" Owen's fingers trail a path down my bare arm. "You don't have to work tomorrow."

"That's true." Owen's touch is getting me hot again. I shift restlessly in my seat, and they both notice. "Are you trying to tell us something, Piper?" Owen teases me.

I flush again. I have no problems arguing with Owen

and Wyatt over restaurant details. But we're not at *Piper's*, and I'm unable to speak.

"Cat got your tongue?" Wyatt's eyes gleam in anticipation. "Let's play another game. Whatever you ask for, we'll do. But if you don't ask for anything, we'll just sip our wine and enjoy the night sky."

"You're joking."

"Not even a little."

Owen grins. "Oh, this is going to be good," he says. "Come on, Piper. Don't be shy."

"You guys think I'm a prude." My cheeks might be flaming at the idea of asking them to go down on me, but I'm definitely not a prude. If I were, I'd be at home, in my rocking chair, with Jasper on my lap. Not sitting naked on a rooftop in the Upper West Side, between two fully clothed men.

"I don't think you are," Wyatt replies. "You need to ask for what you want." His voice softens. "My dick has been hard all evening long, Piper," he says. "There's nothing you can say that's going to change how much I want you."

Oh what the heck. I'm here, and they're here, and I want them. I lift my chin up. "I want Wyatt to kiss me."

Wyatt pulls me toward him. "Kiss you where?" he whispers, his breath tickling my ear. "Here?" He kisses the side of my neck. "Or here?" He pushes the blanket aside and he nuzzles the curve of my shoulder.

"On my lips."

His fingers rest on my chin. "Gladly." His mouth lowers on mine, claiming my lips with a deep, sensual kiss. His fingers skim the sides of my breasts as our tongues dance together. I'm dizzy with need when he breaks free. "What next, Piper?"

This is getting easier. "I want Owen to go down on me," I

say bravely. "And I want to suck Wyatt's cock at the same time."

"Fuck me." Wyatt looks at the stars. "You said cock. I think my heart just stopped."

Owen positions me on the coffee table again. Wyatt unzips his pants and his cock leaps out, hard, long, and thick. I swallow as I look at it. Wyatt's huge. If Owen's the same size, I'm in over my head.

Owen's tongue lavishes my clitoris with toe-curling attention. I twist to the side and reach for Wyatt's cock, wrapping my hand around the base. Wyatt throws his head back. "Piper," he rasps. "You are killing me here."

I look up at him through my eyelashes. "I just wanted to repay the favor," I say sweetly. Then I take his length into my mouth, my tongue swirling around his head.

I'm rewarded by his throaty groan. His hand presses against the back of my neck, but he's letting me set the pace, and I appreciate his consideration. I'm not an expert at this. I don't know how to deep throat. If he forces his cock into my mouth, I might bite him.

Owen slides two fingers deep into my pussy and twists them to find my g-spot. "God," he says, his voice ragged. "You are so fucking tight, and you taste so fucking good." His tongue circles my clitoris while he pumps his fingers in and out of me.

I moan into Wyatt's cock. I'm seconds from losing control again. Blood pounds in my head as my orgasm nears. Owen's skilled fingers and mouth cause me to hurtle to the edge. I bob faster on Wyatt's dick, alternating delicate licks with harder suction. His desperate moans make me feel powerful.

The ache in my pussy intensifies as Owen circles my clit

with the tip of his tongue. His touch feels amazing, but I need more. I need a cock thrusting into me, pounding, thrusting, each stroke making me tremble and quiver. "Please," I pull my mouth free of Wyatt's cock and beg Owen. "Fuck me."

His eyes blaze with heat. "Gladly," he growls. Wyatt tightens his grip on my hair, and I turn my attention back to his cock. My fist slides up and down his length, and I wrap my lips around his thickness.

Owen rolls a condom onto his cock. His hands grip my ankles. "I'm going to fuck you, Piper," he warns. He pushes into me in one forceful thrust.

Oh my God this feels incredible. He fills me completely. After years of celibacy, it's a little painful, but I welcome the burn. It's been so long. I want this.

My gaze meets Wyatt's. His eyes are hazy with desire. "Piper," he warns me. "If you don't want me coming in your mouth, tell me now."

Owen's thumb circles my clitoris. His dick pounds into me. The strokes are thundering, raw and powerful. I'm engulfed in pleasure. I pull back from Wyatt's dick long enough to look him in the eyes. "I want to swallow."

"Fuck me," Wyatt groans. "Piper, what are you doing to me?"

Owen's thrusts are faster now, more uncontrolled. I moan aloud, uncaring that I can be heard. I can't think about anything other than how good this feels. The friction is exquisite. My body is liquid heat. My muscles tighten and clench. I can't hold back; I need to come now.

Wyatt grunts, his hand on the back of my head holding me close. He comes deep in my throat, and I swallow every drop. Owen doesn't let up on my pussy. He slams into me, hard and fast. When his fingers increase their pressure on my clitoris, I come again, screaming my pleasure for all of New York to hear.

"Spend the night," Owen says lazily.

I can't deny I want to. I don't know if the subway's running at this hour and the idea of curling up between the two of them is very tempting.

But sleeping with someone is a far more intimate thing than having sex with them.

"Piper." Wyatt's voice jerks me out of my reverie. "We only bite on request. The bakery downstairs makes an incredible croissant. You'll think you're in Paris. Please stay."

"Okay." Who am I kidding? I don't want to leave.

22

If you know yourself but not the enemy, for every victory gained you will also suffer a defeat.

— SUN TZU, THE ART OF WAR

Owen:

I wake up early. Piper's curled up into a ball in the center of the bed, the blanket wound tight around her. Wyatt's side is empty. He must be up already.

I slide out of bed without making a sound, and head to the kitchen. Wyatt's leaning against the counter, sipping at his coffee. I nod in his direction, grab a mug and pop a coffee pod into the machine. No messy coffee grounds for Wyatt.

"I met Mendez yesterday."

Wyatt snaps to attention. "You did?" he asks warily.

"Yeah. I checked out three restaurants for him. They were all clean. I told him I was done helping him."

"And?" Wyatt knows there's more to the story.

The coffee finishes brewing. I add milk and sugar and take a long sip before replying. "He implied that Seamus Cassidy is in Manhattan."

For an instant, Wyatt's expression is shocked. Then his natural skepticism reasserts itself. "Mendez brought up Seamus Cassidy after you told him you wanted out? Doesn't the timing strike you as suspicious?"

"Of course it does." I give him a steady look. "But if Cassidy is in New York, that explains why Mendez thinks the Westies back in business."

"Hmm." Wyatt considers that carefully. "Wouldn't your uncle have warned you if Cassidy was out of jail?"

"Not necessarily." After my mother had been killed, my uncle had succumbed to his own demons. Even though he'd been part of the mob, he'd been unable to protect his sister and her family. We'd gone into Witness Protection, and the experts had separated us, sending me to America for my protection, and placing him in hiding for his own. I haven't spoken to him since. "I don't know how to reach him."

"I know I should walk away," I continue. "The first round of Piper's contest is next week. Carl's loaning us Linda to work the front all weekend, but that's only a temporary solution. We need to hire someone - Kimmie can't act like a hostess to save her life."

"I couldn't agree with you more."

I grin. Kimmie's gum chewing drives Wyatt insane. If there was any way he could fire her and still make the finances work, he would. Unfortunately, with an accountant auditing the books on a monthly basis, we can't afford to fire her. Yet.

"You said you *should* walk away. Are you going to?" Wyatt asks.

I drink my coffee. The idea of letting my grief go is

tempting. Last night, I saw what my life could be and it was good, filled with a warm beautiful woman, good food and wine, laughter and happiness. For the first time, I have something to lose.

Then I hear my mother's voice, thick with fear, wondering what would happen if the Westies came for us. I see the bodies, sprawled on the floor in a pool of blood. I shake my head. "I'm going to try and reach my uncle to see if he knows anything about Cassidy. But I'm not ready to walk away. Not yet."

Piper:

The insistent ringing of my phone wakes me up. I grope for it, my eyes still closed, and hit the *Talk* button. "Hello?" I say, my voice thick with sleep.

"Piper Jackson?" The guy on the other end sounds irritated.

"Yes?"

"My name is Josh Lewis. I'm the auditor from Grant & Thornton. I was under the impression I was meeting you at ten this morning, but the restaurant is closed."

I sit up, the blanket falling to my waist. "You're supposed to show up on Tuesday."

"No," he corrects me. "Monday."

I'm fairly certain the letter from Grant & Thornton said Tuesday, but I don't want to argue with the guy who's about to audit my books. "I'm sorry, I must have got the dates mixed up. I'll be there in thirty minutes."

"Fine," he snaps. "I'll find a coffee shop to hang out in until you get here."

Damn it. Talk about getting off on the wrong foot. I jump to my feet and look around for my clothes. I find my panties on the floor of Wyatt's bedroom, and my bra on his dresser. Grabbing them, I get dressed, slipping my sundress over my head. I wish I had time for a shower and a change of clothes, but unfortunately, it's not in the schedule.

"I thought I heard you in here." Wyatt appears in the doorway. "Coffee and a croissant?" He takes in my stressed expression. "What's wrong?"

"The accountant called. There's been some kind of mix-up and he's at the restaurant right now."

"Fuck. Okay, we'll come with you."

"You will?" The fear gripping my heart lifts a little. "Really?"

He gives me a puzzled look. "We're your partners, Piper," he says. "Of course we're coming."

Twenty seven minutes later, we're outside *Piper's*. Even though I'm nervous about the upcoming audit, I can't suppress a thrill of excitement as I look at the sign with my name on it. The last month has been so busy that I haven't had any time to stop and just breathe, and reflect on the fact that my dream is slowly but surely coming true.

Thanks to Owen and Wyatt. Who I slept with last night. I hope that wasn't a mistake.

Josh Lewis is waiting for me, with an impatient look on his face. He's a tall, thin guy with dark hair and wire-rimmed glasses. "You must be Piper Jackson," he says tightly when he sees me. "I'm glad you could make it."

I shake his hand. "These are my partners," I tell him. "Wyatt Lawless and Owen Lamb."

The instant he hears their names, his attitude changes. "Mr. Lawless, Mr. Lamb," he stammers. "What a pleasure to meet you. I knew Ms. Jackson had new partners, but I didn't realize..." His voice trails off. "My wife is a line cook at *Paesano's*."

Owen turns on the charm. "My compliments to her," he says. "I've never had a bad meal there."

Wyatt nods in agreement. "Mr. Lewis, you're here to audit Piper's books?"

"I am," the accountant says, his voice more conciliatory than it was when he was addressing me. But hey, I'm just the lowly chef. I'm not Lawless and Lamb. In a minute, he's probably going to offer to blow them. "I hope it's not a bother."

"Not at all," Wyatt says. "Piper runs a clean shop."

Josh Lewis gives me a doubtful look. Grant & Thornton have probably hinted that my books could use extra scrutiny. My cousin Colton would love to find any evidence that would make me lose my restaurant, and my parents seem eager to assist him in the process.

I unlock the front door and we enter. "My office is really just a cubbyhole," I say. "Why don't I bring my laptop to one of the tables and we can do our work in the front?"

"Good idea," Owen says. "In the meanwhile, I'm going to grab us some coffee and breakfast. Josh, you want something?"

The accountant looks surprised that he's being asked. "No thanks, Mr. Lamb," he says. "I should get started."

I fetch my laptop for him and navigate to my accounting software. "Here you go," I tell him. "I'm going to be doing some prep in the back. Call me if you need something."

He nods, his attention on my computer. I don't think he even notices when I walk away.

❧

THE INSTANT I walk into the kitchen, Wyatt pushes me against the freezer and kisses me hard. I whimper at his touch. Damn Josh Lewis. I would have liked a repeat of last night this morning.

"Hi there," he says, smiling at me. "How're you doing?"

I don't know how to respond, so I settle for politeness. "I'm well, thank you."

He raises an eyebrow. "Did you have a good time last night?"

I turn red as I remember yesterday evening. I can't believe I sucked Wyatt off while Owen pleasured me, first with this mouth, then with his thick cock. I also can't pretend I didn't enjoy it. "I had a very good time."

"Had a very good time with what?" Owen comes through the back, holding a tray of coffee and a paper bag. "Just bagels and cream cheese, I'm afraid. We'll have to do croissants some other time."

"Piper was just telling me she had a good time last night."

"Did you?" Owen grins. "That's good, sweetheart. Me too."

I eye them both with exasperation. Part of me wants another go at Owen and Wyatt, and the other part of me is nervous.

"What's the matter, Piper?" Wyatt asks.

I chew on my lip. "Should we have done what we did last night?" I reach for the coffee and take a sip. "We work together. Maybe we shouldn't have been so self-indulgent."

Owen looks up, his expression intent. "Are you concerned that if things end badly, we'll take it out on your restaurant?" he asks me.

"No, of course not." I can't see them being so petty. They're consummate professionals. "But things could get really awkward, couldn't they?" I fix Wyatt with a level gaze. "Have you seen Maisie Hayes since your break-up?"

He doesn't meet my eyes. "No," he confesses.

"Why not? Because it's uncomfortable, right?" I challenge him. The more I'm thinking about this in the clear light of day, the more I'm starting to think I made a mistake. "And Owen? Do you keep in touch with ex-girlfriends?"

"I don't have any," he responds.

That knocks me off my stride. "None? Really? How come?"

He grimaces. "Can we leave my dating history out of this?" His blue eyes lock onto mine. "Piper. Listen to me. All that matters is the three of us. Do you trust us not to screw you over? Do you trust us to be fair to you?"

"Yes." They've more than demonstrated their commitment in the last month.

"And we trust you to be fair too," Owen replies. "So, rather than jumping ahead to the future, can we just take it one day at a time?" His lips twitch. "What are you doing tonight?"

"It's Monday," I reply automatically. "I'm hanging out with my girlfriends."

"Ah yes," Wyatt grins. "The drinking club. We can't get in the way of that. And unfortunately, we have to work the next couple of evenings. Are you free on Thursday?"

Before I can answer, I hear Josh Lewis call my name. "Ms. Jackson, do you have a moment?"

I hurry to the front to see what he wants. The table is scattered with papers, but my laptop is shut. "I've got everything I need," he says when he sees me.

"That was quick."

He nods. "Well, everything seems in perfect order. I can't think of why Mr. Elliott wanted to check your books." He shrugs. "Still, it pays the bills. I'm supposed to audit your books every month, so I'll see you in four weeks."

Mr. Elliott. *Wait, Colton was responsible for this, not my parents?* Guilt stabs at my insides. Maybe I'm being unfair to my mom and dad. The restaurant has been doing better. Maybe they've finally accepted my decision to stay in New York.

I shake his hand and show him out, Wyatt and Owen right behind me. "See?" Watt says, when Josh Lewis is out of sight. "Piece of cake. On to more important things. Will you come over on Thursday night?"

I gaze at them helplessly. I'm not sure if they're being foolish or wise. "The contest starts on Thursday," I point out.

"Good," Owen says. "You'll be stressed out. Dinner will relax you."

I can't help myself. Excitement buzzes through me at the thought of another night with Owen and Wyatt. "Okay."

I hear my mother's voice in my head. *You're being very foolish, Piper,* she sniffs. I'm afraid she's right. I'm am being foolish, but I don't care.

23

I wake up every morning and I surprise myself. I wake up to a new me.

— GINA CARANO

Piper:

"Piper," Gabriella's voice sounds from the monitor. "Spill."

While I've been busy with the changes at my restaurant, Gabby's been making some changes of her own. She's in a relationship now. She moved to Atlantic City a month ago, which is why she's on Skype, not here in person. Though I miss my friend, I'm really happy for Gabriella. She reunited with the two guys she had a one-night stand with. She's got her own mini-family now, complete with two boyfriends and a new nephew, an adorable toddler called Noah.

Unfortunately, Skype or not, Gabby always has an eagle-eye. "I don't know what you are talking about." It's a weak answer. The truth of the matter is, I'm not looking to keep last night a secret. My girlfriends are good at advice, and I need it.

"Piper," she warns me. "There are consequences to keeping secrets from your best friends."

"Shot, shot, shot," chant the others. I smile inwardly as I remember the night Owen, Wyatt, and I sat around a table at *Aladdin's Lamp* and had a drink. That was the moment everything had changed. I take a shot of vodka, coughing from the burn of the alcohol as it flows down my throat. "We miss you, Gabby," I tell her. "There are no sandwiches."

"I'll be in Manhattan in two weeks," she promises us. "Dominic has some kind of work thing, and we are all coming down for the week. I'll bring sandwiches then. And Piper?" She gives me a dirty look. "I know an attempt to change the topic when I hear it."

"Okay." It's confession time. "I may have been inspired by you and Bailey, and done something stupid."

"Wait a second," Wendy leans forward, her mouth open. "You jumped on the ménage wagon?"

"I didn't go all the way." God, that sounds lame, not to mention I'm bending the truth a little. I've decided that in a ménage, going all the way is anal sex. That's my position and I'm sticking to it.

"Who with?" Miki, who's also Skyping in, looks absolutely fascinated. "Anyone we know?"

Oh God, can this be any more embarrassing? Bailey, who knows who the guilty parties are, grins in her corner, but lets me flounder. "Sort of," I whisper, mortified. "It's Wyatt and Owen."

Gabby bursts out laughing. Bailey's grin widens into a smirk, and Miki chuckles. Damn it. I try to change the subject by asking Gabby about her new relationship, but she doesn't let me off the hook. "No, no," she says. "I move to Atlantic City and all of a sudden, you're getting crazy and adventurous? How did this happen?"

"I am being crazy, aren't I?" I wince as I sip at my drink. "What was I thinking?"

Miki frowns in puzzlement. "Why are you crazy? Because you were in a threesome? Two of your best friends are in ménage relationships. You're not going to get a lot of judgment in this room over that."

"Not in this room. But my parents will absolutely lose their minds."

Wendy makes a face. "It seems to me, Piper," she says, "that your parents disapprove of everything you do anyway. So they'll have another thing to add to the list. So what?"

That's true. My mother wants me to move back home, get married, and launch into the business of being a society wife. She'll go ballistic if she finds out about Wyatt and Owen, but it's not as if I'm basking in the glow of parental approval right now.

I still quail at the thought of telling them.

"The timing isn't great." I lift my chin up. "The first *Can You Take The Heat?* round is this week. Shouldn't that be my focus?"

Bailey speaks up. "Life isn't perfect, Piper," she says gently. "It isn't a to-do list where you check off one item, then move on to another. I was really busy when I met Daniel and Sebastian. You just make it work."

"That's the way I've always lived my life," I reply.

"And have you been happy?" Bailey asks pointedly.

For the last six years, I've been alone. I can't lie; it's been tough. I think back to the way Wyatt and Owen insisted on accompanying me to the accountant this morning, the way they'd calmed me down when I was almost overwhelmed with nerves. "It's nice to have someone to share stuff with," I admit.

Katie gets up to refill our glasses and empty a fresh packet of potato chips into the bowl in the center. Jasper, who thinks he's getting fed every time someone goes into the kitchen, looks up hopefully and goes back to sleep when he realizes that fish isn't on offer.

"Talking about the contest," she says, "we're all coming to dinner to *Piper's* on Thursday. Adam and I, Bailey, Sebastian, Daniel and Wendy. I made reservations yesterday."

"You are?" I grin delightedly at Katie, warmed by the gesture of support. "All of you? Including Sebastian Ardalan? I don't know if I'm thrilled or intimidated."

"Be thrilled," Bailey advises. "Sebastian is just a guy, though admittedly, a very hot one." Her smile turns fond. "If you see him bumping into furniture in the morning because he hasn't had a cup of coffee, you'll never be intimidated by him again."

Katie chuckles. "Adam's the same way. He's completely helpless in the morning. Incidentally," she turns to me, "the woman who took my details was a bit of a hot mess."

"Kimmie," I groan. "I know. We're trying to hire someone to act as hostess, but it's been difficult. I can't afford to pay very much, and Owen and Wyatt are being very particular. It's insane. We have someone filling in this weekend, but we need a long-term solution."

"You'll figure it out." Wendy's voice is confident. "You don't give yourself enough credit, Piper."

My thoughts return to last night, and I decide to confide my worries in my friends. "There's something else." My cheeks heat and I keep my gaze fixed on my drink. "Wyatt and Owen asked me out again."

Gabby punches her fist in the air in celebration. "That's awesome. You do like them, don't you?"

"I do, but I don't have a lot of experience, and I'm afraid they're going to get bored of me. They probably think I'm a prude."

"You're definitely not a prude," Bailey says, her voice emphatic. "Like Miki said, two of your friends are in ménage relationships, and you've been nothing other than supportive."

Gabby shrugs. "So fix it." she suggests, her voice unconcerned. "If they think you're uptight, do something that will prove them wrong."

Hmm. That makes sense. The beginnings of an idea start to form in my mind, and I can't hold back my smile. I'm going to give Owen and Wyatt one heck of a surprise.

24

All warfare is based on deception. Hence, when we are able to attack, we must seem unable; when using our forces, we must appear inactive; when we are near, we must make the enemy believe we are far away; when far away, we must make him believe we are near.

— Sun Tzu, The Art of War

Owen:

Seamus Cassidy had ordered the hit on my family to make us an example of what happened when people opposed the mob. I still had a death sentence on my head, but my troubles paled in significance when compared to my uncle.

After the murder of my parents and my sister, Patrick Sarsfield had gone to the cops in Dublin and he'd told them everything he knew. He named names. He provided details of crimes, and more importantly, he had evidence that could be used to jail the ringleaders for life. Almost ill with grief at his failure to keep his sister's family safe, he walked into the line of fire.

In return for our troubles, the police had put us in witness protection. For me, they arranged for a foster family in New York. A cop called Eduardo Mendez and his wife, Nina would take care of me until my eighteenth birthday.

For Patrick Sarsfield, they needed to do more. My uncle's testimony was responsible for convicting six of the Westies' most senior leaders. His life was in acute danger. In order to protect him, the two of us were separated and we were ordered never to communicate with each other.

I've obeyed that order for seventeen years. For seventeen years, Mendez, the man who was supposed to protect me has used me as a pawn in his schemes. In the years when we don't talk, my life flourishes. Whenever he re-enters my life, he sucks me in, and my hard-won peace of mind disappears.

I want Piper to win *Can You Take The Heat?*. I want more nights with her. This morning, when Wyatt had asked me if I was ready to walk away, I'd almost said *yes*.

First, I need to know the truth.

It's three in the morning. In Dublin, it's eight, and the day has just started. And the woman I need to talk to, Aisling Rahilly, would have arrived at work, a large cup of coffee in her hands.

I dial her number. It's time to find out where my uncle is. Who better to ask than the woman responsible for his disappearance?

~

THE PHONE RINGS ONCE, twice, a third time. Fear skitters down my spine. If Seamus Cassidy is out of jail, then none of the people responsible for putting him there are safe. Not my uncle, not Aisling Rahilly, not me.

I'm about to disconnect the line when she picks up. "Constable Rahilly."

I exhale in relief. Aisling Rahilly was kind to me during a very difficult time in my life. She'd comforted me as I'd mourned my family. She'd arranged for a way to keep me safe, and she'd done her best to find me a better life.

"It's Owen Lamb."

It takes a few minutes for her to recognize my name, then she gasps. "What's happened?"

The rules are designed for our protection. I'm never supposed to contact Aisling Rahilly. "Is Seamus Cassidy still in jail?"

No one will talk about the Westies. Their trials were behind closed doors. Their sentencing was shrouded in secrecy. Their locations, once they were jailed, was unknown, never revealed to the public.

Just as I feared, her reply is not helpful. "I don't know."

My uncle will be able to answer my question. For Patrick Sarsfield, this isn't a matter of idle curiosity. It's a matter of life and death. "Then I need to reach Patrick."

She inhales sharply. "That's a foolish request."

"It's not a request." My voice is hard. "For seventeen years, I've done as I've been told. Now I hear that Cassidy might be free, that he might be in New York. I have to know the truth."

Several moments elapse before she replies. When she breaks the silence, she reels off a phone number. "I hope this isn't a mistake," she adds quietly.

I close my eyes in relief. If Constable Rahilly had refused to help, I wouldn't have known what to do next. "Thank you."

She clears her throat. "Are you well, Owen?" she asks, a tremble in her voice. "We sent you away from your home when you were just a child. Did we do the right thing? Has life been kind to you?"

I reflect on her words. My friendship with Wyatt has enriched my life and our partnership has made both of us wealthy. And there's Piper. In her arms, the ghosts are silenced, the past a distant memory.

What would have happened if I'd stayed in Dublin? I'd been heartbroken and angry; reckless in a way only a sixteen year old could be. I'd craved revenge. I would have died before my seventeenth birthday.

I swallow a lump in my throat. At the time, I'd been angry about being sent away, but I realize now that Aisling Rahilly gave me a precious gift. She'd given me a second chance. "Life has been more than kind."

Once I hang up, I stare at the phone number I've scribbled down for a long time. I can't shake off my premonition of doom. The world I've so carefully built will come crumbling down if I dial that number.

You have to know if Cassidy is in New York, I reason with myself.

I punch in the digits and make the call. There's no turning back now.

25

Do not swallow bait offered by the enemy.

— Sun Tzu, The Art of War

Piper:

According to Google, one of New York's ten best sex stores is located in SoHo, which is only a twenty-minute ride on the C line for me. Tuesday morning, I wake up and head there, anxious to put my plan into action.

A young woman is just opening the store as I walk up. "Hello," she greets me, smiling in a friendly manner. If she thinks it's weird that I'm shopping for sex toys at ten in the morning, her expression doesn't reveal it. "Can I help you find something?"

I'm relieved it's a woman at the store, not a guy. As it is, I'm mortified. Of course, I can hear my mother's voice in my head. *Well-behaved Southern women don't shop for sex toys.*

I'm getting better at ignoring that voice. "I'm looking for butt plugs," I lean in and whisper.

"All the way in the back of the store, on the right hand side," she replies. "Call me if you need help."

Pigs will fly before I have a discussion about the best kind of butt plug to buy for first time anal sex. *Piper Jackson, what are you doing?* I ask myself, but I also feel a thrill run through my body. This is uncharacteristic of me, and I *like* it. I'm tired of being the good girl. Wyatt and Owen have awakened strange desires in me, desires that demand satisfaction.

There is a bewildering array of options. There are butt plugs that vibrate, plugs that can be controlled by remotes, butt plugs with bumps of increasing size, even butt plugs decorated with bushy tails. The tails make me blush. *One step at a time, kiddo.*

After a few moments of searching, I find what I'm looking for. A set of three plugs, increasing in size. The package promises that it's perfect for anal beginners. I pick it up, and then my eye falls on a glass butt plug adorned by a sparkling red jewel. Butt plug jewelry. Who knew? Strangely, it's really pretty. It's also sixty bucks, but I can't resist.

I take my purchases to the front, and the young woman rings them up for me. "What about lube?" she asks, her voice matter of fact. "You're going to need lubricant for those."

I can barely meet her gaze. "Right," I mumble. "I forgot."

"Try this one," she advises, pointing to a clear plastic bottle in the front. "It's one of our best sellers."

"Sure." I grab the larger size. I'm sure I'm going to need lots of lube. I pay for my bag of smut, and I almost run out of there, back to the safety of my restaurant.

∾

As soon as I walk in the door, my phone rings. It's my mother. I'm still feeling ashamed at the way I automatically assumed the worst of my parents in yesterday's accountant episode, so I pick up the phone. "Hello mother."

"Piper, what a surprise. I thought I'd have to leave another message on your voicemail."

"I spoke to you on Saturday," I defend myself mildly. "What's up?"

"I hear you're going to be on TV. I'm quite hurt you haven't told me, Piper."

I wince. Damn it, she really does sound upset. I've been avoiding talking about the restaurant on the general principle that the fewer details my parents know, the less they can interfere. Still, I should have known I couldn't keep *Can You Take The Heat?* a secret.

"Sorry, mother." I apologize out of habit. "I submitted my application late, and I wasn't sure if I'd get selected. It's only in the last week that I found out I was in."

"Tell me all the details, dear," she urges. "When does the contest start, and how long does it run?"

I sigh inwardly. "The first round is on Thursday," I reply. "There are sixteen restaurants participating, and it runs for four weeks. Each round, half the restaurants are eliminated, I think. They've been quite vague about the format."

"Well, your father and I were thrilled when we heard the news."

"You were?" I don't think my mother's been thrilled at anything I've done in the last six years. Did aliens abduct my mother and replace her with a kinder clone?

"Of course we were, honey. We ran into Merritt Grant yesterday at the club, and he said you're doing quite well."

My mother sounds almost proud of me. I wonder if I've

misjudged her all along. "Thank you, mom. Things are getting better. Wyatt and Owen have been a great help."

"Yes, your new partners. You haven't told me very much about them, Piper."

I swallow. I'm not ready to talk to my mother about Owen and Wyatt yet. "They're legendary in the restaurant business," I tell her. "I'm very lucky they want to work with me."

"How did you connect with them?"

"My roommate Bailey recommended me to a chef friend of hers," I say vaguely. "One thing led to another."

"That's great, dear. Of course, your father and I are coming up to watch you. We'll be there on Thursday."

A sense of unease washes over me. "You're coming to New York?"

"You didn't think we'd miss your contest, did you?" she asks with a fond chuckle. "Save us a spot at your restaurant, dear. We're quite excited to taste your food."

My parents have never once eaten my cooking, never once taken an interest in my restaurant. I'm not sure what caused their change of heart, and I don't really trust it.

26

Know thy self, know thy enemy. A thousand battles, a thousand victories.

— Sun Tzu, The Art of War

Wyatt:

Before I know it, Thursday is here.

"You look nervous," Owen says as the two of us make our way to Hell's Kitchen. It's a warm sunny afternoon, and we've elected to walk.

"I am." My voice is clipped. Owen gives me a curious look, and I elaborate. "I'm worried about Maisie."

"Maisie? Why?"

"She's an ex-girlfriend. What if she's jealous of Piper?"

Owen shakes his head. "I don't think so," he says confidently. "I know Maisie too, remember? She's far too professional for such emotions. This contest is a major coup for her. She's got a TV crew to film this show. She's on the front page of Yelp. She's not going to fuck that up. Besides, I didn't think you parted on bad terms."

"We didn't."

Owen rolls his eyes. "Don't worry," he says dryly. "Maisie is not going to cause problems. I wish I could say the same thing about Piper's parents."

I sigh. It had taken all the willpower I possessed to keep quiet when Piper had told us her parents were coming into town. But she'd sounded so happy that they were finally being supportive, and I didn't have the heart to shatter her illusions. If the three of us have one thing in common, it's that we have massive blind spots when it comes to our families.

We arrive at *Piper's*. The windows are freshly washed, and flower boxes overflowing with pansies and asters decorate the front. The two of us gaze on it silently for a few seconds.

Less than two months ago, this place was a dump serving indifferent Middle Eastern food. Now, the restaurant is warm and welcoming, and the food is staggeringly good.

It's quiet inside. It's two-thirty in the afternoon, too late for the lunch crowd, too early for dinner. "What time does the TV crew get here?" Owen asks as we head to the back.

"Four," I reply, pushing open the swing doors to the kitchen. "Hey," I greet Piper with a smile. We've exchanged texts and talked on the phone, but I haven't seen her since Monday, and I've missed her. "Ready for tonight?"

She looks up, her expression harried. It brightens when she sees us. "I thought you were my parents," she explains, coming over to hug us. That sweet Southern accent of hers can still harden my dick. "I was a wreck all morning, but it went away when I walked in here." She smiles at us warmly, and my heart skips a beat. "You guys have made this place gorgeous. We're going to kick ass tonight."

"Did Piper Jackson just say ass?" Owen teases. "Forget the contest. I'm looking forward to what's after. All week, I've been dreaming of you, Piper." His lips curl into a smile. "You, me, Wyatt. In a bed this time, maybe? Or do you want to do it outside again?"

I'm prepared for Piper to blush, but she surprises me by winking. "Wait and see," she says airily. "I might have a surprise for the two of you tonight."

I look up, intrigued. "What kind of surprise?"

"The kind that'll be ruined if I tell you what it is," she replies tartly. "Okay, the camera crew is going to be here in ninety minutes. I need to make sure everything's spotless in the kitchen. Want to help me scrub?"

"Sure."

We get to work. "Where's Josef?" I ask her, noticing she's all alone in the kitchen. "Kevin's working tonight as well, isn't he?"

"You just missed Josef," she replies. "He had some errands to run. He'll be here at three thirty. Kevin was here early for prep, and he'll be back again in time for dinner service."

Just then, Owen's phone rings. He frowns at the display and answers. "What's up, Carl?" His expression turns grim as he listens. "It's not your fault," he says. "We'll manage."

"Trouble?" Piper asks as he hangs up.

Owen nods. "Linda, the woman who was going to be our hostess tonight, fell down a flight of stairs and twisted her ankle. The doctors have told her not to put any weight on it."

"Shit." Piper frowns. "What are we going to do?"

The kitchen doors swing open again, and Piper's mother

walks into the room. "Darling, I came to do your makeup before the TV crew got here," she exclaims. She comes to a halt when she sees us, and she gives us an assessing look. "Hello, I'm Lillian Jackson. I don't believe we've met."

"Wyatt Lawless," I say, shaking her hand. "I'm one of Piper's partners. It's good to meet you, Mrs. Jackson."

Owen shakes her hand as well. "I'm Owen Lamb."

"Mother," Piper interjects. "They're here to film my cooking. They don't care what I look like."

"That might be so, Piper," her mother retorts. "But I do." She looks at the two of us in appeal. "Don't you think Piper will look better with makeup?"

I refuse to be dragged in the middle of this. "Piper's beautiful all the time."

Piper blushes at that. "Mom, we need to clean the kitchen. If you give me thirty minutes, I'll do my makeup when we're done. Okay?"

I gave her a wry look when her mother leaves the room. "Yes," she says, sounding a little irritated. "I know I should stand up to my mother. But sometimes you have to pick your battles. What are we going to do about the hostess?"

Owen frowns. "I don't know," he admits. "I'm working on it. Worst case scenario, I'll do it myself."

"That isn't the worst case scenario," Piper says gloomily. "The worst scenario is that my mother hears that we're short a hostess and offers to help."

I glance at Owen. I don't trust Piper's parents. I have to make sure that scenario doesn't come to pass.

～

THREE HOURS LATER, we're no closer to a solution for the hostess problem. Owen and I have called everyone we know, but restaurants tend to be busy on Thursday nights, and nobody can spare such a key staff member.

The film crew is in the kitchen, setting up their cameras and adjusting the lighting. Between calls, Owen makes sure that their presence isn't disruptive. "She still has to cook here," he tells the crew member in charge. "Make sure you aren't blocking anything."

I leave them arguing in the back and head out to the front. Kimmie's walking among the tables, folding the heavy cloth napkins into pouches and inserting a fork, a knife and a spoon in each one. Her jaw moves rhythmically as she works, and I exhale in irritation.

Owen comes out at the same time and notices her. "Kimmie," he snaps at her, keeping his voice low in deference to the five diners who are occupying the table in the front. "For fuck's sake, you aren't working in a tacky diner. This is a nice restaurant. I've told you a million times that you can't chew gum at work. Chef Jackson might be too nice to fire you, but I'm not."

She gives him a sullen look. "The place is empty," she argues.

He looks pointedly over to the front table, and she drops her gaze. "I don't give a shit what you think," he replies. "Go spit it out."

Kimmie scurries off to the washroom, looking resentful. "We can't afford to fire her yet," I point out to Owen.

"I know that, but she doesn't," he replies. "She's not an idiot. No waitress in Manhattan is paid sixty grand plus tips and she knows it. She definitely doesn't want to lose this job."

I'm about to agree with him when the door opens. I look up and my heart stops.

The man who's just walked into *Piper's* is my father.

Though I saw him on the security footage, it's been twenty years since I've seen him in person. Time hasn't been kind to him. In my memories, my father has always been well-dressed. Today, the kindest word to describe him would be slovenly. His shirt is torn and stained and his jeans have seen better days. He's unshaven, and he reeks of stale alcohol and cigarette smoke.

My pulse races. I'm not ready for this confrontation.

"You bastard," my father screams as soon as he sees me. Every single person in the restaurant swivels to watch as my father barrels toward me, his fist raised. At the last moment, he reconsiders and drops his hand, but he doesn't lower his voice. "You're having me evicted? Your own father?"

Up close, the smell of booze almost makes me gag. His eyes are red and bloodshot. He's drunk.

"I don't want you here." My voice is steadier than I feel. "Leave."

"Fuck you," he snarls. "My son thinks he's too good for me, is that what it is? This is a public restaurant. You can't throw me out of here like you can at your office. I think I'll sit here and eat a meal." He draws a chair back and sinks into it. "Where's the fucking menu?"

This is a disaster. There's a crew in the back, ready to film this controversy. The one thing I know about reality TV is that the producers thrive on drama. My father isn't a fool. He's made the same calculation as I have. He knows I'll do anything to get him to leave.

And he's completely wasted. He's swaying in his seat, his head slumped forward. The diners at the front table are still staring, absolutely fascinated at the scene unfolding a few feet from them. *Where's Stone Bradley,* I think angrily. *Isn't there supposed to be a tail on my father to prevent such incidents?*

At least Piper's mother isn't here. She left after putting

on Piper's make-up, promising to be back at six. I have thirty minutes to fix this situation. "What do you want?" I hiss, pulling up a chair next to my father.

In response, he throws up on the table in front of him.

"Did that guy just vomit?" I hear one of the diners ask, her voice tinged with shock and disgust.

"Gross," another one replies. "I don't think I'm going to be able to eat any more of my food."

Owen snaps into action. He hurries over to the front table. "Ladies and gentlemen," I hear him say soothingly. "I'm so sorry for the disruption. Your meals are *obviously* on the house. Please accept our apologies."

There's five of them, and they've ordered food and drinks. Owen's waiving a three hundred dollar tab. That'll buy a lot of forgiveness.

Guilt gnaws at my insides. This is my fault. Stone Bradley warned me not to push my father. He realized that desperate men have very little to lose. My father gambled, coming here, that I'd be too wary of scandal to throw him out by force. And he's right.

Out of the corner of my eye, I notice that Piper's come out of the kitchen, attracted by the commotion. *Great.*

My father raises his head to look at me. Little bits of vomit cling to his face and to his stubble. "What do I want?" he asks loudly. "You're evicting me."

"Will you go away if I call it off?"

He gives me a cunning look. "I need money," he says, slurring the words together. "I've got nothing."

I pull out my wallet and extract all the cash I have from it. "Here's two hundred and fifty dollars," I tell him. "*Leave.*" There's desperation in my voice. The clock is ticking. Soon, Lilian Jackson is going to be back. The restaurant is going to start filling up, and there's a drunk in the middle of the place, and the table he's sitting at is covered with vomit.

Piper's mom playing hostess isn't the worst case scenario. Maisie being upset and taking it out on *Piper's* wasn't the problem I should have been concerned with.

We all have blind spots about our parents. I thought I could make my father go away without seeing him. *I was wrong.*

He takes the notes I hand him, and counts it. "This isn't enough," he says. "My son is a millionaire, and all he can spare his father is two hundred and fifty bucks?"

A small part of me mourns the thirteen year old boy I once was. For days, months after my father left, I'd hoped it was a mistake. I made up all kinds of stories to account for his disappearance. He'd been hurt, and he had amnesia, so he couldn't remember us. He'd been kidnapped by an evil drug lord. Anything to hide from the truth. Anything to avoid facing the fact that he'd walked out on his wife and child without a word of warning.

Owen's gaze is on me. Piper's expression is heavy with sympathy. *I don't want your pity,* I want to scream at them. *I've overcome my past. Wyatt Lawless isn't a neglected child anymore. He's a successful businessman.*

The table in the front rises to leave, still staring at us. My cheeks heat with shame. The control I've fought so hard for is sliding away from my grasp. "It's all I have right now," I tell my father. "Come to my office on Sunday morning, and I'll give you more."

His voice is sly. "And the eviction is off?"

"Yes." *Go away. Please.* This isn't about me anymore. I'm ruining Piper's dream.

He rises to his feet, weaving unsteadily. He's won this round and he knows it. "See you Sunday, *son.*"

PIPER WALKS UP TO ME, but I don't look up. I'm too ashamed to meet her eyes.

When I was fourteen, there'd been a girl at school that I'd liked, Janet Blythe. She would smile at me whenever she saw me, and it was enough for me to be smitten. I'd been trying to summon up the courage to ask her to Junior Prom, when she'd dropped by at my house, unannounced. I'll never forget the look of mingled disgust and horror in her eyes.

This is my childhood all over again. I don't want to see that expression in Piper's face.

Owen joins us. "What's the film crew doing?" he whispers, his voice urgent. "We can't let them to the front before we clean up."

Piper's voice is tired. "Josef showed up to work drunk," she says. "He set a pan on fire. They have enough to keep them occupied." She puts her arm around my waist, and stands on tip-toe to kiss my cheek.

"I'm so sorry, Piper."

Her grip on my waist tightens. "We aren't our parents, Wyatt," she says gently. "We can't control what they do." She moves in front of me so that I'm forced to look at her. "We're partners," she says to me. "We're in this together."

Owen pats my shoulder. "Yes, we are. Wyatt, take a moment to shake this off. I'll clean this up."

"No." I stare down at my hands, trying to forget everything, trying to bring my focus back to tonight's contest, then I address Owen. "If Josef's drunk, Piper's going to need you in the kitchen. This is my mess. I'll clean it up."

The vomit is easy to deal with. The larger mess with my father? That isn't going to be quite that easy to fix.

27

A real friend is one who walks in when the rest of the world walks out.

— WALTER WINCHELL

Piper:

The cameras are recording as an obviously Josef mouths off in the kitchen, and I don't know what to do. I go to the front to enlist Owen and Wyatt's help, only to walk in the middle of Wyatt's confrontation with his father.

Poor Wyatt. My heart aches to see his face, tensed and closed off. He strips the tablecloth off the table, then retrieves a mop and cleaning supplies. "Is he going to be okay?" I whisper to Owen, who's also watching Wyatt with a concerned look.

"I think so," he whispers back, not sounding certain at all. "Let him clean. Restoring order to chaos calms him down." Then he seems to realize I'm not in the kitchen. "You said Josef set something on fire?"

"He's drunk." I shake my head. "He was thickening the gravy and he had some oil going in another pan. Of course, the incident has been captured on camera."

"Of course," Owen says wryly. "Why is Josef drunk?"

"He told me he was nervous about tonight, so he thought a shot of tequila would calm him down." I frown. "I can't babysit him tonight. I'm going to send him home. Can you cook his station?"

"Yes," Owen replies confidently. "I know your menu like the back of my hand."

He's right. In the last month, we've cooked each dish dozens of times, honing the recipes until they're perfect. I heave a sigh of relief. "Thank you," I say gratefully. We walk into the kitchen, where Josef is stirring the gravy with a faraway expression on his face. "Josef," I beckon him over, "I'm sending you home."

Cameras swing in my direction. A bearded young man with a handheld video camera jockeys for a better angle to capture Josef's reaction. "What do you mean, you're sending me home?" Josef asks belligerently. "I'm fine."

"No." I keep my voice calm with effort. "You're not. You set fire to a pan of oil. You're no use to me in this state. Owen's going to take over your station. Sleep it off and come back tomorrow."

Kevin's watching from his corner, his mouth hanging open. Sending Josef home, especially on the first day of the contest, is a slap in the face. I wish I didn't have to do it, but the risk that he's going to hurt himself is too great. Alcohol and the kitchen don't mix.

Josef straightens his shoulders. He's about to protest again when he notices my expression. I'm not going to budge on this and he appears to realize it, because he takes a deep breath and seems to deflate. "I'm sorry, Chef," he says quietly. He takes off his chef's jacket, hangs it on the hook in the corner and leaves out of the back door.

"Can we get that camera out of Piper's face?" Owen asks tersely, as I slump against the counter, drained by the confrontation. I'm not very good at telling people off. Especially Josef and Kimmie, who were running this place until I showed up. "Piper, take a deep breath. We've got this."

I nod, then I stop cold. "If you're working in the kitchen, who's going to play hostess? Wyatt can't do it. I need him to work the floor and make sure everyone's doing okay."

On cue, the kitchen doors open and my mother walks in. "No," I groan, exchanging a look with Owen. But I don't have any other choice.

~

"OF COURSE I'd be happy to help, Piper," my mother says, when I ask her if she can play hostess tonight, sounding quite sincere. I want to believe her. My parents have been supportive in the last few days. They flew into town so they could attend the first round of the contest. My mother got here early to help me with my make-up, and now, she looks excited at her chance to help me.

On the other hand, I can tell that Owen thinks this is a very bad idea. I give him a look of appeal, and he shrugs resignedly. "Sure," he says, his voice distinctly unenthusiastic. "Why don't I run you through what you need to do, Mrs. Jackson?"

They disappear, and I take a deep breath. My nerves are a frazzled mess. I have to get my head in the game. The dinner rush is going to start any minute now. For the next five hours, I can't let anything interfere with my focus. Not my mother playing hostess, not Josef's drinking. Not even Wyatt's reaction at seeing his father again.

Owen comes back. "Okay, Wyatt's coaching your mother on what needs to be done," he says. "And twenty people just walked in, so it's going to get crazy in here in a second. Are you good to go?"

This contest is huge. Winning it will really put *Piper's* on the map of the New York restaurant scene. I won't have to anxiously count tables to see if I've made enough money to pay rent.

I'm as ready as I'm ever going to get. "Yes," I say, attempting a smile. "Bring it on."

As the tickets start rolling in, we get into a rhythm, the three of us functioning like a well-oiled machine. "You're really good at this," I tell Owen with a grin as he brings up an order of fried chicken to me.

He laughs. "Other kids had a misspent youth," he says cheerfully. "My ma made me peel buckets and buckets potatoes to keep me out of trouble."

My smile fades. "I'm sorry," I whisper, cursing myself at my thoughtlessness. Owen's parents were killed.

There's only one cameraman in the kitchen now, and his attention is on Kevin. We have a small moment of privacy. "Don't be," Owen replies. He smiles at me warmly, and he squeezes my hand. Even that brief touch sends heat trickling through my body. "I had a happy childhood."

"Okay."

He leans closer. "What's the surprise you have planned for us later?" he whispers in my ear.

My lips twitch. "It's killing you, isn't it?" I take a step away from Owen as the camera pans the room. "You'll find out later on."

He laughs and walks back to his station. "Yes, Chef Jackson."

I'm still smiling as I ladle some gravy on the plate, On auto-pilot, I dip the tip of a spoon into the liquid to taste it, and I realize that I'm in trouble. The gravy, which goes on the side of almost every dish on my menu, has far too much salt. So much salt that I want to spit out my little taste of it.

Damn Josef. Today of all days, he had to be drunk.

"Owen, I need another order of fried chicken," I call out. This one is coated in too-salty gravy, and all I can do is empty it in the trash. "Kevin, can you chop up some mushrooms, fast, and get a roux going?"

"Yes Chef," he calls out.

Owen can hear the stressed note in my voice. "What's the matter, Piper?"

"Gravy's too salty," I toss back over my shoulder as I head to our temperamental walk-in freezer. "We have to make another batch." As I move, I'm trying to remember if I have enough stock to make the gravy. We make our own stock at *Piper's*, and store-bought is a very poor substitute.

I hear Owen curse as I rummage through the shelves. The freezer is absolutely packed. Our meat supplier delivers every two weeks, and he came yesterday. Finally, I find a dozen mason jars containing frozen stock on the top shelf. Breathing a sigh of relief, I grab six of them and head back out. "Thaw these," I tell Kevin. "We've got to make the gravy in a hurry."

Kimmie comes to check on her food. "Not done yet," I snap at her. "Give me three minutes."

Think, Piper, think. I can't make gravy in three minutes, but can I make a substitute? I open my refrigerator doors and inspiration strikes. Duncan Bright brought me a dozen cauliflowers on Tuesday, and I'd been trying to perfect my cauliflower soup recipe. I have a couple of containers of pureed cauliflower left from that experiment.

I look around and I get lucky again. On the bottom shelf, there's a Tupperware dish filled with caramelized onions. We used most of them in a French Onion soup we served for lunch yesterday, but one lonesome container is left.

It's not gravy, but a buttery onion-cauliflower sauce would work great with the chicken, and I can make it in two minutes. I grab everything and sprint to a burner, putting a saucepan on it and turning the heat on high. I add a generous dollop of butter, then spoon in the onions. Once they've warmed through, I mix in the cauliflower and season the dish.

Thirty seconds with the immersion blender, and it's done. I taste it and nod my approval, just as Owen rushes up to the pass with another perfectly fried chicken. "Thank you."

Kimmie appears again, and loads up her tray.

"Nicely done," Owen says to me.

I look up, almost jolted out of my moment of intense focus, to see Owen watching me, an openly impressed look on his face. "That was very hot, Chef Jackson," he says, with a smirk.

Kevin chuckles. "Stock is thawed, Chef," he says. "You want me to make some gravy? We're out of turkey fat."

"Use the duck fat instead." My heart's still racing in my chest, and as the adrenaline slowly drains away, I start to tremble. Owen's at my side immediately with a glass of water. "Drink this," he says. "Take a deep breath. You did good."

"Thank you." I sip at the water and slowly return to normal.

Then another fresh batch of tickets come in. The brief

moment of tranquility is over. I call out the order and Owen and Kevin repeat it, and we get back to work.

AFTER THAT, it's almost an anticlimax when the judges show up. Wyatt walks back to hand us the ticket. "The cauliflower sauce was a huge hit," he says to me.

"Seriously?"

He nods. "Yeah, everyone loved it. You should add it to the menu."

"Not tonight." I'm done with curveballs for the evening

He grins. "No, of course not. The judges are here, by the way, and so are your friends."

"My friends are here?" I cheer up. "All of them?"

"All six of them," he confirms. "And the instant the judges saw Sebastian, they all acted as if he were visiting royalty." He shakes his head with a grin. "Had I known it would have such an effect, I'd have invited him myself."

I chuckle and call out the ticket Wyatt's handed me.

"Who are the judges?" Owen asks from his station. "Anyone I know?"

"Maisie Hayes, of course. John Page, who heads up the Hell's Kitchen business association. George Nicolson and Anita Tucker."

I feel faint. George Nicolson and Anita Tucker are legendary chefs. Anita Tucker was the first woman in New York to win a Michelin star. George Nicolson has founded more restaurants than I can count, propelling each of them to stardom before moving on. These are not ordinary judges. They are luminaries in the field.

"How's my mother working out?"

"So far, so good," he replies. "She's strangely good at it."

"She's a society wife in New Orleans," I tell him. "Playing hostess is what she does."

Kevin hurries up with a platter of breaded catfish, and I plate them, spooning jalapeno tartar sauce on the side, and adding scoops of rice and collards. Kimmie comes up to take the food out.

When she's gone, I look up at Wyatt. I don't really have time to get into a long conversation with him, but I want to make sure he's okay. The film crew is in the front now, so I'm not concerned that our conversation is being captured for posterity. "How are you?" I ask him.

He shrugs. "Mostly, I'm angry," he says. "I feel ambushed."

I don't blame him. "Let's commiserate over vodka once this madness ends?"

He laughs. "Let's do that," he agrees, a twinkle in his eyes. "Any chance you'll tell me what your surprise is?"

I bite back my grin. My secret is driving both Owen and Wyatt insane, and I love it. "You'll see," I tell him, adopting my most mysterious voice.

Contest or no contest, I can't wait for the night to be over. I can't wait to be in their arms again.

28

For every moment of triumph, for every instance of beauty, many souls must be trampled.

— Hunter S. Thompson

Piper:

Once we get the food out for the judges' table, we get to work on my friends' ticket. "Make this good, you guys," I call out to Owen and Kevin. "This is Sebastian Ardalan's table. The guy has two Michelin stars. Let's show him what we can do."

Owen rolls his eyes.

We've made so much progress here in the last few weeks. The last time Sebastian ate here, he was convinced we'd be out of business in six months. I want to prove him wrong.

Petra takes out that order, then there's a lull. I lean against the counter and glance at the clock in the kitchen. It's almost eight thirty. We're done for the night in the kitchen.

"Kevin, great job tonight," I say, smiling at him. Owen's used to the pressure, but today was Kevin's first day in the major leagues, and he did admirably.

I'm about to add more praise when Wyatt comes back to the kitchen. "The judges want to speak to the chef," he says, winking at me. "You're going to enjoy this, Piper. They loved the food."

"Really?" I untie my apron, swapping it for a cleaner one, and I follow Wyatt out. Applause greets me as I walk up to the table the four judges are seated in. "Chef Jackson," George Nicolson booms. "What an amazing meal."

"Absolutely fantastic," Anita Tucker chimes in. "Creative, well-executed, well-presented. You should be very proud."

I feel myself blush. "Thank you," I say.

Maisie Hayes surveys me curiously. "This used to be a Middle Eastern restaurant when you took it over, wasn't it, Chef Jackson?"

"It was."

"And Wyatt and Owen suggested you change your focus?"

I nod. "I'd added a few Southern dishes when I got here, and they quickly became my best sellers. When Wyatt and Owen pointed that out, it was obvious what I had to do."

Her gaze flickers over to Wyatt. "It's a huge improvement," she agrees. "I ate here four months ago. I liked the food, but the service was indifferent, and the decor was horrendous." She looks faintly apologetic as she speaks. "Now, the service has improved, and the place looks fantastic. And the food is even better than before."

My mother's done with her hostessing duties. She's seated at a table with my father, not too far away, listening to our conversation, her head tilted to one side. I wonder what she thinks of the food.

"Thank you," I say again.

George Nicolson gives me a conspiratorial grin. "I know Maisie's going to kill me," he says cheerfully, "but I see no reason to keep you in suspense until Sunday morning. You're definitely going to make it to the next round."

My heart hammers in my chest. I want to sing and dance, and I want to burst into tears, but most of all, I want to hug the two men who've made it all possible. I couldn't have done it without Wyatt and Owen.

Maisie gives George Nicolson an irritated look. "George," she says archly, "I've worked really hard on this contest. Can we preserve the element of surprise?" She turns to me, and her face softens into a smile. "I guess the cat's out of the bag. A well-deserved win, Chef Jackson. Congratulations."

BEFORE I GO BACK to the kitchen, I need to stop at two more tables. First, I make my way to my parents. "Mom, thank you so much for your help tonight," I say gratefully. "I can't tell you how much I appreciate it."

She smiles at me. "I was happy to help, dear."

"How was the food?" I ask my dad. There's no point asking my mother — she ordered a salad. Lillian Jackson doesn't believe in eating.

"Very tasty," he says gruffly. "You've done a good job with Vera's place." I'm about to thank him for the compliment, when he frowns. "I still think you're wasting your time in the kitchen though."

I should have known. "I'm happy," I say simply, my smile

wry. "The restaurant is doing well. This is what I want for my life."

He snorts. "Dessert?" I ask quickly, hoping to end this conversation. My dad has a sweet tooth. "There's a really good cheesecake on the menu."

My father looks up. "I know you're changing the topic," he says, "but the cheesecake sounds excellent."

I signal Petra and give her the order, then I head to the table by the front window, where my friends are seated. "Piper," Bailey exclaims, jumping up to hug me. "I think that's the best meal I've had in a long time."

Sebastian raises an eyebrow. "Sure," he says dryly. "Break my heart, Bailey, why don't you?" He smiles at me. "Really good food," he says. "A couple of my chefs went to eat at the competition today, and they weren't impressed. I'd be shocked if you don't make it to the next round." He grins. "If you ever want a job..."

Wyatt clears his throat pointedly. "Hands off our chef, Seb," he warns. "We're not letting her go."

Katie and Adam chuckle. "Guys," Wendy says, leaning forward, her glass raised in the air. "Fight over Piper later. For now, let's just drink to her. Here's to Piper."

Katie hands me a glass of wine so I can join in. We all clink glasses, and I take a sip. This is a great end to a very chaotic day.

I CHANGE my opinion once I head back to the kitchen. Owen and Kevin have started to clean up. I shake my head. "No, no, Owen," I protest. "No cleaning for you. You were just filling in for Josef. The place is emptying out. Why don't you head to the front, and I'll finish up here and join you?"

Now that the trials of the day are over, I can't wait to see how Wyatt and Owen are going to react when they see my surprise. I'm grinning in anticipation of their reaction when Kevin clears his throat. "Chef Jackson," he says, sounding unusually tentative. "Can I have a word?"

His voice alerts me that something's wrong. I snap my head up and look at him. "What's the matter, Kevin?"

"It's about the gravy." He looks unhappy. "When Josef set fire to that pan, I was afraid that he'd messed up the gravy, so once he left, I tasted it."

I hear the loud hum of the vacuum cleaner. It appears that Kimmie's actually cleaning up without being asked. *Will wonders never cease?* "And?" I ask Kevin, trying not to sound impatient. It's been a long day. I'm ready for it to be over.

He gives me a grim look. "It wasn't over-salted, Chef. It was fine."

"What are you saying, Kevin?" Blood pounds in my ears and a chill runs up my spine. If Josef didn't mess up the gravy, someone else did, and that can only be...

"Somebody sabotaged you, Chef." Kevin straightens his shoulders and looks at me squarely. "This wasn't an accident."

29

The best and most beautiful things in the world cannot be seen or even touched — they must be felt with the heart.

— HELEN KELLER

Piper:

For a minute or two after Kevin leaves, I stand in the kitchen, completely frozen by his revelation.

I have to tell Owen and Wyatt. We need to figure out who wants to hurt *Piper's* chances in this contest.

My first instinct is to talk to them right away, but I reconsider. It's been a long day for all of us. Wyatt's still coping with the emotional impact of his father showing up at the restaurant. Owen stepped into the breach when I threw Josef out, and has cooked a long shift. We all deserve some down time.

I'll tell them tomorrow. Tonight should be a night of celebration.

THE RESTAURANT's empty when I go to the front. Kimmie's nowhere to be seen. Petra's counting out her tips, looking pleased. "Great job tonight," I tell her. "Thank you."

She smiles. "Thank you, Chef." She clears her throat. "I know I just work the dinner shift now," she says, "and Kimmie covers lunch. But Donny starts first grade in the fall. I'll be available to work the lunch shift as well, if you need me."

I like Petra. She's punctual, neat and tidy, and she's knowledgeable about the food we serve, unlike Kimmie, who forgets what the specials are as often as she remembers them. "I'll keep it in mind," I say, crossing my fingers behind my back. If all goes to plan, I'll need to hire Petra and possibly another waitress to cope with the rush.

I walk over to Wyatt and Owen. Both of them are holding a glass of wine, and they raise their glasses when they see me. "Was one of you vacuuming?" I demand. "That's not your job, you know."

Owen points to Wyatt with a shrug, and I shut up. Wyatt cleans when he's tense. I'm hoping to offer a different kind of stress relief tonight.

Wyatt ignores my comment about cleaning. "Excellent job tonight, Piper," he says warmly. "Everyone loved the food. At one point, you had a line out the door."

"I did? A line?"

Owen grins and pours me a glass of wine. "Forget the line," he says. "Tell us about the surprise."

I wink at them, sipping my drink. I've never had two guys so eager to find out what I have planned. It feels really good.

"Give me five minutes and I'll show you." I wave at the

window. "Can you lower the blinds though? I don't want to be seen from the street."

"Sexy lingerie?" Wyatt sits up, his eyes sparkling. "Bring it on."

I bite back my grin. They think I'm making all this fuss for lingerie? Oh, they are about to be very, *very* surprised.

FIVE MINUTES LATER, I walk out of the washroom. Though I've been practicing since Tuesday, walking with the butt plug feels very weird. It'll be worth it though, just to see the looks on their faces.

"Nice outfit," Wyatt says, looking at my short black skirt and my black tank-top. "Very sexy."

I swirl and the skirt flares out. The two of them swallow as they realize I'm not wearing any underwear. "Fuck," Owen groans. "Come and sit on my lap, baby."

I shake my head. "You're missing the best part of this outfit." My cheeks blaze with heat as I force the next words out. "Do you want to see?"

"Yes." Their replies are instantaneous. "Absolutely."

I'm wearing the jeweled butt plug today. It's made of glass and is the heaviest of the plugs I've worn in the last two days. I can feel it inside me as I move, and the weight of it is turning me on. But best of all is the sparkling gemstone in the handle, blood red in color.

Today, I don't care about well-behaved Southern women. I sashay forward and bend over the table. "Lift my skirt up," I suggest.

Both of them gasp when they see my backside. "Fuck me," Owen says softly.

"Is that a butt plug?" Wyatt asks, sounds astonished.

"It is." I'm glad I'm facing the table and can't see their faces, otherwise I'm not sure I'll be able to continue my speech. "I want you both. I've never had anal sex before, but I thought I'd start planning for it."

A beard prickles at the curve of my ass. *Wyatt*. His lips graze against my cheeks, his touch soft. "Every single time I think I have a read on you, Piper Jackson, you do something that blows me away."

"Does it hurt?" Owen asks, sounding raw with need.

"Not really," I reply. "I bought a training kit. The one I wore on Tuesday was narrower. This is the widest one."

"Piper, if you keep talking, I'm going to explode all over you like a teenage boy." Wyatt sounds like he's teetering at the edge of control. His voice dips lower, and the promise in it causes me to shiver. "Do you want me to fuck you here? At your restaurant? Knowing that Josef, Kimmie, and Petra have keys and can come in at any time?"

"Or do you want us in a bed?" Owen asks.

Could I have both?

It's been a long day. The hint of danger that someone might walk in on me stirs sharp lust in my body, but the temptation of being sandwiched between their hard bodies on a soft bed is too much to resist. "The bed," I choose.

"Then stand up." Wyatt's voice is commanding. "Let's go."

A loud knock at the door causes me to jump. A woman's voice calls out. "Hello, is anyone there?"

Shit. "Deal with it," I hiss at Owen and Wyatt. "I'll go change."

Owen shakes his head, a wicked grin on his face. "Oh no, my pretty little chef," he says, "You don't get to change. I want you to answer the door, just as you are right now."

I give him a worried look. He winks at me as the knock

sounds again. "Damn it. You're really going to make me do this?"

"We're not making you do anything," Wyatt says. "You want to. We're just holding a mirror up to your desires."

He's absolutely right. It was my desire to explore my needs that made me go shopping for a butt plug, that made me wear it at the restaurant to tease Owen and Wyatt. Having come this far, I'm not about to back down. I walk toward the door, adding a sway to my hips as I do, knowing that Owen and Wyatt's eyes are glued to my ass. "We're closed," I say as I open the door.

Maisie Hayes is standing outside. "I know you are," she says apologetically. "I can't find my cell phone anywhere, and I'm wondering if I've left it here." She notices Wyatt and Owen. "Hey," she greets them, sounding surprised. "You guys are here late."

Wyatt holds up his glass of wine. "We were celebrating Piper's victory."

"Ah." Her gaze is knowing as she looks at the three of us. "Of course. Sorry for interrupting."

This is awkward. "Let me look in the lost and found box," I say hastily. "If one of our waitresses found your phone, that's where they'd put it."

I go to the register. Sure enough, there's an iPhone there. I lift it up in the air. "Is this it?"

"Yes," Maisie says, her relief obvious. "Thank heavens. I'm a blogger," she says wryly. "You have no idea how naked I feel without my phone." She takes it from me with a smile of thanks. "Great job again tonight."

There's a gleam in Owen's eyes. "Yes," he says smirking at my slyly. "The restaurant was absolutely *filled* tonight, wasn't it?"

Wyatt's lips twitch. "Absolutely. I'd say the kitchen was *stretched* to the max. Don't you think, Piper?"

I glare daggers at both of them. Maisie clears her throat. "Right then," she says, her voice amused, "I'm going to take off now."

When she leaves, I turn on them. "Seriously?" I ask them. "Butt plug puns? Are you teenagers?"

Wyatt's eyes twinkle with mirth. "That was fun."

"She knows something's up," I moan. "Doesn't that bother you?"

"Why would it?" He frowns. "I'm an adult. My dating preferences are none of anyone's business."

"People will gossip."

Owen snorts. "Piper, we are, at best, minor celebrities in a city that's teeming with them. We're hardly gossip worthy. Besides, who cares? I can't live my life based on what other people are going to think."

I wish I had their attitude. "Shall we leave?" I ask them. "I'll just remove the plug and lock up?"

"Nope." Wyatt overrules me, his voice smooth as silk. "Oh no, Piper. We're going to slide into a cab, and that plug is going to sink even deeper in your bottom. Every pothole we hit, you'll feel it in your core. That's what you want, don't you?"

"Yes," I whisper. I'm going to be a soaked mess by the time I get to their place, but I don't care.

WE GO to Wyatt's place. They lead me to the bathroom and run a shower for me. When I thank them, Owen shakes his head. "I've been standing in front of a stove for four hours,"

he grimaces. "I smell like stale oil and chicken fat. I'm being selfish here, Piper."

I watch with wide eyes as they remove their clothes. I thought I got my fill last time, but I was wrong. Their muscles ripple as they disrobe, and the trail of hair on their abdomens draws my gaze lower. Their cocks jump as they step out of their briefs. "I'm flattered," I quip cheekily, fighting my urge to blush.

Owen chuckles, a low, sensual sound. "It's your turn, sweetheart," he says, his eyes gleaming with lust. "Step out of that short skirt and bend over again."

I take off my top instead, and Wyatt shakes his head. "Piper," he says, stepping up behind me, and pulling my hands behind my back. "I thought Owen was quite clear."

Tension fills me at his words. Wyatt's expression softens when he sees my anxiety. "Anytime you say no," he whispers against my ear, "we stop. That's a promise." His mouth nibbles at my earlobe and my nerves are replaced by a rush of arousal. The shower runs in the background, gallon after gallon of warm water pouring down the drain, and I'm too lost in the haze of my lust to pay attention to it.

Owen stalks in front of me, his eyes heating with desire as he draws near. "Hold her for me, Wyatt," he says. In the position Wyatt has me in, my breasts jut out almost lewdly, but Owen seems to appreciate the view. He bends his blond head to my nipples, and pulls an erect bud between his teeth.

Warmth floods my body at his bite. I press back against Wyatt, who inhales sharply in response. "You like that, don't you, Piper?" His fingers close around the base of the plug, and he tugs gently until my anal ring yields to the pressure. "Do you feel your muscles stretch?" His breath tickles my ear. "They're going to stretch around our cocks tonight, Piper. Is that what you want?"

"Yes."

Owen kisses the side of my throat. "You're so bold tonight," he marvels. "Wrap your fingers around my dick. Show me what you want."

If I give in to my need, we're never going to make it to bed. "Shower first," I say, groaning as I grip the velvety steel of Owen's shaft. "Then I'll do whatever you want."

"Is that so?" Owen slides open the shower door. "In that case, step in, Piper."

I almost moan with lust at the sheer magnificence of that shower. Sharp, hot needles of water pound on my flesh, massaging aches and pains I didn't know I had. Two shower heads on either side of the stall ensure that there's not a single cold spot in the space. "I might never leave," I sigh.

Wyatt's lips twitch. He unhooks the hand-held shower attachment from its spot on the wall, and he approaches me with intent. "Part your legs for me, baby," he urges. "Put one leg up on the ledge." With a wicked grin, he turns the attachment on and directs the spray of water right at my clitoris.

"Aah." My knees buckle. Owen's arms wrap around my waist, holding me immobile. "I want to watch you come," Wyatt says. "I want to hear you scream, Piper."

He shifts the angle of the stream of water, and I gasp, standing on tiptoe to ease the pressure on my core. I don't build to my orgasm, I hurtle toward it, helpless to resist. I try to twist away, but Owen stops me. "No," he says firmly. "Don't move. Don't pull away." His fingers tug at my nipples; his lips rain kisses down on the curve of my shoulder. Wyatt watches, his nostrils flared, as my release claims me, but he doesn't move his hand away. The water still pounds in relentless jets at my sated clitoris. "Stop," I beg. "Please."

"So soon?" Wyatt sounds a little disappointed. "Are you sure you don't want another orgasm or two?"

"I'm saving my energy for your cocks," I tell him. "But if you don't want that..."

They grin. "Well played, Piper Jackson," Wyatt congratulates me, shaking his head ruefully. "Very well played."

They lather soap all over my body and shampoo every strand of my hair. I'm purring like a contented kitten by the time they are done. I shiver as they towel me off, though I'm not cold. Far from it. I'm hot with desire; I'm burning with need.

We stumble to Wyatt's king-size bed, covered in pristine white, cotton sheets whose thread count is so high the fabric feels like silk against my skin. The butt plug has been in my ass for the better part of an hour and I'm getting used to it. Part of me is anxious about the anal sex tonight. The other part is almost trembling with excitement.

Wyatt tilts his head to one side. "I'm assuming you've noticed," He says, "that I like to be in charge."

"You?" I keep my voice innocent and flutter my eyelashes at him. "A control freak? I have no idea what you're talking about."

"Control freak, am I?" His eyes dance with amusement. "Sometimes, I like to take charge in bed."

Anal sex and dominance, all in one night. My horizons are being widened. Whatever well-behaved Southern women are supposed to do, this isn't it. *And I don't care.*

Perhaps Wyatt mistakes my anticipation for apprehension, because he's quick to reassure me. "I'm not going to do anything intense," he promises. "Want to try it?"

"Does Owen listen to you too?" I ask curiously. Somehow, I can't see the big blond man listening to Wyatt's instructions.

Owen snorts. "I don't think so," he says immediately. "Wyatt bosses me enough around the office. Nope, our focus tonight is going to be entirely on you."

Entirely on me. Goosebumps break out on my skin. I'm going to like this. "What do I have to do?"

Wyatt's eyes blaze with heat. "I think that you should give Owen a blow job."

A smile breaks out on my face. "Well," I say, drawing the word out, "I *do* owe Owen a blow job. After all, Wyatt got one on Sunday. We have to keep things fair."

Owen groans. "Piper," he says, his voice hoarse, "you are going to be the death of me." He moves so he's sitting at the edge of the bed, and I sink to my knees on the floor. I run my fingernails over his thighs, and am rewarded by his sharp inhale of breath. His eyes squeeze shut, and he throws his head back as I wrap my fingers around his length and close my mouth over him.

My tongue swirls over his head, licking him and teasing him, before I relent and bob my head up and down over his shaft. I'm captivated by the way his dick feels in my mouth, by the way it twitches when I take him deeper down my throat. As I suck, I let my hand run over his chest, feeling his muscles, tugging him closer to me. "Fuck, Piper," Owen bites out, pulling away with a wild look in his eyes. "I don't want to come just yet."

He lifts me onto the bed and positions me on my hands and knees. "Wyatt, you've got to get in here."

Wyatt nods in agreement. "Do you want me in your pussy, Piper?" The tone of his voice sends desire strumming through my body. "That butt plug is already in your ass. Are you ready to be filled completely?"

Owen positions himself at my mouth. Instinctively, I part my lips for him. The mattress dips as Wyatt climbs on the bed, and moves behind me. His fingers play with my folds. "So wet, Piper." A condom wrapper tears and he rubs his cock up and down my cleft, causing prickles of heat to radiate from me until I'm convinced I'm going to combust from sheer anticipation. *Hurry it up, Wyatt. I need you now.*

His hands grip at my hips, and he thrusts inside me in one long stroke.

Oh my God. I thought Sunday night was amazing. But this? Wyatt's shaft and the butt plug? This is intense and overwhelming, and I'm about to burn with pleasure.

"Please," I sob into Owen's cock, my hands clenching around Wyatt's cotton sheets.

Wyatt stills. "Are you okay, baby?" he asks with concern. "Is it too much?"

I shake my head. "Don't stop," I beg, blood pounding in my head, aching need clawing through my core. "So good."

His strokes resume, forceful and deep. I tremble and moan as I'm filled more completely than I've ever been filled in my life. His fingers twist the butt plug as he moves within me, and that adds another sharp layer of lust to my pleasure.

My insides twist, and my muscles contract around his cock. "Fuck," he moans. "You are so tight, Piper. You feel so good."

He pulls out and throws himself on the bed, pulling me on top of him. "Ride me," he orders, his voice hoarse. "I want to see your face."

I lower myself slowly on Wyatt's dick, gasping at the way my muscles stretch to accommodate him. Wyatt's hands close over my breasts, squeezing them, rolling my nipples between his fingers as I ride him. Owen repositions himself behind me, his hand grasping the butt plug. "As you ride Wyatt," he says, "I'm going to thrust this butt plug in and out of you."

He's true to his promise. As I bounce on Wyatt's hard dick, Owen teases the butt plug in and out. Sensation assaults me and I'm a whimpering mess, overwhelmed by the raw heat that's radiating through my body.

I'm ready. I'm not nervous anymore. I trust Owen and Wyatt to make it good for me. "Please," I beg. "I want both of you."

Owen groans. He removes the butt plug from my ass, and he trickles some lube down my crack. Wyatt pulls me forward so I'm lying down on top of his hard chest. "We're going to take it very slow," he promises. "We're going to make sure you're enjoying yourself." His mouth meets mine in a tender kiss.

My heart squeezes at the caring in his voice. "I'm not afraid," I tell him.

I'm lying. I'm not afraid of anal sex, but I am afraid of the future. I'm not Bailey or Gabriella, steadfast in their convictions. My parents have always been able to bully me into what they want, and they're going to be horrified if they find out what I'm doing.

Owen's fingers trace the ridge of my spine, and he pushes one finger into my ass. "Relax," he soothes. "The plug is much thicker than my finger."

"But not your cock." I bite my lip. Maybe I am a little nervous after all.

Wyatt moves his hand to my pussy. His fingers trace soft circles around my clitoris. "You're so beautiful," he says warmly as Owen adds another finger. "When I saw you tonight with the plug, I was so turned on." He trails kisses down my shoulder. "Did you think of us when you bought the toys?"

My cheeks heat. "Maybe," I mutter.

As Wyatt's words distract me, Owen adds a third finger. I feel a surge of slick, wet heat at his touch. "This feels great," he rasps.

"Piper," Wyatt groans, "you are so wet. You like this, don't you? Such a good girl in public, and so naughty in private."

I blush at his words. I'm really enjoying my walk on the wild side.

Wyatt's thumb moves faster over my clitoris, as Owen thrusts his fingers in and out of me. I'm dangerously close to another orgasm. "I'm going to come," I choke out.

"Good," Wyatt purrs, strumming faster on my tight bundle of nerves. My muscles clench and tighten. I grip Wyatt's shoulders as I near my release. "Come for us, Piper," he whispers.

My climax rushes toward me in a thunderous, explosive wave. When it hits, I scream and erupt, twisting and flailing in Wyatt's arms. Owen pulls his fingers out. My muscles are still quivering when I hear the condom wrapper tear. "I'm using plenty of lube," Owen says, his voice reassuring. "Trust me."

I'm still feeling the aftershocks of my orgasm as Owen's cock pushes into me. I inhale sharply as he enters my ass, and I clench my fingers into a fist as I feel my muscles stretch to accommodate his thickness. Owen strokes my back and Wyatt kisses my lips. Feeling me relax, Owen slides in further, deeper. "You are so tight, Piper."

He pushes deeper, until his entire length is in me. As he pulls out to thrust again, it strikes me that they're both in me. Wyatt's thick cock is buried in my pussy. Owen's hard shaft is stroking in and out of my ass. I'm sandwiched between their bodies. It's wrong and kinky and very naughty, *and I love it.*

"This is so incredible," I breathe.

They groan and pick up the pace. "Touch yourself," Wyatt commands me. "I want you to come again."

I don't need to be asked to come. I've been on the verge of release ever since Owen took my ass. I move my hand down to my clitoris, and pet myself, soft teasing strokes that make me shiver.

They coordinate their thrusts now, both pulling out of me, leaving me feeling empty, then thrusting in unison. I'm filled, *so filled,* that even though I want to prolong my orgasm, I can't. I explode between them, almost sobbing with the intensity of my climax.

They aren't too far behind. Owen's fingers dig into my hips and Wyatt's hands tighten on my waist, and within seconds of each other, they both find their release.

We stay huddled together in one sated, exhausted heap. Their bodies bracket me and warm me, and I never want to leave.

My mother's voice, banished during sex, makes an unpleasant return to my head. *This is not the behavior I expect from you, Piper.* She sounds both disappointed and disapproving.

I don't care, I retort defiantly.

But I'm not sure that's true. I don't think what the three of us are doing is a one-night stand. It has the potential to become a real relationship.

And if my parents find out, they'll go ballistic.

30

It is easier to forgive an enemy than to forgive a friend.

— WILLIAM BLAKE

Piper:

My hopes of a relaxed breakfast are dashed when I wake up, because the first thing I remember is Kevin's revelation. I groan, get out of bed, and wander to the kitchen. I'm not looking forward to telling Wyatt and Owen last night's news.

Sun is streaming into the room. PBS is on the radio. Owen's cooking breakfast and Wyatt's sitting at the table, reading the paper. "Kevin told me something last night that I thought you guys should hear," I say, coming into the room.

They look up. "Good morning," Wyatt says with a smile. "Did you sleep well?"

"No." I can't stop a silly grin from breaking out on my face. "A couple of really hot guys kept me awake all night."

"Really?" Owen's lips twitch. He pours me a cup of coffee, and adds milk and sugar. I give him a grateful smile as he pushes it in front of me. "That sounds terrible."

I laugh. "Are you kidding? It was great. I can't wait to do it again."

"Good." Wyatt sounds satisfied. "You started saying something about Kevin."

I make a face. "You know we had a crisis in the kitchen at the start, when the gravy was too salty?" I ask Wyatt. Owen knows all about it, of course, because he was in the kitchen with me, but I'm not sure if Wyatt is aware of the details.

He nods. "That was the reason you made the cauliflower sauce, right? As a substitute?"

"Yeah. It was going to take about fifteen minutes to get another batch of gravy made, and we had orders queuing up. I couldn't fall behind." I run my hands through my hair. "I thought Josef messed up the gravy because he'd been drinking, but last night, Kevin told me he'd tasted it after Josef left. He said it was perfect."

They both look up at that. "He's sure?" Owen asks, his voice sharp.

I sigh. "He swore that he was." Josef screwing up under the influence is annoying but benign. Somebody deliberately salting my gravy in order to throw me off is far more sinister.

Wyatt frowns. "Somebody sabotaged your gravy?" His voice shimmers with tightly controlled anger.

"That's what it looks like," I reply moodily. "I didn't want to tell you last night."

"I'm glad you didn't," Owen replies. He comes up to me and wraps his arms around me in a comforting hug. "Last night was very special."

Wyatt nods in agreement, but his attention quickly

returns to the gravy incident. "Who could it be?" he asks. "Who was in the kitchen last night?"

"Everyone," I reply. "The two camera guys. Kimmie. Petra. You. Me. Kevin. Josef. Owen. My mother. The kitchen was party central last night."

"Kimmie," Owen says flatly. "She was in a snit because I told her I'd fire her if she didn't stop chewing gum."

Wyatt looks skeptical. "You think she sabotaged the gravy as a result? I can't see it. She's got to be the best paid waitress in Manhattan. If we caught her, she has no reason to think she won't be fired."

"You're being rational," I tell him, sipping my coffee. "Not everyone is as logical as you. If she was pissed off, then she could have salted the gravy in a huff."

"Okay," he concedes. "Kimmie's a suspect. But you're forgetting someone else."

"Who?"

"Your mother."

My head snaps up in shock. "You're kidding."

He shakes his head. "I know you don't want to hear this," he says, his tone gentle. "But think about it. Your parents have never been happy about your decision to be a chef. They ensured you were late for your meeting with us. You even thought they were responsible for the Grant and Thornton audits."

"And I was wrong. Josh Lewis said it was Colton who'd asked for the audit."

"What if Josh Lewis is wrong?"

I glare at Wyatt. I can't believe his accusation. Owen steps into the fray, clearing his throat. "Here's what I see, Piper. Your parents have never taken any interest in your career. All of a sudden, when you're on the cusp of making it, they fly up to support you? Your mother offers to play hostess? Doesn't this strike you as suspicious?"

"No," I say stubbornly. I'm not going to listen to this. I know my parents haven't cared for my choice of career, but that doesn't mean they're going to actively mess up my chances of winning this contest. "You're wrong. My mother did not salt the gravy."

The two of them exchange glances. "Okay," Wyatt says. "As a precaution, we should probably get security cameras installed in the kitchen."

"Fine." I fold my arms around myself and don't look at them. I'm seething with rage. Several angry thoughts chase each other in my head, and I can't keep them contained. "You want to know what I think?" I snap at Wyatt. "You're upset that your dad showed up at the restaurant and caused a scene, and you're projecting. Well, my parents aren't sabotaging me. I had a happy childhood. Stop trying to compare my parents with yours."

Wyatt's face turns expressionless, and a pulse ticks in his jaw. Seeing his reaction, a hot surge of shame runs through me. I know Wyatt's sensitive about his childhood. He only told me about his past in order to comfort me the day I found out I was being audited. The moment I throw those words in his face, I wish I could take them back.

"I'm sorry," I stammer. "That was uncalled for."

Wyatt rises. "I'm going to work." His voice is cool. "See you around, Piper."

Owen doesn't meet my gaze. The silence stretches between us after Wyatt leaves, and he doesn't break it. Not to smirk, not to crack a joke.

"You're angry with me too." I want to lay my head down on the counter and cry.

He doesn't attempt to deny it. "Don't you have to be at

the restaurant?" he asks, the hint clear. He wants me to leave.

"Yeah." I don't look at him as I get up. The sun is still shining brightly, but my day has dulled. Last night's victory seems so far away. "I should go."

"Goodbye, Piper."

31

We must let go of the life we have planned, so as to accept the one that is waiting for us.

— JOSEPH CAMPBELL

Owen:

What a fucking disaster.

Once Piper leaves, I shower, get dressed and head to the office. I know Piper's sorry about what she said, but right now, my priority is Wyatt. He's my friend, he's hurting and knowing Wyatt, he's going to act like nothing's wrong.

"Is he in his office?" I ask Celia as I walk in.

She nods. "He's asked not to be disturbed." Her face twists into a worried frown. "Is everything okay?"

"It will be," I say grimly, knocking on the door and pushing it open.

"I told Celia I didn't want to see anyone," Wyatt says as I walk in.

"I wasn't aware that included me," I retort, sitting down on the other side of him and leaning back in the chair. "How are you?"

"Fine." His voice is clipped.

"Bullshit." I look around, and sure enough, the office is so spotless that I could eat a meal off the floor. "The last twenty-four hours have been crazy, and you're only human. I'm your friend. Talk to me."

He gives me an expressionless look but doesn't say anything.

"Wyatt," I tell him with a sigh. "I have shit to do. I'm not going anywhere unless you talk, but for the sake of my to-do list, I'd be really grateful if you stop stonewalling me."

That causes him to crack a smile. "Okay. I'm pissed with my dad, with Stone Bradley, and with Piper."

"In that order?"

He contemplates that. "I think so," he replies.

"Well, that's good. Start with your dad. Tell me why you're angry with him."

"Seriously?" He gives me a dry look. "I need to explain why? You were there."

"Humor me." I'm sure I'm driving Wyatt insane, but I've learned from experience that it's extremely helpful to peel back the layers to get to the underlying cause.

Wyatt looks exasperated. "Yesterday," he says, "my father deliberately came into *Piper's* to embarrass me. He showed up drunk, because he knew it would bother me. Throwing up on the table? That was a classic Jack Lawless power play."

"So you're angry that he out-maneuvered you."

"Yes. No. I don't know." Wyatt stares into space. "I just want him gone."

"Wyatt," I tell him quietly, "You keep saying that, but are

you sure that's true? If you really want him gone, all you have to do was pay him off. What would it cost you? A million? Two? Five? You have more than enough money."

"What are you saying, Owen?" Wyatt doesn't sound angry anymore. He just sounds tired.

"I'm saying that I've never heard you talk about your mother's hoarding to anyone. Hell, we were friends for ten years before you told me. Yet you told Piper. Maybe you're ready to face your childhood, not hide from it."

He gives me a thoughtful look. "I don't want to pay my father," he repeats. But the words don't have the same venom they usually do. "I need to come up with a plan." He sips at his coffee, his brow furrowed.

"You do that." I rise to my feet. "And call Piper."

"I'm still annoyed with her," he replies mildly.

"She apologized. Get over it."

"Don't you have a to-do list?" he counters. "Perhaps you should get to it."

STONE BRADLEY IS WAITING for me in my office. "Are you sure you aren't looking for Wyatt?" I ask him.

He shakes his head. "It's taken a few weeks, but I finally have something on Michael O'Connor for you."

Piper's landlord. I'd almost forgotten I'd asked Stone to investigate his connections with the Westies. "What do you have?"

He frowns. "It was very difficult to find the details, but Michael O'Connor's driver's license was first issued thirteen years ago. As was his social security number."

A chill travels up my spine. "He's part of a witness protection program."

"Sure looks like it."

When Michael O'Connor had pointed a gun at me, my first thought had been that he was mixed up in something crooked. What if that wasn't the real reason he'd been on edge that day? What if, even after thirteen years, he's still afraid?

Is this what you want to become, Owen?

I thank Bradley for his efforts, and see him out. I pop back into Wyatt's office. "I'm going to see Michael O'Connor," I tell him. "I want to persuade him to install the security equipment we need."

He looked up at me. "Really?" he asks, his eyebrow raised.

I shrug, unable to lie to him, but also unwilling to tell him the truth.

I still haven't been able to make contact with my uncle. I left a message on his voicemail on Monday. It's Friday, and there's been no reply.

I need to find out if Seamus Cassidy is in New York. If Michael O'Connor is so afraid of the reach of the mob that he's carrying a gun, even after thirteen years, then he might know something useful.

Then there's *Emerson's* and *The Pear Tree*. I can't just drop the ball on those while I try and find out if Mendez is lying to me.

MICHAEL O'CONNOR LOOKS wary when I knock on his door. It's early. The restaurant isn't open yet and Piper's nowhere to be seen. It's better this way. I don't want Piper wondering what I'm doing talking to her landlord.

"Mr. O'Connor?" I hold out my hand. "I'm Owen Lamb.

We met before?"

"Yes, you're the guy that likes to root through the trash." He shakes my hand. "What can I do for you?"

I'm the guy that likes to root through the trash. Sigh. *I'm great at first impressions.* "Can I come in?" What I'm going to say can't be said in the corridor of a building where we might be overheard.

He nods reluctantly and steps back to allow me entry. I walk into his sparsely decorated apartment, taking it in. No pictures hang from the wall. The couch is a faded navy blue monstrosity that has seen better days, and the coffee table is littered with empty pizza boxes, beer bottles, and takeout containers. "Sorry about the mess," he says, noticing my gaze. "I live alone. Cleaning doesn't seem worth the hassle."

Wyatt would hate this apartment. "No worries," I say easily. "I wanted to talk to you about Piper's restaurant."

"What about it?"

"Her lease needs to be renewed," I tell him. "And the restaurant needs some basic repairs done that are part of your responsibility. The tiles in the bathrooms are chipped, and I'm pretty sure the emergency features aren't up to code."

He shrugs. "The rent's below market."

"Fine. If that's the trade-off, then we'll draft up a ten-year lease for you to sign, and make the repairs ourselves."

"I can't do a ten year lease," he replies with a sigh. "I'm going to sell the building in the next few months and move away from New York."

I stiffen. "Why?" I demand, abandoning the pretense that I'm here about Piper's bathroom tiles. "What do you know? Are the Westies back in Hell's Kitchen? Is Seamus Cassidy in New York?"

He goes deathly white, and staggers where he stands.

"Who are you?" he asks hoarsely, his eyes wide with fear. "What do you want from me?"

Fuck. I don't want Michael O'Connor to have a heart attack. "Calm down," I say hastily, trying to sound reassuring. "I'm not here to hurt you. You were in witness protection, and so was I."

"What?" His mouth falls open. "Why?"

"The Westies murdered my family seventeen years ago." I swallow the lump in my throat. *The pain never fades.* "Seamus Cassidy ordered the hit. My real name is Owen McKenna."

He stares at me. "McKenna. I know the name. Cian McKenna was going to testify against the mob. The night before the trial, the family was killed."

"Not all the family." I can close my eyes and see the bodies of my da and my ma, my little sister Aileen. All dead. I force the words out. "I lived. I'm Cian McKenna's son. They changed my name and they put me on a plane, and I ended up in New York." I give Michael O'Connor a serious look. "Your story is probably quite similar, isn't it?"

He goes to his refrigerator and pulls out two bottles of beer. Opening them, he hands me one before taking a large gulp from his own. I refrain from pointing out that it's well before noon. "I was lucky," he says. "I was single. No wife, no children. I didn't have anything to lose." He gazes into his beer. "Except my life."

"What happened?"

"It was in Limerick," he says. "I was the bookkeeper of the Ryans." His mouth twists wryly. "I was also a double agent. When I testified, I took down the gang. All the leaders were sentenced to lengthy jail terms. Of course, the Ryans put a price on my head."

"And so the cops sent you to America. Why did you

come to Hell's Kitchen? You could have gone anywhere."

"I was homesick," he replies. "America was new to me and Hell's Kitchen was as close to Ireland as I could find. It was dangerous, but the Westies were gone from this neighborhood by then, and the Ryans had never made it to America."

"Are they back?" My voice is urgent. If the Westies are operating in this neighborhood again, and they find out who either of us are, they will take us out, and they will take out our loved ones as well in a warning that they are not to be crossed. In my case, Piper and Wyatt. I cannot allow that to happen.

He puts his beer down on the coffee table and leans forward. "I keep my ears to the ground, McKenna," he says, looking directly at me. "But I can't be certain of anything. I just don't know."

The silence stretches between us. "I need to leave here," he mutters in the end, his voice low and nervous. "I can't stay in New York if the Westies are back. I've been thinking of moving anyway. I'm tired of Manhattan, of the snow and the crowds and the noise. I want to find a beach in Florida. Maybe even a woman, after all these years." He smiles sadly. "I could never bear to get involved, you know? It never seemed right to bring a woman into my life. I couldn't risk it."

Piper asked me once why I didn't have any ex-girlfriends. *This is why.* When there is a price on your head, you aren't free to fall in love.

"You're going to need to sell the building." The germ of an idea is taking root in my head. Wyatt and I can't buy this building, not without setting off all kinds of red flags at Grant and Thornton. But we have friends, and two of them are real-estate magnates. "I might have a buyer for you."

32

Tread softly because you tread on my dreams.

— W. B. YEATS

Piper:

I expect the kitchen to be empty when I make it into the restaurant, but to my complete shock, Josef is there already, chopping a head of celery in swift, efficient motions. When he sees me, he straightens his shoulders. "Chef Jackson," he says, sounding surprisingly formal, "I want to apologize for yesterday."

I don't want to deal with this. Right now, I'm too heartsick about this morning, too filled with self-hatred at my cruelty to Wyatt, too fearful of the possibility that the two of them could be right about my parents.

"Okay," I say, moving past him to go to the refrigerator so I can get started on prep.

"No, Chef Jackson," Josef contradicts me. "It's not okay." He swallows nervously. "May I explain?"

I sigh inwardly. "Sure."

"I started working at *Aladdin's Lamp* twelve years ago," he says. "Your aunt hired me. I was fresh out of culinary school, and I knew what I wanted to do. I didn't want to work at a large restaurant where I would be a cog in the machine. At *Aladdin's Lamp*, I had a chance to cook my native cuisine, as well as work in a small bistro. It was a dream come true."

His words make me pause. Josef's never shared his dreams, but as he speaks, I realize how close his vision is to mine. He wanted to work in a small restaurant and cook the food he was passionate about. Me too. That's what *Piper's* is all about.

"Then," he continues, "Your aunt left to go back home, and she never came back. She appointed a company to manage the restaurant. For a while, I thought that was going to be good for me. I was the head chef. I believed that I could make this place great."

I feel a pang of sympathy for Josef. He's been here twelve years, and for most of those years, *Aladdin's Lamp* has limped along, losing more money with each passing year.

"But I quickly realized," he says sadly, "that I was the head chef in name only. I wasn't allowed to make any changes to the menu. I begged for better equipment, and my requests were rejected. The management company didn't care about *Aladdin's Lamp*. It was easier to do nothing and bill your aunt for the losses."

Aunt Vera had covered the losses while she was still alive, and *Aladdin's Lamp* had slowly been run into the ground. It was only after her death that things had changed.

"It's hard to walk away from a well-paying job," he confesses. "And there was no doubt, I was making better money than most of my peers. All I had to do was shut up, take my money, and stop caring about my work."

Poor Josef. Overwhelmed with money problems, I'd been too busy to try to get to the root cause of what was bothering him.

"When you started, I was briefly hopeful. You added new items to the menu and you seemed to care." He grimaces. "But after a month, I came to realize it wasn't enough. The restaurant was in dire straits, and you didn't have enough money to save it."

He's right. Had it not been for Owen and Wyatt, I would have failed.

In less than two months, they've turned things around. Last night, George Nicolson and Anita Tucker had praised my food. Maisie Hayes had commented on how much the place had improved. I'd made it through the first round of *Can You Take The Heat?*.

"What was yesterday about?" I ask Josef. "With the changes Wyatt and Owen have made, we have a real chance of success. You know that."

"I can't explain it," he replies. "After so many years of failure, things were finally going to turn around. I panicked." He looks up, his voice earnest. "It won't happen again, Chef."

I've been remiss in my duties as a business owner. I should have tried to understand why Josef was unhappy. "What do you want, Josef?" I ask him now. "What's going to make you jump out of bed in the morning, eager to get to work?"

He takes a deep breath. "I would like a fresh start," he says. "I want to be the head chef in a small Lebanese restaurant in New York, but the offers aren't pouring in."

Comprehension sets in. "If we win *Can You Take The Heat?*, you'll be able to put that on your resume."

He nods. "Yes, Chef Jackson. As you can see, I need you

to win this contest. I promise you, there will be no repeats of yesterday."

He resumes chopping the celery, then moves on to the carrots and onions. I stare into space. One thing becomes clear. Kevin's right; Josef didn't sabotage me last night.

Something nags at me. Kimmie's been around kitchens for a long time. She would know that over-salting the gravy wouldn't do anything other than throw off our rhythm for a few minutes. Gravy doesn't take long to make.

But my mother doesn't know anything about food.

I recoil from that thought. It can't be my parents. It just can't.

33

The truth will set you free, but first it will make you miserable.

— JAMES A. GARFIELD

Wyatt:

After Owen leaves, I contemplate his words for a long time, and I make a decision. I've been avoiding talking to my mother about this situation, but if my father's back in New York, my mother needs to know. Jack Lawless abandoned both of us when he left, not just me.

I dial her work number and she picks up on the second ring. "Wyatt," she says happily, "what a surprise. You're never going to guess what happened."

I rub at my temples. I have a bad feeling about this. "What happened?"

"Jack came by the house to see me. After all these years, he came back. I can't believe it."

The hair at the back of my neck stands on end. "When was this?" I ask carefully.

"On Tuesday."

I do some rapid calculations in my head. I told Stone Bradley to get my father evicted on Friday, exactly a week ago. Almost immediately, my dad had countered. "And you're happy about this?"

She exhales. "I'm not a fool, Wyatt. I know your father left us when we needed him. But I can either be angry at the past, or be happy in the present, and I'm choosing the present."

I'm getting schooled about letting go of the past from a woman who owns three dozen tennis shoes with holes in the soles, because they might be useful one day. *Fucking great.*

"I see." I keep my tone neutral. "What did he want?"

"To help me, dear," she replies fondly. "He knows one of the producers of *Hoarders*. He's going to get me on the show."

I clench my fingers into a fist. I don't want my mother on *Hoarders*. I don't want the world laughing at her, as if she was some kind of strange animal in a zoo. I don't want the cameras zooming in on the piles of torn underwear that she can't bring herself to throw away. I don't want the host of the program making my mother cry in order to titillate the TV-watching public. "If you wanted help, you just had to ask me."

"Is that true, Wyatt?" she asks sadly. "Maybe I'm too proud to ask for help from a son who is obviously ashamed of me. You don't think I know how bad the house is? Knowing that I have a problem is a lot easier than doing something about it." She sniffs, and I can picture her at her desk, her hair in a tight knot, her clothes neat to a fault, all carefully designed to keep her illness hidden from her friends and co-workers. "Your father was kind to me when he visited."

My father is lying scum. "Did he take photos of the house, mother?"

"Of course, dear. The producers of the show need it. He came in with an SLR camera and took enough photos for two rolls of film. I laughed at him about upgrading to a digital model, and he was quite indignant. I'd forgotten what a camera buff he was."

So my father has pictures now. Ammunition to blackmail me, in case his little display at *Piper's* isn't enough. If I didn't hate him so much, I'd almost admire his diabolical cunning.

"Mom." I stare out of the window. "I'm sorry I haven't been very kind." I draw a deep breath. "It was hard for me to grow up in that chaos. It was easier to try and forget about my childhood than to make peace with my past."

My words wound her; how could they not? But I've been silent for too long, holding on to my simmering resentment. If the distance between us is to be bridged, I need to tell her the truth. I can't nurse my anger until it hardens into bitterness.

When I was seven years old, I'd moved a stack of newspapers in the laundry room to reach the washer so I could do a load of laundry, and unwittingly, I'd disturbed a nest of mice. They'd scattered with squeaks in every direction, some running over my feet in their haste to flee. To this day, I remember how terrified I'd been, all because my mother couldn't bring herself to throw away a pile of old papers.

She doesn't reply. I hear a click on the other end of the line. She's hung up on me.

Yet I'm not sorry. I've finally stopped pretending, and it feels like a huge weight has been lifted off my shoulders.

34

Just as water retains no constant shape, so in warfare there are no constant conditions.

— Sun Tzu, The Art of War

Owen:

I've spent more time thinking of the Westies and Seamus Cassidy in the last few weeks than I have in years. I can't seem to focus on anything. A thousand thoughts chase each other in my head.

Wyatt's right. Mendez isn't good for my peace of mind.

Getting a hold of my uncle is turning out to be more difficult than I thought. Michael O'Connor doesn't know anything. No one is giving me a straight answer and the truth seems impossible to find.

The images flash through my head constantly. My father's body sprawled on the floor. My mother's hand linked in his, fear and horror etched on her face. Aileen looking puzzled, not understanding why someone would want to kill her. The blood seeping out of their bodies, staining the faded shag carpet.

I will never allow that to happen again to someone I care about. If Seamus Cassidy is out of jail, then I'm prepared to do whatever it takes to neutralize him as a threat. I don't care how bloody my hands get. This time, I *will* protect the people I love.

The people I love. Piper? Can it be true that I've fallen in love with her?

A slow smile breaks out on my face as I search my heart. We've only known each other for a few weeks, but even in that short time, she's become precious to me. When I'm with her, the ghosts of the past recede and my pain fades.

She makes me happy. She makes me feel whole, undamaged.

I draw a deep breath. I didn't think I was capable of falling in love. I was too wary of letting people in. My heart had been ripped into pieces once — I couldn't risk that kind of pain again.

But Piper slid into my life when I wasn't looking. When she let her walls down and cried to us, she destroyed my barriers.

I will do anything to keep her safe.

There are two restaurants on Mendez's list that I need to investigate, *Emerson's* and *The Pear Tree*. It's time to get to work.

I SPEND most of Saturday with Carl Marcotti, working with him on the design and layout of his new kitchen. Once we're done, he asks if I want to grab a pint of beer at the local pub. "How about *Emerson's* instead?" I ask casually. "The last time

I talked to Max Emerson, he boasted that he was going to win *Can You Take The Heat?*. He talks a big game. I want to see if he can back it up."

Carl frowns with distaste. "If you insist," he replies. "I personally don't want to give that thug any of my money."

I raise my eyebrow, alerted by Carl's tone of dislike. "I didn't know that you knew him."

"I don't. A couple of my waitresses used to work there. I hear things."

"What kind of things?"

"Emerson has a private room in the back of his restaurant. Tammy was assigned to work it, and she hated it. The customers would grope her and she was expected to put up with it. Max more or less told her that those men were his high-rollers and if she complained, she'd get fired."

"High-rollers? Is Emerson running a gambling ring there?"

Carl gives me a confused look. "I thought that's why you decided to pass on him," he replies. "Everyone knows Lawless and Lamb run a clean shop, and *Emerson's* is dirty as shit."

I shake my head. "We only met Max Emerson once," I tell him. "He was too cagey about his numbers, and Wyatt and I didn't get a good vibe from him." I'm cursing myself as I speak. I've been so busy fixing Piper's restaurant that I've missed the obviously illegal activity at *Emerson's*. *What else have I overlooked?*

We get to the pub. Even though it's six in the evening on Saturday and the neighborhood is packed with people enjoying the warm weather, *Emerson's* is almost empty. "Max told me on the phone that this place was doing great," I remark. "It sure as hell doesn't seem like it."

Carl rubs his chin but doesn't say anything. We settle in

and order pints of beer, nachos, and chicken wings. Carl checks his phone while I look around discreetly. There's only one waitress working the place, and she's so surly that she makes Kimmie look friendly and welcoming. The place smells like stale beer and depression.

Max Emerson himself is nowhere to be seen, but that doesn't surprise me. Max doesn't cook and he doesn't manage the front either. He's an absentee owner, someone who wants the rewards without doing the work. I have no respect for people like him.

In comparison, Piper's in her restaurant every single day, working her ass off so she can be successful. When we're done here, Carl will go back to his restaurant and work for another five solid hours, making sure everything's okay.

Our food arrives. The nachos are lukewarm and the chicken wings are bland. Carl grimaces in disgust as he eats. "How did this place even get on *Can You Take The Heat?* I can name a dozen places that are more qualified than this one."

Another interesting question, and this time, I know who to ask. Tomorrow morning, I'm going to have a long chat with Maisie Hayes.

35

Sometimes, you have to get angry to get things done.

— Ang Lee

Wyatt:

Owen threatened to beat me to a pulp if I didn't take him along when I went to see my father. I'm fairly sure he was joking, but I still knock on his door Sunday morning.

He opens it, barely glancing up from his phone. "Have you read Maisie's blog post today?" he asks me.

I shake my head. I've been so stressed out at the thought of meeting my father that it's completely slipped my mind that the results of the first round were going to be announced today on Maisie's blog. "Piper made it through, didn't she?" I demand.

"She did." He gives me a pointed look. "You still haven't called her."

"Not yet," I confess. "I want this mess out of the way first."

He rolls his eyes at me. "Wyatt, do you like Piper?" he demands.

"Of course," I reply automatically. I don't just like Piper. *I really like her*. Whenever I think of her, I smile like a silly fool. Every time I hear someone with a Southern accent, I'm reminded of her. When I see someone on the street with curly blonde hair, my heart starts to pound.

"Then call her, because I don't want to lose her." He looks at me seriously. "For the last seventeen years, I've resisted getting involved. But I'm in love with Piper, and I think you are too." He takes a deep breath. "I don't want to mess things up with her."

Am I in love with Piper? I ask myself that question and the answer is instantaneous. Of course I am. I'm madly, crazily, head-over-heels in love with Piper Jackson. I'm also, unfortunately, a control freak who likes to compartmentalize his life in tidy little boxes. "As soon as this situation with my dad is sorted out, I will."

"She's too important to risk, Wyatt." Owen's voice is urgent.

He's absolutely right. I don't want Piper to think I'm still angry with her. I've known Piper for a little over two months, and I've been happier than I've ever been in my life. The three of us have attended restaurant auctions together. We've painted her restaurant and chosen the dishes on her new menu. All the hours we've spent together in the evenings after her restaurant has closed has brought us together. I can't imagine my life without her in it.

"I agree." I don't intend to fuck this up. I care for Piper too much. "What were you saying about Maisie's blog?"

"I was looking at the list of winners," he says with a frown. "*Piper's* beat *Soul Kitchen*, no surprise there. But *Emerson's* beat *The Queen's Beaver,* which seems strange to me."

My lips twitch involuntarily. *The Queen's Beaver* is a cheeky name for a British pub. "You didn't expect that?"

"No," he replies. "I've eaten at *The Queen's Beaver* before. Their chef is very concerned with local and seasonal ingredients. The food there is light years better than *Emerson's.*" He gives me a troubled look. "Carl Marcotti told me yesterday that Max Emerson ran a gambling ring in the back of his restaurant."

I grow still at that. "Mendez put *Emerson's* on the list for a reason," I say slowly. "Max Emerson is a sleazeball, but I didn't think he was dangerous."

"Someone picked *Emerson's* as a contestant on *Can You Take The Heat?*, even though there are better choices. Max has advanced to the next round, though he shouldn't have. None of this makes sense, and I want answers." His voice is hard. "I need to talk to Maisie."

"Good idea. Let's visit her after I deal with my father."

Owen seems surprised. "You're coming too? You don't approve of Mendez."

"No, I don't," I agree grimly. "I think he's lying to you about Seamus Cassidy, and I don't think the Westies are operating in Hell's Kitchen. But if *Emerson's* is in the contest, then eventually, Max Emerson will be competing against Piper. I want to know what we're dealing with."

THE SECURITY GUARDS have been instructed to escort my father upstairs. He shows up precisely at ten, and a guard brings him up to the conference room I'm waiting in. Owen's seated at my side. On our way here, I've filled him in on the most recent developments. He knows my father took photos of the chaos in my mother's house, and he's reached the same conclusion I have.

Embarrassing me isn't enough. I'm about to be blackmailed.

"Hello son."

His greeting sends a fresh surge of rage through me, but I take a deep breath and calm down. I know that my father is needling me deliberately. He's trying to make me angry and throw me off my game.

Jack Lawless notices Owen and he stiffens. *Good.* He expected that we'd be alone today. In this game of cat and mouse, I'm done being chased and I'm ready to be the predator. "Who's this?" he asks, unable to keep the edge out of his voice.

"Owen Lamb, meet Jack Lawless." I perform introductions blandly.

They don't shake hands. My father takes a seat at the table. "I thought you'd want us to have this discussion in private."

"On the contrary, I'd like Owen to be part of this discussion." I feel a faint sense of satisfaction at my father's consternation. Let's see how well he does when he's off balance. He thought that I'd meet him in secret and he'd make his demands. He's counted on my sense of shame about the way I grew up.

He takes a deep breath and launches into his spiel. "I know you want me gone from your life, but I'm broke. If you could help me with that, I'll leave New York, and you won't hear from me again."

"How much?" From the start, I knew this was about dollars and cents. The Wall Street Journal article had spoken admiringly of our financial successes, and my father had thought he could make some easy money.

My bluntness takes him by surprise. "Three million."

At my side, Owen stiffens with outrage. "You're fucking insane," he snaps.

I hold up my hand. "What's the '*or else?*'"

"What do you mean?" my father blusters.

I meet his gaze squarely. "Let's lay our cards on the table. You're trying to blackmail me for three million dollars. Why do you think I'm going to agree to your demands?"

Is he going to mention the photos?

He does. "If you don't," he says, "I will sell photos of your mother's house to the tabloids. The entire world will know that Wyatt Lawless' mother lives in squalor. Everyone will whisper and talk." He sneers at me. "I don't think you're ready for that, Wyatt."

Owen's hands clench into fists.

When I hear the threat, my heart breaks. A small, stupid part of me had hoped that it wouldn't come down to this. But to Jack Lawless, I'm nothing more than a walking wallet.

"I don't have ready access to that kind of cash," I reply, lying without a twinge of guilt. "My money is tied up in investments. It'll take me a few weeks to free it up."

"How long?" Greed is making my father stupid. He doesn't stop to think that I might be bluffing.

"Three weeks." I want Piper to win *Can You Take The Heat?* before I see my father again. We promised her we'd be there for her and I intend to keep my word.

"I can't wait that long," he argues.

I get to my feet. "That's the offer," I say flatly. "Take it or leave it."

He gives me an assessing look. Perhaps he's trying to figure out how much he can push me. After a long pause, he gives in. "Okay. I'll meet you here in three weeks."

"There's a condition." Owen cuts in, his voice hard. "If you try and contact Wyatt before then, the deal's off."

My father opens his mouth to protest, then thinks better of it. He nods tersely, rises to his feet and leaves the room.

Jack Lawless thinks I'm going to pay him.

I'm not.

What I need is a plan.

I've bought myself some space. This is a chess game, and I have twenty-one days to figure out my next move.

Owen:

"What are you going to do?" I ask Wyatt as we head to Maisie's apartment.

"I don't know." He walks forward, his hands in his pockets. "My father hasn't apologized for abandoning me. He hasn't once said he was wrong to walk out on a thirteen year old child. All he cares about is himself." He shakes his head, looking frustrated. "If it were just me, I'd tell him to go to hell. But I have to think about my mother. She's spent her entire life trying to hide her illness from her friends and her co-workers. How is she going to feel when her house is being mocked in the tabloids?"

I'm surprised that Wyatt cares about his mother's reaction. In all the time I've known him, he's barely mentioned her. They only see each other a handful of times a year and Wyatt always returns from these meetings tense and angry. "So you're going to pay him off?"

"Two impossible choices," he mutters. "I need to find a third one."

"Can Stone Bradley help?"

He shakes his head. "Stone won't do anything illegal."

"Will you?"

His lips twist. "I'd prefer to stay within the law. We've built a successful business over the years, you and me. We have restaurants that depend on us. I'd hate to risk all of that for my father."

We walk the rest of the way in silence. When we reach Maisie's building, Wyatt presses the buzzer.

"Hello?" Maisie's voice sounds from the speaker, tinny and crackly.

"Maisie, it's Wyatt and Owen. Can we chat with you for a minute?"

She sounds surprised to hear from us. "Umm, sure. Come on up."

She buzzes us in and we make our way up to her apartment. Maisie's standing in the doorway, waiting for us. "This is unexpected," she says, surveying us with narrowed eyes. "To what do I owe this pleasure?"

"I want to talk to you about *Emerson's,*" I reply.

"Oh boy." She steps aside. "You better come in." We follow her inside, and she waves to the couch. "You guys want a cup of coffee or something?"

We both decline. "What do you want to know?" she asks.

"I read your article this morning," I tell her bluntly. "I also ate at *Emerson's* last night. How did it make it into the contest, and how on earth did it beat *The Queen's Beaver?*"

"The first question is easy to answer," she says, flopping into an overstuffed armchair. "There were sixteen restaurants in the contest. I picked eight. Yelp, as one of the sponsors, chose four, and the Hell's Kitchen Business Association, as the other sponsor, chose four more. Yelp was transparent in their selection process; they put up a poll on their website, and the four restaurants with the most votes were chosen. The association wasn't. John Page gave me four names with no explanation on how they were picked. *Emerson's* was one of them."

Interesting. "How did it advance to the next round?"

"That," Maisie sighs, "I can't explain. I eat at *The Queen's Beaver* all the time, and I love the food there. But when we showed up on Friday to judge them, the kitchen was off its game so badly it was unrecognizable. There's no explaining it." She grimaces. "They might have still made it through, but *Emerson's* won the public vote by a landslide."

"What?" The contest has been designed quite carefully to make sure the only people that can vote on a restaurant are the people that eat there during the week. At *Piper's*, we've been given a stack of comment cards to hand out to our patrons, each with a unique identifier to prevent fraud. "*Emerson's* was nearly empty last night."

She nods dourly. "They've got to be cheating."

"Aren't you going to do anything about it?" Wyatt demands in outrage.

"What do you want me to do?" she snaps, giving us an irritated look. "Do you expect me to stand outside *Emerson's*, counting the number of guests each night, and making sure only the diners get a comment card?" She shrugs. "It sucks for *The Queen's Beaver*. However, in the final round, there's no popularity contest. The winner will be decided by the four judges and no one else."

Wyatt frowns at Maisie. "You're awfully calm for someone whose contest is being fucked with," he growls.

"You should have seen me last night," she retorts. "There was screaming."

~

"It doesn't add up," I tell Wyatt as we head back to our offices. "Why did *The Queen's Beaver* screw up? Greg Tennant has thirty years of experience. Maisie's contest isn't going to throw him off his game."

Wyatt glances at his watch. "Let's go ask him," he suggests. "And I want to call Piper after that."

"That's good," I tell him with a smirk.

"Shut up," he grumbles, but a smile plays about on his lips. He raises his hand for a cab and we make our way to Hell's Kitchen. With any luck, we'll talk to Greg, then head back home in time to cook Piper a nice meal.

When we get to *The Queen's Beaver*, everything's oddly quiet. The restaurant is busy, but the waitresses, normally cheerful, are walking around in hushed silence. Something's the matter.

We take a seat at the bar and Wyatt pulls a business card out of his wallet. "Is Chef Tennant working today?" he asks the bartender, handing her his card. "If he is, could you tell him I'd love to see him?"

She barely looks up. "The chef is extremely busy this morning."

"We're old friends." I give her my best persuasive smile. "We only need a minute."

"Fine." Reluctance drips from every syllable. "I'll see if he's available."

In about three minutes, Greg Tennant appears, wiping his hands on his apron. When he sees us, he gives us a strained smile. "Wyatt Lawless and Owen Lamb. I'm honored."

Greg and I had lunch together only a few weeks ago. He looks tired this morning, a lot greyer than the last time I saw him. Something's going on and I'm determined to get at the root of the matter. "Greg, can we talk to you in private?"

"Let's go to my office."

Greg's office is tiny. The two of us squeeze in and take a seat. I eye the piles of paperwork threatening to overflow the battered wooden desk with amusement, but at my side, Wyatt flinches in discomfort. The place probably reminds him of his mother's home, and after this morning, he's especially vulnerable to chaos.

As soon as the door shuts behind us, Greg opens his mouth. "What'd you guys want to talk about?" he asks bluntly. "Forgive me for hurrying you, but I was on my way to the hospital."

"The hospital?"

He takes a deep breath. "Can you guys keep something quiet?" he asks. "Max Emerson came to my kitchen last week and told me to throw Maisie Hayes' contest."

"What?" I lean forward, shocked.

He nods. "Of course, I told him to fuck off. As if I'm going to let a punk like Emerson tell me what to do. Then on Friday night, hours before the judges showed up, some guy ran a red light and t-boned my wife's car."

"No." Wyatt sounds horrified. "You think Max is involved?"

"I don't know," Greg admits. "But after the accident, I had to take him seriously. Donna broke two ribs and a leg." He spreads his hands, looking helpless. "What would you have done in my place?"

Cold fear grips my heart. After her outstanding performance in the first round, Piper is the front-runner in *Can You Take The Heat?*. I can't be worrying about Mendez's shadow threats right now, not when there's a real risk that Emerson might hurt Piper to win the contest.

"We have to tell her," I tell Wyatt. "We can't keep her in the dark."

Wyatt looks grim. "You're absolutely right."

36

Holding on to anger is like grasping a hot coal with the intent of throwing it at someone else; you are the one who gets burned.

— BUDDHA

Piper:

By the time Sunday rolls around, I'm tired, cranky, and completely miserable. I haven't heard from either Owen or Wyatt since Friday morning, and I have only myself to blame.

I could call them. A thousand times, I've picked up my phone to dial their number, but my shame prevents me from following through. Without Wyatt and Owen, I'd be teetering on the verge of failure. I owe them everything, and this is the way I reward them?

There is, however, a silver lining. After our talk on Friday, Josef is a new man. He's raised his game considerably. On Friday and Saturday, the kitchen ran like a well-oiled machine. So much so that when my mother calls and suggests eating lunch together, I agree without too much reservation, and meet my parents in a pretentious little bistro on the Upper East Side, steps from their five star, six-hundred dollars a night hotel room.

Once the three of us are seated at an outdoor table, my mother smiles warmly. "The restaurant was busy Thursday," she remarks.

"It was." My voice is neutral. Wyatt's accusation echoes in the back of my mind. "Thank you again for your help."

She waves aside my thanks. "Angelina said you wrote to her telling her you couldn't be a bridesmaid." Her lips turn downward into a frown. "That's disappointing."

Ah. We're on much more familiar ground. I'm used to my mother's unhappiness. "She wanted me to fly to New Orleans every second weekend from now until May," I reply, scanning the menu instead of facing her accusing glare. "I just can't afford to do that."

My dad changes the topic. "I read about the contest on that woman's blog this morning. What's her name? You know, the one who's in charge of the show?"

"Maisie Hayes." I've been so depressed the last two days that I've completely forgotten that the official results would have come out this morning.

"Right, that's her. She was very impressed with your restaurant."

"Was she? I haven't read her blog post yet."

"Really?" He raises an eyebrow, pulls out his phone and hands it to me. "Why not? You've officially moved to the next round."

"I've been busy," I mutter, not ready to discuss Wyatt and Owen.

I skim the article. Maisie's raved about the food,

declaring it to be the best meal she's eaten in a long time. She says a lot of flattering things about the decor at *Piper's,* and the atmosphere, warm, friendly, and unpretentious. She closes with advice for her readers. *As soon as the world discovers Piper's,* she writes, *there's going to be a months-long wait to get in. So go now, citizens of New York! Go before the crowds show up, and enjoy Chef Piper Jackson's inventive twist on Southern comfort food.*

My heart jumps at that last line. We're going to be busy this week, thanks to Maisie Hayes. I want to text Wyatt and Owen to ask them if they've read the article.

Then my smile fades. I can't do that. "That's a nice review," I say flatly, handing the phone back to my dad.

My mother gives me a piercing look. "Your partners, Owen and Wyatt," she says, her voice deceptively casual. "You seem close to them."

Panic fills me. Lillian Jackson has always been good at ferreting out the things I'm trying to hide from her. If she suspects the nature of our relationship... I can't let that happen. I just can't. Even though I'm an adult and I don't need my parents to approve of my relationships, when I even think of revealing the truth, the words freeze in my throat.

I settle for a half-truth. "Their help has been invaluable."

"You mean their money," she says. Her nose wrinkles in distaste. In Lillian Jackson's world, talking about money is just not done.

"Actually, no." To my surprise, I contradict her. "Anyone could have invested money, but they did so much more." Owen and Wyatt have been with me every step of the way. They cheer me up when I'm down, deliver bracing words of encouragement when I doubt myself, and when I need their support, they're always there with a shoulder for me to lean on.

They're more than my partners, and they're more than just friends. Though I wanted to slap them the first time I met them, I can't imagine my life without Wyatt and Owen in it.

I think I've fallen in love with them.

Shit.

"They're quite unsuitable, of course," my mother sniffs. "I'm assuming you know that, Piper."

I ignore the warning in my mother's tone. We finish our lunch in silence.

AFTER THAT STRAINED MEAL, I'm ready to talk to someone normal. It's Sunday. I'm assuming Bailey is doing something with Daniel and Sebastian. Gabby is a two-hour drive away and I don't own a car. Katie's busy with the monster twins and Miki's in Houston.

I call Wendy and beg her to hang out with me. An hour later, the two of us are huddled in a booth in a bar in West Village, looking at a beer list that's three pages long, trying to make up our minds what we want to drink. "I really shouldn't," I say regretfully, looking longingly at the pints of beer on the tables all around us. "I might have to go back to work."

Wendy grimaces. "Me too." We order glasses of orange juice, ignoring the eye-roll the waitress gives us. Once she's gone, Wendy gives me a piercing look. "You look glum," she says. "Which is odd, because I read what Maisie Hayes had to say this morning. You should be over the moon."

"I'm having boy troubles," I say moodily.

"How come? The three of you looked pretty close on Thursday."

I look up at her. "You noticed that too? My mother remarked on it today."

"I'm not surprised," she says. "Neither Wyatt nor Owen could take their eyes off you. So what happened between Thursday and now?"

"I did something really stupid." I take a sip of my orange juice and wish it were something stronger. Drowning myself in drink might not solve anything, but it will at least numb my misery. "I said something really mean to Wyatt."

I tell Wendy the story of the ruined gravy. "Wyatt and Owen thought it was my mother who did it," I finish. "I lashed out at Wyatt." I grimace. "I was so angry, but that's no excuse. I shouldn't have."

Wendy frowns. "Didn't you apologize to him? You don't typically sit on your high horse when you're in the wrong."

"I apologized right away. But I haven't talked to them all weekend."

My friend shakes her head. "In other words, each one of you is waiting for the other to call," she says dryly. "That's very grown-up of all of you. Why are you avoiding them?"

"What if they want nothing to do with me?" Gulping nervously, I voice my deepest fear. "I really like them. I don't want it to be over."

"Oh for fuck's sake. Don't be ridiculous. Call them now."

"What?" I look up at her. "I can't do that."

My phone's on the table. Before I can react, she grabs it, finds Wyatt on the list of my contacts, and dials his number, ignoring my outraged squawk. "Stop that," I say indignantly, but it's too late. Wyatt's picked up.

"Is that Wyatt Lawless?" she asks. "This is Wendy, Piper's

friend. We've met before. Piper wants to talk to you." She hands me the phone. "Do it."

My hand trembles as I reach for the instrument. "Hey," I say, crossing my fingers behind my back. "I'm so sorry. I should have never said what I did. Please don't be mad at me."

Wyatt's voice wraps around me like a warm embrace. "Okay," he says.

"Wait, what?" Of everything I expect to hear from him, this isn't it. I'm prepared for a cold shoulder, or angry words of recrimination. I'm not ready for a calm *okay*.

"Okay," he repeats, and this time, there's a note of amusement in his voice. "Okay, I won't be mad at you."

"If you aren't angry, why didn't you call me?" The moment those words leave my mouth, I want to take them back. I sound like a whiny girlfriend, and God knows I don't have any claim on either Wyatt or Owen. We've had sex twice. That does not give me the right to make demands of them.

Wyatt doesn't seem to think my question is out of line. "I'm sorry about that," he says regretfully. "I was just about to call you. Are you at *Piper's* right now?"

"No, Josef's working today. I'm taking the afternoon off."

"Good." He sounds relieved. "Owen and I need to talk to you. If you don't have to be at work, can you come over?"

"Now? I'm having a drink with Wendy."

Wendy rolls her eyes and snatches my phone from my hand. "No, she's not," she tells Wyatt. "She's finished here. She's heading over right now."

I glare at Wendy, but my outrage lacks conviction.

37

Love is friendship that has caught fire.

— Ann Landers

Piper:

Both Owen and Wyatt are at the curb waiting for my cab. The instant I pull up and open the door, they jump forward. Wyatt encloses me in a hug, while Owen pays my driver. "Hey, I can do that," I protest, to no avail. "What's going on? You guys are being weird."

"Come upstairs," Wyatt replies. "We'll explain."

Something is wrong. An old lady rides the elevator up with us, preventing me from questioning them. I wait impatiently until we get to the top floor.

Owen pushes the door open to his place and gestures me in. The instant the door shuts behind us, Wyatt's tension seems to drain away. "Hello, Piper," he says, his voice low and intent. "I've missed you."

The way I see it, I have two choices. I can either demand

that they tell me what is happening, or I can fall into bed with them and have some mouth-watering sex first. Falling into bed wins by a landslide.

"I've missed you too." I'm wearing a short sleeved button-down shirt, and I reach for the first button, and undo it. My lips quirk into a smile at their reaction. Wyatt sits down on the couch and leans back with sharp interest, his eyes fixed on the slivers of skin slowly coming into view.

Owen is more proactive. He takes a step toward me. "Do you like your shirt?" he growls.

"I hate it." I sound like I've been running a race. My voice is breathless, layered with need.

"Good." His fingers grip the fabric, and he rips. Buttons fly everywhere, and I gasp as he yanks the shirt free. The bra follows. I stand in my pencil skirt and my pumps, lust raging through my blood.

"Two nights," Owen says, his voice controlled, his breath tickling my ear, "we slept without you. Tell me you want to make it up to us."

The violence of my need almost causes my knees to buckle. "I want to make it up to you," I whisper.

"Get on your knees."

I sink to the floor, my eyes on Wyatt, loving the way he's watching me. I'm prey and these men are the predators, but though my heart hammers in my chest, I have no desire to be anywhere but here.

"Crawl toward him." Owen's instruction almost makes me combust. My insides tighten. On my hands and knees, I move to Wyatt.

When I reach him, I sit up on my haunches and my fingers find his belt. "I want you," I say boldly.

His eyes darken. "I'm all yours, Piper," he replies as I undo his belt and unzip his trousers, almost tearing his clothes away so I can touch him. His cock jumps out, hard and ready, and I close my hand around him, sliding up and down on his thick length before taking him in my mouth.

"Fuck, Piper," Wyatt groans, his head thrown back on the couch, his eyes closed.

I love this reaction. I can feel my pussy drip; I'm so turned on.

Owen comes up behind me, wrapping his arms around my waist. "I missed these breasts," he growls into my ear as his hands slide up my chest to cup my globes. "I missed these nipples." He rolls my erect nubs between his thumb and forefinger, then he pinches them hard. I gasp onto Wyatt's cock as a slice of raw heat cuts through me.

He grabs the hem of my pencil skirt and tugs up, smoothing the fabric over the curve of my hips until it's bunched up at my waist. He yanks my panties down to my knees. "Part your legs for me, baby," he urges.

His fingers slide deep into me. "So wet," he marvels. "I've been starved for this pussy, Piper. You offered us a feast and you took it away." His other palm smooths over my ass, then he spanks me.

Oh, that was nice. We *have* to do that again.

I pull my mouth from Wyatt's cock. I lick the underside of his shaft, and cup his balls gently. "So fucking good," he moans, staring down at me. "So fucking beautiful."

Owen's fingers find my clitoris, and he pets me in little teasing strokes. "More," I gasp out, trying to push back into him so there's more contact, more friction. I need this; I need them. Before I met them, I went without sex for five years. Now, I can't seem to last five hours. My desire, so long on the back-burner, is now ablaze. I quiver and tremble for their touch.

"You're in full sight of the window," Wyatt says, staring at me with hungry eyes. "It's daytime. Anyone can look in and see you on your knees, with your pretty little lips wrapped around my cock."

"I don't care," I say defiantly. "Let them look." Right now, it wouldn't even matter if people were standing in a circle around us, staring down at the tangle of bodies. All I want is for Owen to stroke me, just a little harder. My thighs tremble as my climax dances, just out of reach.

"You don't care?" Owen asks. "Really?" His tone is deliberately casual. He's plotting something.

Wyatt's lips curve into a smile. "Get up, Piper."

Owen helps me to my feet. I strip off my panties while Owen's fingers work at my skirt, undoing the button and sliding the zipper down. "Step out of it," he orders.

If this is a test, then I'm going to ace it, because I will do anything to for my orgasm. If they ask me to spread my legs and touch myself in front of them, I will. If they order me to fuck myself with a dildo, I'll comply with pleasure. I ache with throbbing need; I'm trapped in a net of powerful lust.

Wyatt strips efficiently, unembarrassed by his nakedness. I shamelessly check him out. Owen disappears for a minute and returns with condoms and lube. He removes his clothes as well, and wraps his hands around my wrist. "We're going to push you against the window and take you in full sight of the city, Piper."

I bite my lower lip, but my pussy floods at the thought. "Okay," I whisper.

Their eyes blaze with heat. "What a naughty girl," Wyatt says, his hands gripping my wrists as he inches me back toward the glass.

"She is," Owen agrees. "I should pull you over my lap, Piper, and spank you hard."

There's no doubt; my body likes the sound of that. I

watch with greedy eyes as they roll condoms on their cocks. Owen slicks a generous amount of lube on his shaft, and fists himself, pumping up and down to coat every hard inch.

Wyatt reaches for me. I lift my right leg off the floor and wrap it around his hip, standing on tiptoe as his thick length penetrates me. "Fuck yes, he says through clenched teeth. "You are so tight, Piper."

Owen's dick nudges at my bottom. I gasp as he penetrates me, filling me completely. My body tingles as they thrust into me. At first, they hold on to their control, but it doesn't take long before they unravel. Their strokes get harder, faster. "Touch yourself," Owen rasps. "I want to feel you come, Piper."

My fingers strum at my clitoris. I'm not gentle. My body is shaking with raw desire. I rub myself, pleasure radiating from my core. I'm so close. Just a little more, just a little harder...

And I'm there. My climax washes over me in a thunderous wave. I see stars; I touch the skies. When my quivering tremors have barely begun to subside, Wyatt and Owen groan out within seconds of each other as they explode, their fingers digging into my flesh.

"So tell me something," I ask them, as we collapse on the carpet, the fibers tickling my skin, "did the whole of New York just watch us?"

Wyatt chuckles. "You liked the idea of that, didn't you?" he teases. "No, the glass is coated. You can't see in."

"I thought as much," I lie, but neither of them falls for it. Their gazes are knowing, and my cheeks flush. I'm turning out to be some kind of sex-crazy fiend.

But I like it.

∾

"Are you going to tell me what's going on?"

The sun is lower in the sky. The bright lights of the city are flickering on as the daylight recedes. It's as quiet as it gets in Manhattan, as people start the Sunday night routine of getting ready for the week ahead.

Wyatt takes a deep breath. "Where should we start?" he asks Owen.

Owen looks nervous, which startles me. I don't think I've ever seen Owen Lamb at a loss for words. "Can I ask you something?" he says to me.

"You're freaking me out."

He doesn't crack a smile, though he takes my hand in his. "Where do you see this relationship going?"

"Are you breaking up with me?" I ask bluntly.

Wyatt snorts. "Oh for fuck's sake, Owen," he says with fond exasperation. "Piper, Owen's trying to tell you he's in love with you." He rolls his eyes in Owen's direction. "He's doing an excruciatingly bad job of it."

Owen glares at Wyatt. "I don't see you saying anything," he points out. "It's harder than it looks."

I look from Owen to Wyatt, disbelief and the beginnings of joy warring in my heart. "Wait, you're in love with me?" I ask Owen. "Is that true, or is that something Wyatt made up?"

"It's true." His clear blue gaze never leaves mine. "I love you, Piper Jackson. And I know we haven't talked about the future, and I know a threesome is unorthodox, but I also know that the last eight weeks have been the happiest of my life." He turns toward Wyatt. "Your turn."

Wyatt actually blushes. The look on his face tugs at my heartstrings. "You probably know where this is going," he says, rubbing the back of his neck. "I love you too Piper. I think I've loved you from almost the first moment I met you." He reaches for my other hand, the one Owen isn't holding, and he continues, his voice soft with memory. "You put your hands on your hips, and you demanded to know why we'd eaten at your restaurant for the last two weeks. You were so feisty and so spunky that I couldn't help but fall in love with you." He swallows. "I was hurt by your words on Friday," he admits, "but when you left, I realized that it didn't matter. If we fought, we'd make up, because I can't imagine my life without you in it."

I grin widely. "I love you too," I reply, sitting up straight and throwing my arms around them. "I love both of you so much. And I know a threesome can be complicated, but two of my best friends are in them. If they can make it work, so can I."

My mother's face dances before me, her eyes blazing with anger and disapproval. I shake my head and push it away. *I don't care what my parents think,* I tell myself defiantly. *I'll find a way to make it work.*

But there's a small voice inside me that's calling me a liar, and I think that voice might be right.

"HANG ON," I say, after another extended round of cuddling that predictably, leads to sex, "That's not the reason you guys were acting so strange when I pulled up."

Owen sits up with a sigh. "It's a long story," he says. "And you might be furious with us once you hear it. You remember the day we first met? You asked us why we picked *Aladdin's Lamp*."

I nod. "Because Sebastian told you to, right?"

"Wrong." Wyatt shakes his head. "Sebastian just suggested we try your food. And we did, for two weeks. But

I was pretty convinced *Aladdin's Lamp* wasn't a good fit for us."

"There's a cop called Eduardo Mendez," Owen continues. "Mendez and his wife were my foster parents when I first moved to America. I've helped him out with his cases from time to time."

Wyatt lifts a single eyebrow, but doesn't interrupt. "Anyway, Mendez is investigating a gang that's operating in Hell's Kitchen, using local restaurants as a front. Drugs, mostly. *Aladdin's Lamp* was on his list of suspects. I promised him I'd look into it."

"Wait a minute." My mouth falls open. "That's why you invested in my restaurant? Because you thought I was dealing drugs?"

Owen squeezes his eyes shut. "Only at the start."

"Your innocence was obvious to both of us in less than a week," Wyatt adds, giving Owen an exasperated look.

"So hang on," I say slowly, "when you helped me paint, did you think I was guilty?"

"No, of course not." Owen's gaze is tender as he looks at me. "You remember the night we sealed our friendship over the better part of a bottle of vodka?"

How can I forget that night? It was the first time I'd wanted them. I'd gone to bed, my body aching with longing, desperate to feel the press of their bodies against mine. "Yes."

"I knew you were clean that night," Owen says.

"So everything that came after, the painting, the sign, all the help you gave me, that was real? Not because of your investigation?"

"No, Piper. We didn't lie when we said we were there for you."

"Okay." I lift my shoulder in a shrug. "We're cool. Continue the story."

"What?" Wyatt props himself up on his elbow to stare at me. "You're okay? You're not furious?"

I shake my head. "I thought you were assholes when we met the first time," I tell him. "I wanted to punch both of you. First impressions aren't always right. Besides, you didn't know me, and *Aladdin's Lamp* had lost money for a very long time. I'm not surprised the cops suspected me of illegal activity."

Wyatt gives me an astonished look. Owen kisses my cheek. "Thank you," he mutters into my ear. "Back to the story. I've been checking out the restaurants on Mendez's list. One of them is participating in *Can You Take The Heat?*."

They fill me in on their conversation with Greg Tennant. "So you see," Wyatt finishes, his voice serious, "why we were worried for you this afternoon."

I hug my knees to my chest, feeling chilled to my core. Restaurants aren't above sabotaging each other, of course. It's a brutal and competitive world.

But Wyatt and Owen aren't describing a simple act of sabotage. They're talking about someone deliberately targeting Greg Tennant's wife. Hurting her, sending her to the hospital with broken bones.

"Surveillance cameras will be installed tomorrow," Wyatt says. "Both outside the building and inside the restaurant."

I've almost forgotten the original reason Wyatt wanted cameras in the kitchen. The incident of the salted gravy seems trivial now. "Can we afford it?" I ask automatically.

"Yes," Owen replies. "You're getting a new landlord soon. They'll be covering the cost."

"Are you buying my building?" I demand. They're very

rich, I know and I wouldn't put it past them. "I don't want any special favors."

Wyatt shakes his head regretfully. "As much as I'd have liked to do that," he says, "I'm sure that'll violate one of the million terms and conditions of your aunt's will. No, a couple of our friends invest in real estate. We just connected them with Michael O'Connor."

"Of course." My voice is dry. I'm slowly beginning to understand how their world works.

"Also," Wyatt says, "we've arranged for you to have a bodyguard at all times, at least until this contest is over. His name is Tomas."

"Really? You don't think that's overkill?"

"No." Owen's voice is hard. "I've lost people I love once. I won't let it happen again."

My gaze softens as I look at him. I can't even imagine how hard this must be for Owen. "Okay," I agree, not wanting to cause him any more pain, "Bodyguards it shall be. I know I sound like a stuck record, but can we afford it?"

Wyatt growls. "If you think keeping you safe is a business expense, Piper," he says, his eyes blazing with fire, "you're very wrong. You're the woman we love. Protecting you is personal."

I didn't think I was the type that got turned on by growling possessiveness, but color me corrected, because at that tone, heat snakes down below. I wriggle against them and bat my eyelashes. "Say that again."

Owen smirks and Wyatt chuckles, and they proceed to make me forget Max Emerson, my parents, the contest, and everything else.

38

A part of kindness consists in loving people more than they deserve.

— JOSEPH JOUBERT

Wyatt:

The next few days are idyllic.

At *Piper's*, Josef has turned over a new leaf. He shows up to work early; he leaves late. "If this keeps up," Piper says thoughtfully, "Maybe he can manage the pass on Tuesdays. I could even take some time off in a couple of months."

"That's a great idea," I tell her and Owen is quick to agree. We both know that the risk of burnout is real. Piper needs to drastically cut down the hours she works if she wants to run her restaurant for more than just a year or two.

Not yet though. Maisie's article has brought a fresh rush of diners to Piper's. On Tuesday, we get lucky and are able to hire three new much-needed employees, a hostess with a warm smile called Sasha, a waitress called Gina, brisk and competent, and a line cook called Salim, who proves his worth in the kitchen right from the start. The extra help comes in handy as we grapple with the sudden crowds. For a couple of dinner services, Owen even rolls up his sleeves and pitches in to cook. I'm an utter liability in the kitchen, but I work my magic in the front.

To my relief, I don't hear from my father. Owen's threat has worked and gives me a much needed breather.

Our relationship flourishes. We spend as much time as possible together. It doesn't take long before Jasper, Piper's cat, is brought over in a cat carrier. He promptly scratches my furniture and pees on my rug as a protest for being uprooted from his home. Piper stammers out an apology but I just smile and throw away the rug. Nothing can tarnish my happiness, not even the insanely strong odor of cat pee that lingers for three days.

"Move in with us," Owen mutters one late night, when the three of us are sprawled on the sectional on the roof, sharing a bottle of wine after a hard day at the restaurant. "We can knock the wall down between our apartments and make one really big space."

"Really?" Piper asks, looking surprised. "Aren't we moving too quickly?"

"I don't think so," I reply. "Besides, how many nights have you spent at your apartment lately?"

She laughs. "There is that," she agrees. "And Bailey is leaving next week for Argentina. The place is going to be empty all the time. Okay. If you're serious, I'll look for a sublet."

"Oh, we're absolutely serious," I tell her, and Owen and I proceed to show her exactly how important she is to us.

This time, when she screams her pleasure to the stars, she doesn't even blush.

The second round of *Can You Take The Heat?* is a cakewalk. Piper makes it through easily. Again, the judges lavish praise on her cooking. The only person silent is John Page, the head of the Hell's Kitchen business association, who glares at Piper the entire time the judges are complimenting her food.

Unfortunately, that's when the good times come to a screeching halt.

The third round has eight contestants, but in a twist made for reality TV, only three will advance to the finals. Piper's one of the eight semi-finalists. Unfortunately, so is *Emerson's*. And in a quirk of fate that causes my heart to sink, they're matched up against each other.

My phone rings on Sunday morning. I've just received word of the third round match-up and I'm in shock. I pick it up without even looking at the display. "Hello?"

"Wyatt?" My mother's voice echoes back at me. "Is this a good time?"

I haven't spoken to my mother for two weeks. The last time we talked, I told her my childhood had been difficult, and she'd hung up on me. "Of course, mom," I answer automatically. "Is everything okay?"

Piper, Owen, and I are sitting in Owen's living room. Jasper is curled up on the most comfortable chair, fast asleep. When I answer, they both look up, alerted by my tone.

There's a sigh on the other end of the line. "I've been thinking about what you said the other day," she says. "And I owe you an apology." My mother sounds sad. "You'd have been better off if your father had taken you with him when he left."

So many times, I'd wished for that exact scenario. When Janet Blythe had showed up at my house and had been horrorstruck at the mess, I'd wanted to run away and find my father. When I had to move my mother's old sweaters off my bed in order to be able to find a spot to sleep, I'd prayed that my dad would come back to rescue me.

But those were the dreams of a child. As an adult, I see things I missed when I was younger. I used to play Little League baseball, and my mother never missed a game. I was clean; I was clothed. There was always food in the house for me to eat. My mother had an illness, but she did the best she could.

And she's never once tried to blackmail me. For that, I can forgive *everything*.

"I wouldn't have been better off with him at all." My voice is emphatic. "Look, mom, can we just let bygones be bygones? I've hung on to my resentment for a very long time, and all it's done is make me miserable."

Piper squeezes my hand in support. *Should I go?* She mouths at me. I shake my head instantly. Even last week, I would have excused myself and taken this call in private, but I find I want her to stay. I don't want to hide my secrets from her, not anymore. We're together, warts and all.

My mother sounds a little choked up when she replies. "A fresh start," she says wistfully. "Is that possible, Wyatt? I'd really like that."

I resolve to do the best I can to let my anger go. If it requires hours on a therapist's couch, then so be it. "Me too," I tell her.

As much as I'd like to end this call on a positive note, I

need to warn my mother about my father's blackmail. She's going to be more affected by my father's actions than I am. "I have to tell you something. You remember when my father came over to your house to take photos?"

"For the TV show?"

I shake my head. "There's no TV show. He told me he'll sell the photos to a tabloid unless I pay him off."

"How much does he want?" My mother doesn't sound shocked, just tired and disappointed.

"Three million."

She inhales sharply. "Wyatt, I'm sorry. This is all my fault. I should have never let him into the house."

"Don't be sorry." My voice softens. "You aren't blackmailing me. Jack Lawless is. He's the only one at fault here." I draw a deep breath. "I just needed to warn you. If this comes out, your friends will find out. Your co-workers. Everyone."

She laughs harshly. "I wanted to be on a reality TV show, Wyatt. You don't think it struck me that everyone was going to find out when I went on TV?" Her voice lowers. "I'm tired of living like this, Wyatt. My entire life is a lie, but I'm finally ready to tell the truth."

She pauses, and when she resumes, she sounds angrier. "Don't pay your father on my account," she says. "I don't need protection. Not anymore."

No, she doesn't. For the first time, I'm hopeful that my mother will seek help for her hoarding problem.

But I'm no closer to determining what I'm going to do about my father when I hang up. Yes, she's told me she doesn't care about the photos being made public, but I do. I'm unprepared to let my mother become a laughing stock.

39

A lie can travel half way around the world while the truth is putting on its shoes.

— CHARLES SPURGEON

Owen:

I've been keeping a very close eye on *Emerson's* in the last two weeks, looking for signs that something's amiss. Wednesday morning, I get the breakthrough I've been searching for.

I'm nursing a cappuccino in the cafe opposite *Emerson's,* when I see a familiar yet unexpected face. John Page, the head of the Hell's Kitchen Business Association, walks up to the pub and raps on the front door with his knuckles.

My pulse starts to race. *Emerson's* isn't open yet, so John Page can't be going there for an early lunch. He's not a co-owner, because that's a conflict of interest that Maisie would have flagged. There's no reason for him to be here.

The front door opens for a second, and Page slips in. I've

just enough time to wonder how long he'll be when he steps back out, carrying a navy blue backpack he didn't have when he entered. Slinging it over his shoulders, he starts to walk away, his gait rapid.

The hair on the back of my neck rises. I know I've witnessed something significant here, but I can't confront John Page directly. He's seen me at *Piper's* more than once; he knows that Piper, Wyatt, and I are partners. If I confront him, I might be putting them in danger.

As much as I'd like to investigate personally, to do so would be foolish and irresponsible. There's only one thing to do. I call Mendez.

"What do you have for me?" He snaps as soon as he picks up the phone.

"I heard through the grapevine that Max Emerson is running a gambling ring out of his back room."

"I need evidence, not rumors." Mendez sounds irritated. "What is it with you these days, Lamb? You've lost your edge."

Mendez can sneer all he wants. I've lost the desire to be crazy and suicidal, because I've found someone to live for, and I wouldn't trade that for anything in the world. "Here's something for you. John Page, the guy who heads the local business association, just walked into *Emerson's*, and walked out carrying a backpack."

"The guy who heads the Hell's Kitchen business association?" Mendez's voice sharpens with interest. "Are you sure?"

"I saw him with my own eyes. He's on foot, heading east toward Times Square. If you hurry, you can intercept him before he has time to dump the bag. That is, if you want to know what he's carrying."

"Got to go," Mendez says tersely and hangs up.

Piper:

"This is unacceptable."

Wyatt's on the phone with Maisie Hayes, his voice rising in anger. "Maisie, you admitted to us that Max Emerson is cheating. Well, he's up against Piper now, and this has become my problem. You need to do something about the public votes, otherwise your contest is a farce."

"Thank you for that, Wyatt." Maisie's voice comes through the receiver, loud and clear. Her tone is dry. "Fortunately, I have a solution."

I lift an eyebrow. What's Maisie going to do?

"Piper's here," he tells Maisie. "I'm putting you on speakerphone."

"Hi Maisie." I quite like Wyatt's ex-girlfriend. She's smart, funny, and most important to a chef, she's passionate about food.

"Hello Piper," she says calmly. "Listen, there's going to be a change in the way we do the comment cards this time around. My team is going to be handing them out to diners at the end of their meal. We're not going to rely on the restaurants to distribute them."

"About fucking time," Wyatt growls.

I frown at him. "I want to win the contest," I tell him. "Stop antagonizing Maisie. She's a judge."

Maisie Hayes laughs. "You heard that, Wyatt?" she teases. "You have to be nice to me. Okay, I have to call the other restaurants and tell them about the rule change. Piper, good luck on Friday."

"Thank you." I've been floating on a love-induced high, savoring each and every moment I get to spend with Owen and Wyatt, and I've forgotten to be nervous about *Can You Take The Heat?*. But if I win Friday's round, I'll be in the finals.

Josef's relying on me to win so he can find a better job. Owen and Wyatt are confident that I can pull this off. My friends are rooting for me. If I triumph, the exposure I'll receive will cause my worries about *Piper's* finances to be a thing of the past.

If I win. Suddenly, my nerves come rushing back. My palms dampen with sweat, and my skin feels cold and clammy. So much is riding on Friday's dinner service.

I'm about to go into full-fledged meltdown when Owen pushes open the front door. "I have news," he says, his eyes gleaming. "Guess who just walked out of *Emerson's* with a backpack that I'm willing to wager is filled with money?"

Wyatt looks up. "Who?"

"John Page." At my blank look, he elaborates. "The guy who runs the business association."

I grow cold. "He's one of the four judges," I say out loud. "And if I'm going up against Emerson, he'll see to it that I lose."

"You don't know that," Owen soothes, putting his arm around me. "Besides, there are three other judges." But he exchanges a worried glance with Wyatt, one I don't miss. They're nervous about tomorrow as well.

Greg Tennant's wife is in the hospital. Max Emerson's reputation precedes him. I've had a bodyguard, Tomas, shadow me ever since we realized what lengths he'll go to win, but I still can't help feeling like we're missing something.

Owen's phone rings and he grabs it. "Mendez," he says. "Tell me you have good news."

His face hardens as he listens to whatever the cop is

telling him. "You fucked this up," he says finally, his voice flat. "I gave you the intel you needed. All you had to do was nab the guy."

Mendez says something that causes Owen's expression to darken. "Are you fucking kidding me?" he snarls into the phone. "That's breaking and entering. I'm not doing it. Find someone else."

"What was that all about?" Wyatt asks when Owen hangs up.

He looks disgusted. "Mendez opened the backpack and found wads of cash, and he arrested Page. Except he forgot to read the guy his Miranda rights. John Page called his lawyer, who showed up and screamed bloody murder."

"Page got off?"

Owen nods bleakly.

"You told Mendez you weren't going to break and enter," I say, looking at Owen curiously. "What did you mean?"

"Mendez wants me to break into *Emerson's* and steal their computer. After today's debacle, he's not going to be able to get a warrant from a judge, so he's hoping to circumvent the system."

"Can you pick a lock?" There's so much I don't know about my boyfriends.

Owen grins. "My uncle was a pro," he says. "He taught me how." He winks at me. "Want to know what other skills I have?"

A familiar heat builds in my body. I pull my t-shirt over my head and move toward Owen. "Show me," I purr.

Owen sucks in a breath, his eyes glued on my bare breasts. "Come closer, Piper," he says, "And I will."

Wyatt stalks toward me with a chuckle, his fingers working on his shirt buttons. "You're very bold today, baby," he says, his voice low and sensual.

My lips curve into a smile. "Are you going to do something about it?"

He's about to reply, to tell me exactly what he's planning to do to me, when my phone rings. *Great.* Today is the day of the never ending calls. I mutter an apology to them and pick it up. "Hello?"

"Hello Piper," my mother says.

Shit. She can't see me, but I've very conscious that I'm half-naked. One hand instinctively covers my breasts. "Hi mom."

She's in a chatty mood. "I'm here with Angelina, dear," she says. "We're eating breakfast, then we're all going to look at wedding dresses. Are you at the restaurant already?"

My brain goes blank. I can't tell my mother the truth about my relationship with Wyatt and Owen. I know I should, but the words catch in my throat. "I'm hanging out with Wendy," I lie.

Wyatt's head jerks up at that, and he gives me a displeased look. Owen shakes his head, looking somber.

"That's good, dear. I called because Angelina just thought of the best idea. We're going to fly to New York on Friday to eat at your restaurant. This way, you can feel like you're part of the wedding party, even though you can't make it home."

"What?" I squeak out. "Mom, Friday night is the third round of the contest. It's a really bad time."

She makes a scoffing sound. "Don't be silly, Piper. I know you can manage. There's going to be twelve of us for dinner. Can you make a reservation for us?"

She hangs up, ignoring my attempts to protest. I shake my head, trying to process the bombshell she threw at me when I realize that neither Wyatt nor Owen have said anything. Suddenly anxious, I look up at them and take in their implacable expressions. "Is everything okay?" I stammer.

"You lied to your mom," Wyatt says. "Why didn't you tell her where you were?"

Damn it. I haven't confessed to Wyatt and Owen that I'm keeping them a secret from my parents.

"Are you ashamed of us, Piper?" Owen asks quietly.

"No." I give him a startled look. "Of course not."

"Then why did you tell her you were with Wendy?" Wyatt demands. "Have you told them you've moved in with us?"

I shake my head, feeling miserable. "I can't tell them. You don't know my parents. They won't understand."

Wyatt doesn't look angry. He just looks *sad*. "Do you want to know why Maisie and I broke up?"

I nod wordlessly.

"I thought I could stay away from kinky sex," he says. "I couldn't. I suggested a threesome with Owen, and she took us up on it. For a couple of weeks, things were good." His mouth twists. "One day, out of the blue, she broke up with me. With us. She didn't want her friends and family to know what she was doing. She wasn't prepared to deal with the gossip. She wanted something easier."

A long time ago, Bailey had warned me that a threesome wasn't all fun and games. She'd asked me if I could see myself telling my parents the truth. I hadn't listened. I'd been too distracted by the prospect of a date with Owen and Wyatt and too excited by the possibility of sleeping with them.

I can't bury my head in the sand anymore.

"What do you want me to do?" I whisper.

"We're here for you, Piper." Owen gives me a steady look. "But are you here for us? When it comes down to it, will you choose us, or will you please your parents?" He throws my t-shirt at me. "You probably should put this on."

His words feel like a slap in the face. I'm seconds from bursting into tears, but I can't blame Owen or Wyatt for this mess. I can only blame myself. "I'm going to work," I choke out. "I'll be there all day."

They don't say anything. They just watch me leave.

This time, the rift between us might not be healed by an apology.

40

Only you can control your future.

— Dr. Seuss

Piper:

I'm avoiding going home to Owen and Wyatt after dinner service. I dial Wendy's number. "Want to meet me for a drink?"

She meets me at *Piper's* in twenty minutes, by which time I've cleaned the kitchen and done the accounts for the day. The two of us settle down with a bottle of red wine in the deserted space. "Another lover's tiff?" she asks me as we sip at our drinks.

I nod, a lump in my throat. "My mother called this morning when I was with Wyatt and Owen, and I lied and told her I was with you. Then the three of us had a fight about me coming clean to my parents." My emotions are still raw from this morning's conversation, and I don't want to think confusing thoughts about Owen and Wyatt.

"Can we talk about something else? What's going on with you?"

She makes a face and takes a long sip of her drink. "Work. All week, I've had to deal with a couple that are snarling at each other. Each of them makes more than a million dollars a year, but they're fighting over who gets to keep the wedding china." She shakes her head. "It's enough to make me lose my faith in people."

I tilt my head and survey her. I've been so busy with my own woes that I've failed to realize that Wendy hasn't been her usual cheerful self. I think she's right — she has lost faith. She's been down and dispirited for weeks. "Why don't you take a vacation?" I suggest gently. "Get away from it all for a couple of weeks? Even a month? You sound like you need a break from your clients."

She shrugs. "Maybe. I know it's the right thing to do, but I can't seem to get excited by it."

"A one-night stand then? How long has it been? I don't think I've heard you talk about a guy in months."

"Too long," she admits. "I've given up on men."

"You have?" I look up, startled. Wendy is the bawdiest of us, the least likely to give up on sex. "Why?"

"All the guys I meet are intimidated by me." Her voice is bitter. "I'm the ball-busting divorce lawyer. The only guys who are interested in me are the deadbeats who are looking for a sugar-mama."

"That's horribly cynical," I argue.

"But true."

I gaze at her, troubled. "Wendy, that's not fair. You can't dismiss all the guys in the world based on a small handful of losers. Remember how we all tried to talk Gabby out of it when she was doing the same thing? There's lots of nice men out there. You just have to have a little faith."

She tosses back her drink, and pours herself another from the bottle. Her hands shake slightly, and I realize she's well on her way to getting drunk. I'm worried for my friend. "Wendy? What can I do to help?"

She doesn't answer my question. "You're one to talk about faith," she says. "You have everything in front of you for the taking, and you don't even see it. Owen and Wyatt are crazy about you, and you're here drinking with me because you can't acknowledge how important they are to you. Through this entire competition, they've been by your side, and rather than confront your parents with the truth, you're acting as if the relationship between the three of you isn't real." She snorts and drains her glass. "You might as well move back to Louisiana and become the socialite your mother wants you to be."

My first, instinctive response is to lash out at Wendy and tell her she's a bitch when she's drinking.

It takes effort, but I fight that urge, because though her words are harsh, there's truth to them.

I've hidden my relationship with them from my parents.

Wyatt was brave enough to open himself up to me. He told me about his childhood, and he trusted me enough to expose his wounds to me.

Owen has, as well.

But I've put nothing on the line, the way they have. I've been the biggest coward in the world.

Not any more. I make myself a solemn promise. As soon as *Can You Take The Heat?* is over, I will tell my parents about Owen and Wyatt.

"You're right." I rise to my feet. "Come on. You've had enough to drink. I'm hailing you a cab, then I'm going to apologize to Owen and Wyatt."

"You are?"

"I am." I hug my friend. "And Wendy, I've been afraid, but I'm not the only one. You're beautiful and successful. You can have any man you want. All you need is faith."

"Faith," she repeats. She's a little unsteady on her feet, but for the first time in a while, she sounds hopeful.

OWEN AND WYATT are watching a basketball game on TV when I walk in. "Hi," I greet them tentatively.

They look up and Wyatt smiles at me. "Come sit down," he invites.

I sit between them, and Owen pats his lap. "Want a foot massage?"

"I thought you were angry with me."

"A little," he admits. "But people can get angry in relationships, and still be very much in love."

"You aren't Maisie," Wyatt adds. "It's a sensitive topic for me, and I over-reacted. You're an adult. I trust you to handle your parents as you see fit."

"I'm going to tell them," I vow. "As soon as the contest is over." I stifle a moan of pleasure as Owen's hands knead my inner arch, and I lean on Wyatt's shoulder. "I'm not ashamed of you. I've just never been good at standing up to them."

"That's not true," Owen says calmly. "You think you aren't capable of asserting yourself, but when the stakes are important, you are more than capable of it. You attended culinary school despite their refusal to help you with tuition. You took over *Aladdin's Lamp* and you persisted with it, even though your parents never valued your efforts. You entered into a partnership with us, despite your mother's disapproval."

Hope trickles through me. They're right. When the

stakes are high enough, I've managed to defy my parents. And nothing is more important than this relationship.

41

My sun sets to rise again.

— Elizabeth Barrett Browning

Wyatt:

There's a long line of people waiting to get into *Piper's* on Friday. Normally, that should fill me with joy, but I'm nervous and I can't understand why.

"What do you think Max is planning?" Owen mutters at my side.

I don't know. Piper's been protected at all times, and Maisie has taken away the loophole in the public vote process. Part of me hopes that Max has decided to give up, but I don't really believe it. If Max wins tonight, he'll be in the finals. Someone ruthless enough to put an innocent woman in the hospital isn't going to roll over at this stage of the contest.

Sasha, our new hostess, greets each group of people

with a smile and seats them promptly. She's put Piper's cousin Angelina and her wedding party at the table in the front. They're loud and giggly and even though they've only just got here, they're already running Gina ragged.

"How are things in the kitchen?" I ask Owen.

"They're ready," he replies. "It's the calm before the storm."

"I hope so," I say, as the first of the orders starts to makes its way to the kitchen.

I can't shake off my feeling that something bad is going to happen.

~

Piper:

I've just finished calling out a ticket when Gina, the new waitress, walks up to me with a plate in her hand. "Chef Jackson," she says nervously. "One of the diners sent back their food. He said the meat tasted off."

I slice off a piece of the offending fried chicken and taste it. There's absolutely nothing wrong with it. I frown at her. "What's his problem?" I mutter. "Fine, we'll make him another. Salim, one order of fried chicken, please. Right away."

"Yes Chef," he calls out calmly. I watch him work for a second, then turn my attention back to the pass. Kevin's brought up two orders of the jambalaya, overflowing with chicken, smoked ham and Andouille sausage. I plate them up with sides of collard greens, and hand them to Kimmie. "Table Nine doesn't seem to like the catfish," she remarks as she takes the plates of jambalaya.

Sure enough, in about five minutes, she's back, carrying three plates of catfish. "They say the fish smells fishy."

"Seriously?" I bite into the battered fish, and it's perfect.

Owen pushes the double doors open and comes in. "What's with the returns?" he asks. "I've never seen so much food get sent back. Do you guys need a hand here?"

"Taste this." I hand him a fork. "Table Nine sent it back because it smells fishy."

He brings the plate up to his nose. "Smells fine," he remarks, cutting off a piece of the fish and chewing. "Tastes better." He grins at me, though there's concern in his eyes. "Let me go sort them out. I'm good at pouring on the charm."

I chuckle. "I know."

But the problem doesn't go away. The food keeps coming back all evening long. Fried chicken, battered fish, grilled lamb chops, the strip steak, even my mac and cheese. Whatever we serve, it gets sent back to the kitchen.

Something's wrong. This has to be Max Emerson's doing.

$\sim$

Wyatt:

"I am going to kill Emerson."

Owen's voice is low and fierce, his face tense with anger. I feel exactly the same way. Rage fills me at Max's move. He couldn't threaten Piper, and he couldn't stuff his ballot with fake customers. So he's resorted to this.

There can be no other reason for the returned food. I've tasted the dishes sent back to the kitchen, and so has Owen. Over the last couple of months, I've eaten many amazing meals at *Piper's*, and the food is even better today than it usually is.

"He's got to be spending thousands of dollars on this stunt. What's the point? He might get the customers through the door if he wins *Can You Take The Heat?*, but he's not going to keep them. His food is garbage."

Owen doesn't reply. His eyes are fixed on the judges' table. Three of the judges, Maisie, George Nicolson and Anita Tucker are digging into their meals with every sign of enjoyment, but the fourth, John Page, has just raised his hand to attract Gina's attention.

"The fucker," I rage helplessly, as John Page sends his food back.

We've underestimated Max Emerson. I knew he was sleazy, but I didn't think he was capable of devising a plan this devious. The judges aren't going to question the low public scores when they come out. Why would they? All evening long, they've seen food get sent back to the kitchen.

Owen speaks up, his voice grim. "I think we've lost."

Though I don't want to face that truth, I'm afraid that Owen's right.

42

None of us is as smart as all of us.

— KEN BLANCHARD

Piper:

There's total silence in the kitchen at the end of the night. We're not fools. We can all read the writing on the wall. We've been out-maneuvered tonight.

"I'm sorry," I tell Josef, knowing it isn't just my dreams that have been dashed tonight.

"The contest was just a shortcut, Chef Jackson," he says, calmer than I expected. "I'll go home and drown my sorrows in drink, and tomorrow, I'll be prepared to take the long way around." He lifts his shoulder in a shrug. "We played by the rules and the other guys didn't. How can you win when your opponent is prepared to lie and cheat?"

I pat his shoulder. We wipe the counters down in silence. Josef, Kevin and Salim file out through the back when they are done. I remove my apron, wondering where Owen and Wyatt are, when they step through the doors.

"We've lost, haven't we?" I ask them.

Wyatt nods grimly. "I'm so sorry, Piper," he says, his voice gentle. He reaches for me, and the two of them envelop me in their arms. We stay in a three-way hug for a very long time.

Finally, we break apart. I turn to the freezer and extract my bottle of vodka. We drank half of it the night we became friends. Tonight seems a perfect time to finish the other half. "Josef said he was going to get drunk tonight," I tell them. "I think there's something to that idea."

"Sláinte," Owen says with a twist of his lips. "Shall we head home first? Jasper will be wondering where we are."

I snort and grab the parcel of fish I've saved for my cat. "I'm ready to bet good money that Jasper will be fast asleep when we get home. But he'll wake up to eat this catfish." My tone is wry. "He might as well. No one else ate it tonight."

Wyatt puts his arm around me. "I want to beat Max Emerson into a bloody pulp," he says.

"You'll have to wait in line." Owen's voice is hard. "One way or another, Emerson is going to pay for tonight." He looks up at me. "Oh, I almost forgot. Your mother said that your cousin Angelina and her friends will be drinking in the Four Seasons bar tonight, and you should come and join them when you're done here."

I'm exhausted. I don't have either the energy or the desire to deal with my family right now. I want to sit on the roof and look at the stars, drink a couple of shots of vodka with Owen and Wyatt, and numb the sting of failure. And when I've done that, I want nothing more than to curl up between their warm bodies and fall asleep.

Angelina can wait until tomorrow. "Screw that," I say

decisively. "Let's go home. I have a cat to feed and vodka to drink."

Owen:

We've each done two shots of vodka and are contemplating a third when my phone rings. I frown at it. It's almost two in the morning. Who would be calling this late?

"Owen?" The voice at the other end is hesitant. "Is that you? It's me, Patrick."

Patrick Sarsfield. The uncle I haven't spoken to in seventeen years.

I have so much to ask him. Is he well; is he safe? Does he have a family now? But I bite those words back. My uncle has waited almost three weeks to return my call. I have to believe that he's nervous about talking to me.

"How are you?" I ask instead. A bland, generic greeting.

"Alive."

Talk about stating the obvious. "Yes, I see that." My voice is dry.

"Why did you call?" my uncle asks bluntly. "How did you get my number?"

I leave Aisling Rahilly out of this. There's no point getting her in trouble. "I heard a rumor that Seamus Cassidy is out of jail."

"No," he replies at once. "Your source is wrong. Everyone's locked up."

I exhale. Wyatt's been telling me from the start that Mendez has been lying to me. Now, there's proof.

"That's all I needed to know. Thank you."

"Don't call me again," he says harshly. "I have a wife and a daughter now. I want them to stay alive, Owen."

"It won't happen again." My voice is soft. I understand my uncle's feelings. I wouldn't risk talking to him if it meant endangering Piper and Wyatt.

For a while after I hang up, there's silence. Then Piper breaks it hesitantly. "Was that your uncle?"

I nod. "Mendez lied to me," I say wearily. "There's no gang activity in Hell's Kitchen. Whatever he's looking for has nothing to do with the Westies. He's been lying to me so that I'll do his dirty work for him." My voice is bitter. "Honesty seems to be a thing of the past."

Piper links her hand in mine. "That's what Josef said tonight," she says. "He said there's no way to win if your opponent is prepared to lie and cheat."

"He's right." I gaze into the distance, angry at Mendez's betrayal, and at the way I let myself be played by him.

"Here's a thought." There's an intensity to Wyatt's voice that causes both of us to start. "What if Josef is right? The deck has been stacked against us right from the start, because we've insisted on playing by the rules. What if we break them?"

"What are you talking about, Wyatt?"

"For Piper to make it to the finals, *Emerson's* needs to be disqualified from the contest. How do we achieve that?"

The realization of what needs to be done dawns on all of us at the same time. "Mendez wanted Max Emerson's computer records," Wyatt says. "If we break in and get a hold of them, I guarantee you Maisie Hayes will kick him out when she finds evidence of wrongdoing. Especially if John Page is involved."

I nod at Wyatt, excitement coiling in my belly. "Now?"

"Are you crazy?" Piper jumps to her feet and glares at

the two of us. "John Page was stopped by the cops two days ago. Everyone's going to be on edge. Don't you think Max Emerson is going to have guards watching his restaurant?"

Wyatt shrugs. "That's a risk we're willing to take."

"No" She shakes her head. "It's not worth it." Her lips turn up in a smile, and her eyes gleam. "There's a better way."

"There is?"

"Yes." She paces back and forth, her gait slightly unsteady from the vodka. "Max Emerson just screwed me over. What if tomorrow morning, just before his restaurant opens, I'm at his doorstep making a scene?"

Wyatt catches on. "You're going to be a distraction?"

"Exactly."

"No." My voice is flat. "I won't risk your safety."

She glares at me. "I won't be in any danger," she says. "Max Emerson will be expecting me to react in some fashion. He won't be surprised when I show up and yell. And while everyone's busy dealing with my temper tantrum, the two of you can sneak in through the back and grab what you need."

"This is crazy."

"It could work." Wyatt sounds thoughtful. "You remember how *Emerson's* is laid out? The back door opens into a corridor which leads to Max's office. We won't even have to go past the kitchen to get to his computer. We'll only need five minutes to get his data."

"Listen," Piper says. "If you don't think I can distract them for five minutes, you don't know me. I'm great at tantrums. Really."

My lips twitch at her passion. "Are you, honey?" I ask her. "Show me."

"Are you going to let me help you tomorrow?" she demands.

I exchange a glance with Wyatt. I don't like it, but Piper and Wyatt are right. Piper won't be in any danger.

"We're in this together, Owen," she says softly. "All of us. We're a team. Let me help, please."

"Okay," I concede reluctantly. "If we wake up in the morning and still think this is a good idea, you can be our decoy."

Wyatt chuckles. "Now," he says, with a suggestive leer, "shall we head to the bedroom and do something more fun?"

Piper:

Lovemaking between the three of us is often intense and explosive. Tonight, it's quieter and more contemplative. When we touch each other, it's with tenderness. There's still desire; there's always desire, but as we make love, our connection seems to deepen.

When Wyatt goes down on me, I feel one with him. When I suck Owen's cock, it feels essential. When I'm lying back on the bed, moaning with need as their hands and mouths touch me everywhere, I feel cherished.

I once told Owen and Wyatt that I didn't enter this relationship because I wanted a threesome. It was because I wanted them, both of them, and I couldn't separate my need and choose just one man.

The feeling that the three of us are meant to be together amplifies with each passing day. At the start, I thought that a threesome was something strange and different. Now, it feels right.

As I shudder out my climax, Owen's face contorts with his release. Wyatt comes a minute later, and we lie there, legs and arms all tangled up in each other, breathing hard as we slowly return to earth.

And I realize something. I've been nervous about telling my parents about my relationship, but there's no need to be fearful. No matter how my parents react, it isn't going to change the outcome. I can't imagine life without Owen and Wyatt.

43

The world needs anger. The world often continues to allow evil because it isn't angry enough.

— BEDE JARRETT

Piper:

O wen doesn't like this plan. Wyatt's not thrilled about it either, but I'm absolutely set on helping them. We're in this together.

Besides, as I've pointed out to Owen and Wyatt, my bodyguard Tomas is never going to be more than five paces from me, and he's carrying a gun. I won't be in danger.

At ten-thirty, we set off to *Emerson's*. As we get closer, we separate, as planned. Owen and Wyatt duck into the alleyway that runs behind the pub, and I march ahead, my spine straight. Tomas hovers just out of sight.

With each step I take, I get angrier. Max Emerson is an asshole. I understand the desire to win, but I'd never stoop to this level. Gaming the public vote portion of the contest by hiring people to show up at my restaurant and send back food? When I see him, I'm going to punch him.

I march up to the pub door and try to push it open. It's locked, so I take out some of my frustration by banging on it with my fists, as hard as I can. In less than a minute, the door swings open and a big, beefy blond man steps out. "Hey," he says indignantly, looking down at me. "What's the matter with you? Do you want to break the door down?"

"Yes," I snap. "As a matter of fact, I do." I deliberately try to push past him. "Where the fuck is Max Emerson? I want to see him."

I only swear when I'm very, *very* angry. I'm furious now. Maybe I won't punch Max Emerson. Maybe I'll knee him in the groin.

"Mr. Emerson isn't expecting anyone," the blond hulk says.

"You think I care about that?" I snarl at him. "Let me in. I need to see Max Emerson, and I need to kick his ass."

Drawn to the commotion, two more men appear. I bite back my grin. Good. Wyatt's arranged for someone to watch *Emerson's* all morning. They've reported that there are only four people in the pub, the three guards and Max Emerson himself. All I need to do is draw out Max and the way will be cleared for Owen and Wyatt to get what they need.

"You're going to kick his ass?" One of the newcomers, a guy with greasy black hair, gives me a scoffing look. "Really, honey? Shouldn't you pick on someone your own size?"

I show him my middle finger. "Either you find Max Emerson," I tell him, giving him my best glare, the one I've learned from my mother, "or I'm pushing my way in and finding him myself."

My scowl is remarkably effective. All three of them draw

back instinctively. "I'll fetch Mr. Emerson," the blond guy says, hurrying off.

"Piper Jackson." Max Emerson shows up in less than a minute, his lips curled into a sneer. "Shouldn't you be at your restaurant? Oh wait, there's no reason for you to be there. You've been knocked out of *Can You Take The Heat?*."

"You asshole," I yell at him. "How dare you send your goons to my restaurant?"

He smirks. "I don't know what you're talking about, Piper." His voice is mocking. "Did your diners not like the food last night?" He throws his head back and laughs. "Did they send the food back to the kitchen?"

His gaze hardens. "When you talk to your precious partners, Owen Lamb and Wyatt Lawless, do tell them I sent my regards."

I give him a steady look. "You cheated."

"If you can't take the heat, Piper," he says, "get out of the kitchen."

How long has he been talking to me? Long enough for Owen and Wyatt to get what they need? My phone buzzes in my pocket. That's our pre-arranged signal. They're done.

"This isn't over, Max." I step right up to him, my expression cold. "You will regret crossing me."

He laughs in my face. "Go home, Piper. You're done here."

I can't take the heat? Max Emerson has no idea what's about to hit him.

44

It always seems impossible until it's done.

— Nelson Mandela

Wyatt:

"Disqualified."

Two days later, *Piper's* is back in the contest, and *Emerson's* is out.

Max Emerson's computer was chock-full of information. The NYPD was exceedingly interested in the illegal gambling activity at *Emerson's*, and is getting ready to indict Max Emerson, John Page, and a dozen other people.

Maisie Hayes, on the other hand, honed in on the emails exchanged between Max Emerson and John Page. The messages showed the two of them plotting to get *Emerson's* to win *Can You Take The Heat?*. When Maisie read the communication between the two of them, she was furious, and she acted immediately.

John Page has been fired as a judge, and *Emerson's* has been thrown out of the contest.

And *Piper's* is in the finals.

The producer was gleeful about the drama. I've no doubt that when the show finally airs to the public, this will serve as a big reveal. "I bet we'll get a huge ratings boost," he said to me, his eyes gleaming with excitement. It took effort not to punch him.

"What's going on with your father?" Piper asks me, once the dust settles. "We've been so busy with the contest that I've hardly had time to ask you."

I shrug. "He's disappeared. He hasn't been back at the apartment he was staying at in two weeks. Stone Bradley's looking for him."

"Have you made any decisions?" she asks. "Are you going to pay him?"

"I don't know." The twenty-one days I had to form a plan has shrunk to seven. It's Monday today. On Saturday, Piper will compete in the final round of *Can You Take The Heat?*. And on Sunday, I'll have to either give into my father's blackmail, or let the pictures of my mother's house go public.

She frowns. "I hate the idea that your father might win," she says. "The bad guys shouldn't succeed. It's not fair."

"Life isn't fair, Piper," I reply philosophically. "I don't like it either, but I don't want my mother hurt. Even though she says she's prepared for the gossip that'd break out when the photos are leaked to the tabloids, I don't think she is. All her life, she's kept her illness hidden from her friends and co-workers. I can't out her. If it costs three million dollars to keep her secret, then so be it."

"I understand what you're saying," she concedes, frowning. "But I don't have to like it."

"You're not the only one, baby."

I<small>T'S</small> the night before the final round of *Can You Take The Heat?*. The three of us are having a late dinner when my phone rings. Stone Bradley's number shows up on the display and I pick up the call. "Hello?"

"Mr. Lawless," Stone's voice is crisp. "You asked me to let you know as soon as we located your father."

I sit up. "You know where he is?"

"He signed a short term lease on a studio in Harlem, and he moved in today." He reels off an address. "He's at a neighborhood bar right now. Do you want me to put a tail on him?"

"Yes." If I'd had my father watched right from the start, he'd have never been able to ambush me at *Piper's*. He'd have never been able to approach my mother without my knowledge. I'm not going to make this mistake twice. Not when the final round is tomorrow. Who knows what Jack Lawless could decide to do after a few drinks?

I hang up and stare into space. In less than twenty-four hours, the contest will be in full swing. A few hours after that, I'll meet my father and give him three million dollars, whether I like it or not.

Owen clears his throat. "Are you okay, Wyatt?" he asks me.

"I guess so. Stone called to tell me he's located my father. He's in an apartment in Harlem."

I turn to ask Piper if she needs more wine, only to see her staring at me as if I've grown a third head. "What's the matter?"

"Whatever you do on Sunday," she says slowly, "I want you to do by choice. If you want to give your father some money, you should do it. But not this way. Not because he's forcing you to." Her eyes gleam with anger. "You're calmer about this than I am, Wyatt. I'm furious. And you know what I've just realized?"

"What?"

"Owen knows how to break into places. I know how to be a good distraction, and you know how to do computer stuff."

Owen straightens. "Are you suggesting what I think you are?"

Piper nods resolutely. "We're going to break into this apartment in Harlem and we're going to steal the photos."

I've got to stop this nonsense before either of them get more excited. "Piper, the final round of *Can You Take The Heat?* is tomorrow. Our focus should be on the contest, not my dad's bullshit."

She shakes her head. "You're wrong. You both helped me when I had no hope. No matter what happens tomorrow, you've given me the most precious gift of all. You made me believe in myself. I used to lie awake at night, worrying myself sick about money. You guys gave me peace of mind, and Wyatt, it's time I returned the favor. Please. Let's get the photos back."

"There's a flaw in this plan," Owen cuts in. "It's a set of photos. Wyatt's father could have emailed it to himself, he could have uploaded it on the internet, he could have posted them on Facebook. We could delete them from his computer, but there will be copies."

Something nags at me. I struggle to remember what my mother told me. "No, there won't be," I correct him as the memory returns. "My mother told me he used an SLR camera. He's old-school. He doesn't believe in digital cameras."

"Excellent." Piper jumps to her feet, looking excited. "Let's go steal your photos, Wyatt."

WE FLAG down a cab and the three of us squeeze into the back seat. I try to protest, but neither of them is listening to reason. "It killed me to give Mendez Max Emerson's computer files," Owen says grimly. "I felt like I was rewarding bad behavior. Mendez lied to me and I had to help him so that *Emerson's* would get disqualified. But I'll be damned if I'm going to let your father get away with blackmail, Wyatt. Not if I can prevent it."

"I agree," Piper says. There's a stubborn look on her face, and I sigh when I see it. There's not the slightest chance she's going to change her mind.

The cab pulls up outside the building. We do a casual walk-by. The first thing we see is the desk in the center of the lobby, with a security guard seated behind it. "I see he's already spending my three million dollars," I remark wryly.

Owen assesses the layout of the building. "The elevators are behind a locked glass door. I'm assuming that residents have keys, and the security guard buzzes guests in."

Piper straightens her shoulders. "Here's what I'm going to do," she says. "I'll go in and tell the security guard that I'm looking for my uncle, and I'll convince him to let me in."

Her blouse shows a generous amount of cleavage. "By flashing him your boobs?" I growl.

She ignores my comment. "You guys just walk in like you own the place." She gives me a mocking look. "You're good at that. And I'll hold the door open for you."

Strangely, though this plan has a lot of potential to fall apart, it works exactly as we hope. The security guard lets

Piper in after ogling her breasts. We stride in behind her, our timing perfect. I hold my breath, waiting for the guard to challenge us, but he's gone back to fiddling with his phone.

We enter the elevator. "Do you know the apartment number he's in?" Owen asks.

"Thirteen-forty-two."

Owen hits the button for the thirteenth floor, and the doors slide shut. "Are you going to be able to pick the lock?" Piper asks him.

He nods. "I'm rusty, but this is an old building in Harlem. Unless your father's installed new locks, getting in should be a piece of cake."

Sure enough, Owen has no trouble opening the door. We enter, our eyes darting around the small studio.

A half-dozen moving boxes are stacked up haphazardly in the middle of the room. There's an unmade bed against the far wall, and a small bedside table next to it. The room doesn't have any furniture.

"There." Piper points to an opened suitcase on the bed. "That's the camera, isn't it?"

I move inside and grab it. "He might have got the film developed," Owen says. "Look around for prints."

"Here." Piper holds up a bright yellow envelope with two flaps, one holding a set of photos, the other containing the negatives.

I take it from her and flip through the photos quickly. It's my mother's house alright. The sink overflows with dishes. The dining room table is completely covered with clothes and piles of books and newspapers. When I see the chaos, my throat starts to close. I shove the photos back in the envelope. "Yes, this is it."

Owen does a quick and efficient search of the room,

making sure there isn't another copy of the pictures. Nothing turns up. "No computer?" Piper asks.

"He doesn't seem to own one."

"Okay." We've been here for five minutes. It's time to go. "We're pushing our luck. Let's leave."

We head downstairs without incident and hail a cab. When we're safely away from the apartment, Piper starts to giggle. Owen shakes his head with a grin, and even I have to chuckle. "I can't believe we did that," I tell them.

"I can't believe we didn't think of it sooner," Owen replies.

"We didn't know where my father was," I remind him. "Not until this evening."

Piper just smiles happily and squeezes my hand. I'm about to pull her toward me and kiss her when all of our phones beep at the same time. "What the heck?" I swear, looking at the display. It's an automated message from the cameras we installed.

It's an intruder alert.

Someone is trying to break into *Piper's*.

Owen exchanges a hard look with me. It's past closing time at the restaurant. The place should be empty. And the timing, one day before the *Can You Take The Heat?* finals, that can't be an accident.

We're facing yet another act of sabotage.

I lean forward and tap at the glass partition to catch the attention of the cab driver. "Change of plans," I tell him. "Take us to Hell's Kitchen instead."

45

Let no such man be trusted.

— WILLIAM SHAKESPEARE

Piper:

The cab races toward my restaurant. Our phones beep again; the intruders have triggered the motion detectors inside the kitchen. "They're inside."

The kitchen cameras have been set up to stream to our phones. We watch three people enter my restaurant, but they're wearing hoodies and I can't make out who they are.

"What's he holding?" Owen wonders, his eyes glued to his phone.

"Who?" I stare harder at my screen and notice what Owen's seen. One of the intruders is taller and broader than the other two, and he's carrying a case in his hand.

"How far away are we?" There's a note of fear in my voice. What if they destroy my freezer or my range? We'll be hard pressed to get a replacement in time for the contest tomorrow.

"Five minutes," Wyatt replies, sounding absolutely livid. "And when we get there, I'm going to make these clowns regret that they ever decided to break into your restaurant."

In four minutes, we pull up at the back door. Wyatt hands the cab driver a hundred and doesn't wait for change. Owen's already jumped out and is running full tilt toward the door. Though he growls something about danger, I'm hot on his heels.

I don't care about my safety. I'm done with this nonsense. First the over-salted gravy, then Max Emerson's stunt. I'm tired of the unending acts of sabotage. Like Wyatt, I want to kick some ass.

Owen unlocks the door and charges in, only to come to a dead halt. I almost slam into his back, then I look up to see what's caused him to stop.

There are three people in my kitchen. One of them is opening a metal cage containing wriggling white mice. That's not why I freeze. It's because I recognize the intruders.

My father's just let the mice out. My mother stands behind him, her expression nervous as the animals escape confinement and make a mad dash for freedom. And Kimmie leans against a counter, watching the proceedings with a peculiar look of satisfaction on her face.

All three look up with an expression of shock as we enter.

But their surprise is nothing compared to the betrayal that I feel.

"Mom? Dad?" My voice is low; my skin feels cold and clammy. I don't want to believe my own parents are capable of such an act. It doesn't take a genius to figure out that with mice on the loose in my kitchen, someone will phone in a tip to the health department, who will promptly shut *Piper's* down.

This time, the sabotage will be fatal to my restaurant. Once the public finds out why we were shut down, they'll avoid *Piper's* like the plague. We'll lose money, hand over fist. We won't be able to survive this.

Wyatt hurries in and takes in the scene in front of us. He turns to me, and there's sadness on his face. "I'm sorry, Piper," he says softly. Wyatt understands, more than Owen, how deep this act of betrayal cuts. He too has been betrayed by a parent.

A mouse skitters by us in search of a place to hide. Owen swears. "How many?" he snarls at my parents. "How many mice were in that cage?"

My parents don't reply, but Kimmie does. "A dozen."

Wyatt spares her a glance. "You let them in tonight?" he demands. "How much did they pay you?"

"Two hundred bucks," she gloats. "I've worked here for twelve years and the three of you waltz in and order me around? I'd have done it for free."

"You're fired," Wyatt snaps. "Leave."

Owen makes a sudden dive and comes up with a wriggling mouse. "Eleven to go." His voice is grim. "Piper, can you run home and grab Jasper? Let's make that cat earn his keep."

I should act, but I can't. My heart is heavy and my throat's choked up. "You did this?" I whisper to my parents. "You wanted me to fail so badly that you'd resort to this?"

My father doesn't look me in the eyes. My mother stands erect, her spine stiff. "I just want what's best for you, Piper. I want you to come back home, find a nice man and get married. Not spend the rest of your life doing menial labor."

My control shatters at her words. "I don't need to find a nice man," I hiss at them. "I have two. You hear that, mother? I'm dating both Wyatt and Owen. At the same time."

She looks horrified. Earlier this evening, I would have been devastated by her reaction, but not any more. I'm far too heartsick to feel anything other than numb. "I think you should both go," I continue. "You've done your damage. Please. Just go."

THREE HOURS LATER, all twelve mice have been found and the kitchen has been scrubbed down. Jasper was great at finding the rodents, but he didn't realize he was supposed to kill them. Instead, he wanted to play with them, and was quite disappointed when Owen took them away from him and put them in the cage.

"They're from the pet store," Owen says in disgust, looking at the trembling creatures. "Poor things, they're frightened out of their minds."

Wyatt's looking a little green as well. "Are you scared of mice?" I ask him.

He shudders. "I found a nest of them once in a pile of newspapers. Ever since then, I've been terrified of them." He frowns. "I know it's a ridiculous fear."

I put my arm around him. Owen makes sure the cage is latched shut, and comes around to hug me. "I'm sorry," he mutters into my hair. "Your parents suck."

I half-laugh, half-sob. "They really do." I cling onto them, seeking comfort in their strength. "What happens now? I'm assuming a health inspector will show up to check on *Piper's* tomorrow."

"There's no sign that anything's amiss," Owen responds. "They can't shut you down unless there's evidence that something's wrong."

"Kimmie could say she's seen mice in the kitchen," I point out. "She's a waitress here. They'd believe her."

Wyatt shakes his head. "I talked to her before she left." His voice is cold as ice. "We have her on the camera feed helping your parents let the mice out. That's a criminal act. I made Kimmie aware that if I ever heard from her again, I'd call the cops on her."

"Oh." That's good news, but I don't know if I have it in me to be hopeful. Not anymore.

"Come to bed," Owen says. "It's really late. Let's stop worrying about what's going to happen tomorrow and get a good night's sleep." He grabs the cage of squealing animals. "Where's Tomas?" he says with a grin. "He seems like a competent sort. I'm sure he'll sort these guys out."

I exhale. Tomas is a softie, and in addition, he's vegetarian. The mice will be just fine.

But me? I'm not sure.

46

Every strike brings me closer to the next home run.

— BABE RUTH

Owen:

The next day, the three of us are on tenterhooks. Every time someone walks into the restaurant, we brace ourselves, thinking they're from the Health Department. But the hours tick by, and an inspector doesn't appear.

The format of the final is different from the prior rounds. The good news is that there's no public vote. The bad news? The final round is about being able to cook under pressure. In forty-five minutes, the kitchen must make as many dishes as they can from their menu, and they'll be judged for speed as well as taste.

I've eaten at the two restaurants that are Piper's competitors today. *Katsura* is a Japanese restaurant that has one of the best tasting menus in the city, and *Cava* is an eatery with

Spanish and Central American influences. At both places, the chefs are top-notch, and they genuinely care about their food. Win or lose, Piper is in very good company.

The cameras have been set up in the kitchen and on the restaurant floor. Josef, Kevin, and Salim are doing some last minute prep. Piper walks back and forth, her nerves impossible to conceal. I'm not worried. The moment the cooking starts, she'll snap into the zone.

The front door opens. I look up, thinking it's one of the judges, here to start the countdown. Instead, Piper's parents enter.

Both Wyatt and I walk toward them immediately. Wyatt's face is a mask of anger. "You're not welcome here," he says to Piper's father. "Didn't you do enough damage last night?"

He flinches, but doesn't waver. "I want to speak to my daughter."

Fuck. I'd happily throw the two of them out on the street, but there's no guarantee that they won't come back when the cameras are running. As much as I'd like to spare Piper the trauma, I'm helpless. "Stay here." I glare at them. "I don't want you anywhere near the kitchen."

Going to the back, I signal to Piper. "I'm sorry, baby," I tell her in a low voice when she nears. "Your parents are at the front. They say they want to talk to you."

∾

Piper:

I should have known this wasn't over.

I count to ten to calm myself, and follow Owen out. I'm still angry. Sleep hasn't lessened my bone-deep rage at the extent to which my parents would go to sabotage me.

"What do you want?" I ask them bluntly as soon as I see them. I note with faint satisfaction that they look terrible this morning. Guilt does not suit my mother's complexion.

My dad speaks up. "Piper," he says, looking uncomfortable. "I want to apologize." He continues hastily, as if he's afraid I might throw them out at any moment. "We went too far, your mother and I. We were so concerned about your life in New York that we forgot that it is *your* life to live."

My mother nods in agreement. "I saw Angelina and Janice plan the wedding, and I wanted that for you and me," she confesses. "I went a little crazy."

"You salted the gravy when you played hostess, didn't you?"

"Yes," she confesses. "Before these two," she says, giving Owen and Wyatt a withering look, "you would have come back home when your restaurant failed. Merritt Grant gave it four or five months. Then you met these men and you started to turn things around. I thought I was going to lose you to New York forever, and I panicked."

Bile rises in my throat.

My dad takes a step forward. "We were wrong," he repeats. "We shouldn't have interfered. I'm sorry, Piper." He takes a deep breath. "I don't approve of this relationship of yours." He glares at Wyatt and Owen.

My voice is hard. "I don't care whether you approve."

"I can understand that." His lips twist into a grimace. "I know we haven't behaved very well, but you're still our daughter. I hope you can find your way to forgiving us one day. Good luck tonight, Piper."

I watch them leave, frozen with shock. Wyatt puts his arm around me. "Are you going to be okay?" he asks, his voice gentle.

"You guessed it was my mother from the start," I reply quietly. "I didn't want to believe you."

His hand rubs my back, up and down, in a soothing, comforting stroke. "I didn't want to believe me either," he admits. "I wish I could have spared you the pain."

Owen's head swivels toward me. He's been keeping watch for the judges. "Anita Tucker is walking up the street," he warns. "She'll be here in a minute."

The hurt I feel will take a while to fade, but for now, I have to refocus. I've endured one act of sabotage after the other. The best revenge would be to win *Can You Take The Heat?*. And tonight, I intend to give it all I've got.

47

Fall seven times and stand up eight.

— Japanese Proverb

Piper:

Three hours later, we're lined up in the boardroom of Yelp's Manhattan office. In true reality-TV fashion, Maisie's assembled the friends and family of each chef in the audience. In my corner, I have Owen and Wyatt, Gabby, Dominic, Carter and Noah, Wendy, Daniel, and Sebastian.

"Bailey sends her love from Argentina," Daniel tells me when I give him a questioning look.

Sebastian grins. "And she told us we had to be here."

I chuckle. "You know Maisie Hayes is going to gush over you? It isn't every day we have a two-Michelin star chef in our presence."

"Will you knock that off?" Sebastian says, aggrieved. "In any case, you appear well on your way to your first star." He gives Wyatt and Owen a dry look. "Feel free to thank me when that happens, you two."

Wyatt snorts. "Don't hold your breath."

We're just chatting to ease the strain. The crew is setting up the stage. Each of the chefs will have a long table in front of them, with each dish they made during the forty-five minute time frame. Right now, a couple of guys in black t-shirts are arguing over lighting. *Tell me who won,* I want to scream. *Just get the suspense over with.*

Of course, if they did that, they wouldn't have much of a show. Maisie has some pretty sharp showbiz instincts. I'm willing to bet that in six months, she's going to have her own show on TV.

"Alright," Maisie calls out after about ten minutes. "Chef Jackson, Chef Garcia, Chef Nakamura, will you please get in position? We're ready to get going."

My heart beats faster. *It's only a silly contest, Piper,* I tell myself, trying to calm down. *You're with Wyatt and Owen. You've already won.*

But I'm lying. I have professional pride, and I definitely want to win.

～

FORTY MINUTES LATER, I'm ready to hit Maisie on the head with a piece of battered fish. She's drawing out the tension, building up the suspense, and I'm ready to scream. So far, she's made each of us introduce ourselves and our dishes. Then the judges have pretended to taste each dish, even though the food is cold by now, and even though they already did their real tasting earlier. "It's for TV," the producer explains when we gets restive.

Finally, the judges are ready to make their decision.

George Nicolson steps forward. "This was a hard choice," he says solemnly. "We have to choose between three exceptionally talented chefs today."

"Chef Nakamura," he turns to the Japanese man. "Every meal I've eaten at *Katsura* has been impeccable. The presentation is beautiful, and the food, superb."

My heart hammers in my chest. I'm so nervous I can't breathe.

"Chef Garcia." Anita Tucker addresses the head chef of *Cava*. "What can I say? Throughout the contest, we've come to identify *Cava* with bold, innovative cuisine, and today, you knocked it out of the park."

My palms are sweaty. I try to wipe them discreetly on my chef's whites. My knees quake. What are they going to say about me?

"Chef Jackson." Maisie Hayes smiles at me. "*Piper's* was our dark horse entry. We knew the other restaurants in the contest, but you came out of nowhere with your modern take on Southern food."

I'm not sure if Maisie's praising me or damning me. I paste a fake smile on my face. My stomach churns.

"Three very deserving restaurants," she says to all of us. "And if we could award three winners, we would. Unfortunately, we're forced to choose."

"George, Anita, and I have conferred and we've made our choice," she continues. "Our winner demonstrated, week after week, that they had what it takes to succeed in a very competitive field. They dealt with one obstacle after the other, and they kept going in the face of adversity. And never once did they take their focus off the food."

I want to throw up.

The lights in the studio dim, and a drum-roll begins to

play. A wide smile breaks out on Maisie's face. "Piper Jackson, you're the winner! Congratulations!"

The spotlight shines down on me, and confetti rains from the ceiling. I barely notice. I'm looking at Wyatt and Owen. A huge smile breaks out on Wyatt's face; Owen pumps his fist in the air.

I'm sure there's something I'm supposed to do right now for the TV show, but I don't care. I run toward them and throw my arms around them. "You did it," Wyatt says, and there's so much pride in his voice that tears prick at my eyelids.

My friends are jumping up and down, cheering. Gabby's hugging Noah. Daniel and Sebastian high-five each other. Wendy dances a little jig, laughing with happiness. Josef looks shocked while the rest of my team, Kevin, Salim, Gina, Sasha, and Petra, beam with joy. Scenes of celebration are all around me.

I feel a momentary pang that my parents aren't among the audience, then I dismiss it. They made their choice. I've made mine. In time, the rift between the three of us might heal, but their many acts of sabotage are too fresh in my mind.

"You're wrong," I tell Wyatt. "*We* did it."

48

Every battle is won before it's ever fought.

— Sun Tzu, The Art of War

Wyatt:

I'm still grinning when I show up the next morning to see my father, Owen and Piper at my side. "Funny," Owen remarks dryly. "I thought you'd be angrier about this meeting."

Piper puts her arm around me affectionately. "Leave him be," she tells Owen, a smile in her voice. "This is a much better reaction than I expected."

I look down at her. "Well, thanks to you, my little lawbreaker, I hold all the cards. Why shouldn't I be in a good mood?"

I feel strangely at peace. A huge weight has been lifted off me. My entire life, I've been ashamed of my mother's hoarding. For as long as I can remember, my parents have been a source of tension, not comfort. Today marks an end to that.

Both Piper and Owen have, in their own way, learned to leave their past behind in the last few days. After they tried to destroy her restaurant, Piper's realized the futility of trying to please her parents, and doesn't want anything to do with them anymore.

For seventeen years, Owen has kept the wound of his family's deaths alive. By telling Mendez he never wants to hear from him again, Owen has finally accepted that it's time to heal.

And I'm ready to tell my dad to fuck off.

As before, my father shows up promptly, a security guard at his side. "Well?" he demands, as soon as he sees me. "Do you have my money?"

My father would make a good poker player. The photos have been stolen; the negatives are gone. He has no leverage on me anymore, but he hides it well. I guess he's hoping he can bluster his way through this meeting.

I don't want a long conversation with Jack Lawless. There will be no negotiation.

"No." I give him a cold look. "The photos are gone, aren't they? You've lost your only weapon." I stand up. Though I try, I can't conceal the sadness. "All you had to do was say you were sorry once, and I would have given you everything. All you had to do was take responsibility for abandoning a thirteen year old child, but you didn't care about me. You never did. It was always about Jack Lawless and nobody else."

My father opens his mouth to say something, but I shake my head. I'm done listening. Nothing he can say can change anything. "You don't have any power over me anymore," I tell him. "If you show up here, you'll be asked to leave. You can get drunk and follow me around; I don't care. All your power came from the fact that I gave a damn." I look down on him. "No more."

Owen rises to his feet as well. "The security guard will escort you out."

As I watch Jack Lawless leave, I take a deep breath. Piper and Owen are at my side.

The past doesn't weigh me down anymore, and the future is bright.

EPILOGUE

Life can only be understood backwards; but it must be lived forwards.

— Søren Kierkegaard

Piper:

Thanksgiving Day...

Piper's is officially shut for the holiday, but you wouldn't know it from the number of people at my restaurant. For the first time in my life, I've decided not to go to New Orleans for the weekend. Instead, I'm hosting a celebratory party, and I've invited all my friends.

The three people that know how to cook — Sebastian, Owen, and me - have spent all morning in the kitchen cooking a feast for the people we love. The tables are loaded with food. The roasted turkey jostles for room with the vegetarian pumpkin lasagna. There's stuffing and gravy, my macaroni and cheese, mashed potatoes, green beans, steamed broccoli, and cranberry sauce. In addition, Gabby's brought sandwiches, because it wouldn't be a party without them.

The place is packed. Bailey's flown up from Argentina for the holiday weekend. Apart from Sebastian and Daniel, she's brought Daniel's mother and sister. "Thank you for inviting us," Daniel says to me as he walks in. He winks at his mother and lowers his voice to a conspiratorial whisper. "You saved me from my mother's cooking."

Bailey chuckles as Daniel's mother digs an elbow into her son's side.

Gabby's men, Carter and Dominic show up. "Where's Noah?" I ask them. I like that little kid.

"With his father," Carter replies. I know from listening to Gabby that Carter and Noah's dad have a rocky relationship, but Carter seems pretty calm at the moment.

"We've got a room in the city," Gabby confesses with a grin. "We're going to make the kid-free night count."

Six months ago, I would have blushed. Now, I just chuckle and look around to make sure Katie's twins aren't listening to this conversation. They aren't. They're at the table holding the pies, and they're eyeing them like they haven't been fed in weeks.

Katie and Adam are talking to Miki, who I haven't seen in months. She's here without her husband, which is an ominous sign. I pull Wendy aside to ask her about it. "Where's Aaron? How come he's not here?"

She grimaces. "I think Miki's leaving him," she says. "She walked in on his secretary blowing him in the office."

"What?" I gape at Wendy. "I'm going to kill him."

"Get in line," she replies. "Miki almost sounded relieved. I think things have been rocky for a while."

"Why didn't she say anything?"

Wendy shrugs. "You know Miki," she says. "She doesn't really say much at the best of times."

"She's not the only one." I give Wendy a questioning look. I haven't seen much of you either. What's going on?"

She doesn't meet my eyes. "Work," she says vaguely. "You know how it is."

Wyatt walks up to the two of us carrying a couple of flutes of champagne. "Ladies," he says gallantly. "You need drinks."

I smile and take the offered glass. Wendy hesitates for an instant before reaching for the champagne. "Aren't the two of you friends yet?" I ask them. Wyatt and Owen have told me about Wendy threatening to hurt them if they broke my heart, but given that I'm deliriously happy, everyone should be getting along just fine.

Wendy grins. "Of course we are." She punches Wyatt lightly on his arm. "Unless you hurt Piper..."

"At which point you'll chop my balls off and use them in a stir-fry," Wyatt quips. "Don't worry," he winks at me. "I take *very* good care of Piper."

My face heats. "Stop that," I mutter, embarrassed, but he just chuckles.

Just then, Owen taps his fork against his glass. "It's time for thanks," he says quietly. "And I have many things to be thankful for." He lifts his glass in my direction. "Let's drink. To laughter, to love, and happily ever after."

I take a sip of my champagne, and turn to Wendy to continue our conversation, when I notice she's not drinking. Her glass is untouched. I open my mouth to ask her why, then I realize that Wendy might not talk with Wyatt nearby. "Excuse us," I tell him, clamping my fingers around my friend's wrist. "Wendy and I need to go to the bathroom."

I drag her through the kitchen doors. "This isn't the washroom," Wendy jokes.

I'm not distracted. "You're not drinking," I tell her. "What's going on?"

She takes a deep breath. "I was going to tell everyone on Monday," she confesses. "Almost two months ago, the day before my birthday, I decided to have a one night stand with two men." Her mouth twists. "It was just one night, no strings attached. What could possibly go wrong?"

I know what's coming, but I wait for her to speak the words.

"Except the condom failed. I was in a ménage, and there were two of them, and now I'm pregnant." She gives me a bleak look. "And I don't know which one of them is the father."

Oh dear. I stare back at her, totally lost for words. "I'm going to be a mother," she continues, her voice a mere whisper. "And Piper, I'm terrified."

∽

THANK YOU FOR READING PIPER, Owen, & Wyatt's story! I hope you love them as much as I do.

∽

THE MENAGE IN MANHATTAN SERIES

WANT MORE? *Wendy's story - The Wager - is next.* Read on for a free extended preview, or check out the other books in the MENAGE IN MANHATTAN SERIES.

The Bet - Bailey, Daniel, & Sebastian
The Heat - Piper, Owen, & Wyatt
The Wager - Wendy, Asher, & Hudson
The Hack - Miki, Oliver & Finn

DO YOU ENJOY FUN, light, contemporary romances with lots of heat and humor? Want to read *Boyfriend by the Hour (A Romantic Comedy)* for free? Want to stay up-to-date on new releases, freebies, sales, and more? (There will be an occasional cat picture.) **Sign up to my newsletter!** You'll get the book right away, and unless I have a very important announcement—like a new release—I only email once a week.

A PREVIEW OF THE WAGER BY TARA CRESCENT

CHAPTER ONE

For time and the world do not stand still. Change is the law of life. And those who look only to the past or the present are certain to miss the future.

— John F. Kennedy

Wendy:

I've been a divorce lawyer for six years, and in that time, I've learned one thing. All men are lying, cheating bastards.

Okay, *okay*. Maybe not all men. Maybe I'm wrong, and maybe my profession has skewed my perception of the gender. Divorce lawyers don't exactly see couples at their best, after all.

Take Howard and Sandi Lippman. They've been married twenty-five years, and in that time, Sandi raised three kids and was the perfect wife and mother. Then

Howard Lippman decided to cheat on her with his twenty-two-year-old assistant. To add insult to injury, he hid the bulk of his assets so he wouldn't have to pay his ex-wife her fair share in the divorce.

My goal today? Find the hidden money with the help of my uber-awesome hacker friend Miki. Demonstrate to the judge that Howard Lippman is a cheating son of a bitch, and my client Sandi deserves half of his assets. Win, and win big.

The streets of New York are almost quiet as I make my way to work. It's a little after seven in the morning, and when I push open the frosted-glass door to the reception area of Johnson Nash Adams, I'm expecting to find the place to myself. To my surprise, Beverly, the assistant I share with two other lawyers, is already at work, as is Lara Greaves, who sits next door to me.

I raise my hand in greeting, and head to my office. Five minutes later, there's a knock on my door and Lara sticks her head in. "Hey Wendy," she says. "A few of us are going to *Nerve* tonight to celebrate Pam's birthday. Do you want to join us? All of New York's rich and famous will be there."

"That's not exactly a selling feature," I reply dryly, thinking of Howard Lippman.

She rolls her eyes. "The drinks are excellent. Dante is the best mixologist in the city."

I'm tempted. I've been working crazy hours in the last couple of months, and I'm overdue for a night out. *Nerve* is Manhattan's newest lounge. It's very exclusive, and I'm dying to find out what the buzz is about.

Unfortunately, there's a large mound of paperwork in front of me that needs to be dealt with. "I can't," I tell Lara regretfully. "Jonathan Stern's lawyer just dumped several boxes of evidence on me before Amber's first hearing next week."

She shakes her head but doesn't try to argue. Lara's trying to make partner too. We both know that work comes first; it always does, and it always will. "I'll put you on the list," she says. "Just in case you change your mind."

Before I can reply, my cell phone rings. It's Miki. "I have to take this," I tell Lara, who nods in understanding and shuts the door. Once I'm alone, I pick up the call. "Tell me you have good news for me, Miki."

We're down to the wire here. Miki is a financial hacker, and she's excellent at what she does, but Lippman's systems have stymied her so far. She's been working around the clock to find me proof of Lippman's missing four hundred million dollars.

"I hit paydirt, Wendy," she announces, her voice layered with triumph. "Shell corporations, offshore bank accounts, you name it, I found it. I'm emailing you the details right now."

"Yes." I punch the air in delight. The idea of Lippman getting away with his ruse has been gnawing at me. Now, he won't. "You," I tell my friend, "are a fucking goddess. A rock star. This is fantastic."

She laughs. "Sorry it took so long," she says. "The company Lippman hired to hide his assets are pretty good at covering their tracks. In fact, I'm fairly sure that my snooping has been detected."

That could be a problem. "How long do I have before Lippman moves the money?"

"A day or two," she replies. "The trial's this afternoon, isn't it? You should be fine." She hesitates for a brief moment, then continues. "This is the third guy in the last two months I've investigated for you. You're making enemies, Wendy. Please be careful."

Miki is rarely paranoid, and this behavior is unlike her. "Miki, this is my job. If I do it right, the ex-husbands want to punch me. It goes with the territory. I'm used to the hatred."

This *is* my job, and I *am* used to the hatred, but this time, it's a little more personal. Sandi reminds me of my mom. They're the same age. Same honey brown hair, fading to gray, same caramel brown eyes. Same lousy taste in men.

Thirty years ago, my father swept my mother off her feet in a whirlwind affair, conveniently forgetting to mention to her that he was married. Then Janet Williams found out she was pregnant. When she told Paul Hancock, he'd given her ten thousand dollars and told her never to contact him again. Too poor to hire a lawyer and fight for child support, my mother raised me on her own, sacrificing everything to give me a stable, loving home.

I have no power to change the past. I can't help my mother, but I can help Sandi. "Don't worry," I repeat. "I've got this."

Judge Hadid takes one look at the evidence Miki has secured for me, says several stern things to Howard Lippman and his lawyer Katrina Schroeder about lying to the court, and rules in Sandi's favor.

Outside the courtroom, Sandi hugs me tight. "Thank you, Wendy," she says, her voice thick with gratitude. "I didn't think you'd be able to pull this off, but I should have had more faith."

I shrug, uncomfortable with her praise. "I'm just doing my job," I tell her with a smile. I watch her leave, then turn on my phone to check my messages. There is no voicemail for me to deal with, but there's a news alert that stops me dead in my tracks.

Paul Hancock has died.

I scan the article for details. My biological father has succumbed to cancer caused by the tumor growing in his brain. His wife Lillian died six years ago, but he's survived by a son, Thorne Hancock.

My good mood evaporates. Paul Hancock never once acknowledged the daughter he conceived. I never met him, and now, I never will.

I don't know how to process the complicated cocktail of emotions I'm feeling, but if I go home, I'll just end up brooding all night. I dial Lara's number. "You guys still going to *Nerve*?" I ask her when she answers. "I'm joining you."

Dante had better mix up a mean drink. I'm going to need alcohol tonight.

~

CHAPTER TWO

Open your eyes, look within. Are you satisfied with the life you're living?

— BOB MARLEY

Asher:

I'm staring at my schedule, wondering why on earth I'm supposed to be at Miguel's new lounge on a Monday night, when my assistant Vivian knocks at my door. "You have a visitor," she says, sounding harassed. "A Mr. Engels. I tried telling him you don't see people without an appointment, but he wouldn't leave."

I go very still. The last I heard, Levi Engels was in jail,

locked up for a year for his role in a scheme involving bad checks and forgery. He's lucky it wasn't longer. My childhood friend has become something of a career criminal, and we haven't spoken to each other in almost fifteen years. Why is he here now?

I force a smile on my face. "Is he waiting in Reception?"

She nods. "Do you want to see him?"

Not really. Levi Engels is trouble with a capital T. I don't have a good feeling about this at all. "Yes, please. Could you send him up?"

"Ash Doyle," Levi's voice booms out as he walks in. He looks around my office, taking in the expansive space, the large windows that overlook Manhattan and the modern art on my walls. "You're a big shot now, aren't you, buddy?"

There's a trace of hostility in his voice. I ignore it. "Long time, Levi. How've you been?"

"I'd have been better had my lawyer been any good," he says. "All lawyers are fucking thieves, am I right?"

Bullshit. His defense lawyer was a genius. It was Levi's third arrest, and he should have been locked away for five years. I disregard Levi's dig at my profession; he's trying to get a rise out of me, and I refuse to let it work. "What can I do for you, Levi?"

His expression turns serious. "I need a place to stay for a month or two, Ash. Just until I'm back on my feet." He swallows, sounding vulnerable. "I want to clean up my act, but it's hard when I'm surrounded by temptation."

For years, I've been waiting for him to ask for help. "Of course," I reply instantly. "I can arrange..."

"No." His voice is vehement. "I don't want your charity. Can I crash at your place? You have a spare bedroom, don't you?"

Several. Bedrooms are not the problem. As much as I want to believe Levi's change of heart, there's always a chance that he's going to get seduced by crime, by the promise of easy rewards. And I can't be involved with that. I won't risk everything I've worked for.

But Levi's expression is hopeful, and I can't turn him away. "Sure," I reply. "My place isn't far away. If you have some time now, I'll get you a key, introduce you to the doorman and show you around."

"Thanks, buddy," he says fervently. "You want to grab a beer later?"

I look up at that, surprised. "Can you go to a bar when you're on parole?"

He shrugs indifferently. "My parole officer's an idiot. He'll never find out."

Trouble already. Thankfully, I have an excuse to avoid Levi tonight. "I can't," I reply. "A client just opened a lounge in SoHo. I promised him I'd drop by."

Levi doesn't look too put out by my refusal. "No worries," he says. "Some other night, yeah?"

"Sure."

I'm pretty sure I'm going to regret this decision.

Hudson:

"Want to bet that we're getting fired today?"

Nadja Breton, my second-in-command, and the only woman I truly trust, frowns at me. "That's defeatist," she chides. "We could be reading this situation wrong."

The two of us are in the small conference room in our

SoHo office. The floor-to-ceiling windows give us a great view of the city while shielding us from the noise and the chaos. We moved into these offices four years ago, and when I signed the lease, I knew I'd made it. I'd grown Fleming Architecture from a one-man operation to a prestigious design firm that had twenty-five employees and was projected to make fifty million dollars by the end of the year.

On the glass table in the center of the room, there's a scale model of the skyscraper I've designed for Jack Price and Ian Schultz. It's gorgeous, among the best work I've done. I eye it dispassionately. "Jack Price received box seats to the Knicks yesterday, courtesy of Kent and Associates. I'm not an idiot, Nadja. I can read the writing on the wall."

"Doesn't it bother you?"

"I'm not going to bribe Price for this job," I say flatly. Fleming Architecture is extremely successful, with an abundance of happy clients. While I'd prefer not to lose this account, my intuition tells me the Clark Towers project is bad news.

There's a lot more I could add. I could remind Nadja that after Megan, my gold-digging ex-wife, I'm leery of people that are only interested in me for my money.

Nadja, who's been staring out of the window, takes a seat at the table. "Some of the newer architects are restless."

I raise my eyebrow. "Why?"

"They think you should be bidding more aggressively for work. Branch out in new directions."

This argument again. I'm willing to bet money that Colin Cartwright is behind the discontent. Colin believes I should have picked him over Nadja to be my second in command, and he's doing everything in his power to undermine me. I'm getting tired of it. "We're a boutique firm, Nadja. We only bid on projects that are a good fit for us."

She sips at her coffee. "I'm not the one you need to convince," she replies.

I make a mental note to have a conversation with Colin. If he doesn't stop his bullshit, his days at Fleming Architecture are numbered.

Jack Price and Ian Schultz frown when they see the model of the skyscraper in the middle of the room. Nadja, noticing their discontented expressions, exchanges a look with me. *Fired,* she mouths.

She's right. Ian Schultz looks up. "I have to be honest, Fleming," he says bluntly. "This isn't working."

Translation: I didn't bribe them. "You seemed perfectly happy with our design during the last meeting."

Jack Price has the grace to flush. "Things change," he mutters. "I'm sorry, Hudson. We're going to have to let you go."

The two of them watch me warily. If they're waiting for me to react, I'm not going to give them the pleasure. "That's your call to make, gentlemen." My voice is pleasant, but underneath, I'm simmering with fury. "Have you decided on a replacement firm?"

They look away, unable to meet my gaze. "Kent and Associates come highly recommended," Price says finally.

I doubt it. Kent and Associates doesn't have much of a track record when it comes to delivering projects on time and on budget. In a few months, when Clark Towers starts to fail, Jack Price is going to regret his decision. "Give my regards to George. I assume you'll see him at the Knicks game tonight?"

Price's head snaps up in shock. I rise to my feet. "I'm not

a fool, Jack," I say evenly. "Don't ever take me for one. You know the way out."

Once they've left, Nadja sighs heavily. "What a day," she says with a grimace. "I think I'm going to leave early, Hudson. This mess will be waiting for us tomorrow morning."

She looks dispirited. We've both put in months of work into this project, and it sucks to see it go to waste. Still, there will be other clients. "The new 3D printer finally came in," I tell her, in an attempt to cheer her up. "If you're looking for a new toy to play with, it's all yours."

My attempt works. Her eyes sparkle with excitement. "Oh good. I've been dying to load up our designs on it and test it out. Remember the all-nighters we used to pull in college when we had to assemble models?"

"Oh God. Don't remind me. Glue, craft sticks and cold pizza. I'm glad those days are behind us."

She chuckles. "Me too. See you in the morning, boss."

I get back to work, losing myself in a preliminary sketch for a museum. I don't notice the setting sun or the darkening sky. Nothing disturbs my concentration until a knock sounds at the door. "I was afraid I'd be interrupting you," my friend Asher says, stepping into my office and giving the crumpled up sheets of paper on the floor a pointed look. "But you look ready for a break. Want to get a drink?"

"Sounds good." I stand up and stretch, my muscles creaking with protest. "What's the plan?"

"One of my clients just opened a new lounge." He grimaces. "I'm duty-bound to make an appearance. It'll be loud and pretentious."

"You're doing a great job selling this." I stuff my laptop into its bag and sling it over my shoulder. "Fortunately for you, a beer sounds pretty good at the moment."

"Don't hold your breath," Asher advises. "Miguel told me he hired the best mixologist in the city. I doubt they serve anything as uncomplicated as a beer."

"Damn it, Doyle," I grumble. "You owe me for this. You're buying tonight."

Asher laughs in agreement. "It seems the least I can do."

Chapter 3

> We must let go of the life we have planned, so as to accept the one that is waiting for us.
>
> — JOSEPH CAMPBELL

Wendy:

The door to *Nerve* is guarded by a burly bouncer in a black suit. He gives me the once-over, taking in my shimmery gray silk dress and my silver hoop earrings before he nods and allows me entry.

I make my way inside, trying to find Lara. The club is beautiful. I'd been expecting black and chrome, but instead, the walls are a soft burnished gold. Hundreds of glass globes hang from the ceiling, filling the space with a warm light. A jazz band plays on a corner stage, but the acoustics are perfect, and the music isn't too loud. It's half past nine, too early for the dance floor to be crowded, though the bar area is packed with people, all waiting for Dante the *mixologist* to make them some fancy concoction.

My bra digs into my sides, and my toes, squeezed into a

pair of painful Louboutins, feel like they are on fire. I scan the crowds for my coworkers and don't see them. I'm debating going home to Netflix and ice-cream when I hear Lara call out my name from a table at the far corner. "Wendy," she greets me with a broad smile. "I'm so glad you changed your mind about coming."

There's one empty chair, and I sink into it with a sigh of relief. Damn shoes.

"What happened with the Lippman case?" Matt Vella, who's sitting next to Lara, asks me. He's also a lawyer at our firm, though I don't know him very well.

"We won," I reply absently, trying to catch the eye of the bored looking waitress who's taking drink orders a couple of tables away.

"Excellent." Pam Prickett turns to Matt, holding out her hand. "Come on, Matt. Pay up."

Matt grumbles as he takes a hundred dollar bill out of his wallet and passes it to her. I give Pam an astonished look. "You bet on the case?"

She tucks the bill in her purse. "Of course I did," she chuckles. "A fool and his money are easily parted. Matt, next time, don't bet against the Barracuda."

Matt grins lazily. "I should have known better," he agrees. "Wendy, you want to dance?"

I shake my head. "Not in these shoes," I say ruefully. "And not before I get a drink."

Matt wanders off to try his luck on the dance floor. Pam, Lara, and I gossip rather aimlessly about work as we wait for the waitress to acknowledge our existence when Lara suddenly grabs my arm. "Oh my God," she breathes. "Look who just walked in. That's Asher Doyle."

I turn around. Asher Doyle is something of a legend in our profession. He started out his career as a district attorney, and then he changed direction and became a corporate lawyer. His hourly rate is two thousand dollars, and his firm supposedly has more work than they can handle.

"He's wasting his time as a lawyer," Pam mutters. "He should be a model."

"An underwear model," Lara adds. "Can you imagine?" The two of them dissolve into a flood of giggles.

I might not trust men, but I'm still human. I like eye candy as much as the next woman *and damn.* Asher Doyle doesn't look like a lawyer. His shoulders are broad; his dark hair is tousled, and his cheeks are covered with stubble.

"Sex on a stick," Pam says dreamily.

I'm staring at the man with my mouth open. I snap it shut hastily, lest I start drooling. "He's probably very boring," I say dismissively. "The hot ones usually are."

Lara shakes her head. "Haven't you heard the stories?" she asks me, lowering her voice. "He's not boring at all. The word is that he likes to share women with his best friend, Hudson Fleming."

"Who just walked in as well." Pam looks like she's about to faint. "Wendy, check him out."

Damn again.

Asher Doyle looks like a bad boy. Hudson Fleming, on the other hand, is smooth and sophisticated. He's wearing dark jeans and a gray button-down shirt with the sleeves rolled up to his elbows. My eyes fly immediately to his strong forearms. Yeah, forearms. I have a thing for rolled-up sleeves, okay? *Sue me.*

The two men go up to the bar, and space clears for them instantly. The bartender, a blonde wearing a very low cut blouse, smiles seductively as she pours them their drinks.

I can't stop staring. I notice the way Hudson rolls his eyes at Dante's contortions. I notice the way Asher Doyle's strong fingers curl around the crystal base of the glass he's holding, the way his thumb almost seems to caress the cool surface. When he laughs at something Hudson says, my stomach clenches with desire. It's their body language. These men are confident and powerful, and unexpectedly, it's turning me on.

Lara says something to Pam and me; I barely listen. The two of them join Matt on the dance floor. The waitress finally notices that I need a drink, and bustles up to take my order.

An hour later, I'm ready to go home. I've lost sight of the eye-candy, and Lara, Pam, and Matt show no sign of slowing down. The glass in front of me is empty, and I'm fighting the urge to check my phone for further updates on Paul Hancock.

You can't leave already, I scold myself. *You came out to have fun, so have fun, damn it.*

What I need is another drink.

I get up and make my way to the bar. Dante's making blush-pink cocktails for a giggling group of women. I find an empty spot and wait for someone to notice me. Next to me, a woman in a red cocktail dress is thumbing through her phone. She catches sight of Dante and rolls her eyes. I bite back a grin at her reaction, so similar to my own.

"Hi there, honey." A man with gel-slicked hair sidles next to her and gives her what he thinks is a winning smile. "Can I buy you a drink?"

"No thank you," she says politely, drawing away from him as he inches closer. "I'm waiting for someone."

Hair-Gel Guy is oblivious to her body language. "No harm having a drink while you wait, is there?"

She gives him a tight smile. She obviously wants to be

left alone, but the guy's not picking up on her signal. "No thanks," she says again.

"Are you waiting for a boyfriend?" He lays his hand on the woman's ass, and she flinches. Her eyes dart around the room, looking for someone to help her out of this situation.

That's my signal to intervene. There's a special place in hell reserved for guys who refuse to take a hint. "She said no," I tell him, not bothering to conceal the disgust in my voice. "Which part of that wasn't clear?"

He turns red. He moves right next to me, hovering threateningly, inches from my face, and I can smell the booze on his breath. "No one was talking to you, bitch," he snarls.

I position myself in front of the trembling woman. "Leave her alone."

He grabs me by the wrist to yank me out of the way. When I first moved to New York, I'd taken self-defense classes. Our instructor had taught us how to handle this. As his fingers clench around my wrist, I twist my hand, hard. His shoulder wrenches, and he grunts and lets go, stumbling back a few paces, pain etched on his face. "That was a big mistake," he says. "You're going to pay for that."

Shit. I'm in trouble now.

Suddenly, two men appear out of nowhere. Asher Doyle and Hudson Fleming fill the space between my assailant and me. Asher grabs the guy by the collar and pushes him back. "I believe the lady told you to leave her alone," he says icily. He seems to make a gentle movement with his fists, and the man goes flying across the room, landing in a heap next to a black leather couch.

The band stops mid-note; a hush falls over the room. People scramble out of the way of the fight. A couple of people take out their phones to take photographs. Of course.

Hair-Gel Guy rises to his feet slowly, shaking his head. I'm hoping he's had enough and is ready to walk away, but instead, he bellows with rage and charges for Asher. I inhale sharply, but my concern turns out to be entirely unnecessary; Asher repeats his movement and the man goes down again.

"Once more?" Asher's eyes gleam with anticipation. He almost appears to be enjoying himself.

Before the man attacks for the second time, a bouncer appears and grabs him by the collar and drags him to the door.

Hudson Fleming, who's been watching the fight intently, turns to me once the threat of danger has passed. "Do you want to press charges?" he asks. "We saw him grab your wrist. We're happy to be witnesses."

I shake my head. It seems more trouble than it's worth.

The band starts playing again, and the dance floor fills with people. Asher approaches the two of us. "Thanks for the help," he grumbles to Hudson.

Hudson laughs. "You seemed to have the situation under control," he responds. "Besides, two on one doesn't seem sporting."

Asher flips him off with a grin. He signals to the bartender, then turns to me with a probing look. "Are you okay?"

My heartbeat, slowly returning to normal after the fight, speeds up again. I thought they were good looking. Up close, they are so much more. They're gorgeous. "I'm fine," I stammer.

Pull yourself together, Wendy. Tongue-tied is not a good look.

The bartender appears in front of Asher. "Mr. Doyle,

what's your pleasure?" she simpers, thrusting her boobs into his face. Subtle.

Asher doesn't appear to notice. "Can I buy you a drink?" he asks me.

"No," I protest. "This round's on me. Thank you for your help."

Asher shakes his head. "It was nothing," he replies. "Honestly."

The bartender's waiting for us to order, so I ask for a glass of their house red. Asher orders a beer, as does Hudson. Once she's moved away to get our drinks, Hudson gives me an amused look. "If you're going to pick a fight with a drunk guy," he chides, "Pick one your own size. That guy weighed two hundred pounds."

I'm grateful for their help. Really, I am. I'm not going to lie—it felt good having two guys charge to my rescue. But I can't get used to it. Men cannot be trusted to stick around. *Just ask my mom.* "I could have handled the situation," I insist.

"Is that so?" Hudson looks amused.

"I've been taking boxing lessons," I tell them solemnly.

Asher's eyes twinkle. "Really?" he drawls. "And how many lessons have you attended so far?"

Busted. "None," I admit sheepishly. "I signed up for the classes but I haven't had time to buy a pair of gloves."

Asher chuckles; Hudson laughs openly. "We haven't introduced ourselves," he says. "I'm Asher Doyle. And this is Hudson Fleming."

I feel the urge to laugh hysterically. Everything about these two men is gossip-worthy. Where they went. Who they were seen with. Who they're sleeping with at the moment, and *oh, did I know they like to share women?*

With heroic effort, I keep my tone neutral. "Wendy

Williams," I reply, shaking their hands, first Asher's, then Hudson's. A tingle runs through my body at their touch, and my insides do a little flip. *Whoa there.*

"Wendy," Hudson says, not letting go of my hand. His thumb strokes my palm; his gaze remains on my face. "Do you come here often?"

Our drinks appear, and I take a big gulp of my wine to try and calm myself. "No, it's my first time here," I admit. "I only got in today because my colleague put me on the list."

"Your colleague?" Asher asks. "What do you do?"

"I'm a divorce lawyer."

"You are?" His eyebrow arches and he surveys me openly from head to toe. "You don't look like one."

He's checking me out blatantly; they both are. I should be offended. I should walk away before I do anything I might regret. These men have a reputation that precedes them.

But the arousal that washes over me is so very unexpected. I can't remember the last time I was this turned on. Hudson's touch on my skin sets my body throbbing. My cheeks are flushed, my nipples hard underneath my dress.

I shift my weight from one foot to another to keep my raging hormones at bay. *Say something, Wendy. You're just gaping at them.* "What do divorce lawyers look like?"

Hudson coughs. "Asher, I beg you, don't answer that question." He grins at me. "You'll have to excuse my friend. He's not the most tactful person in the world."

My lips twitch. "He gets a pass," I tell Hudson. "After all, you guys did save me. My heroes."

The wine is going to my head. I'm flirting with them. If my anthropologist friend Bailey were here, she'd tell me that my body language is giving me away. I'm leaning toward them, smiling into their eyes. I haven't pulled my hand free of Hudson's grip.

I should go back to my table. I don't.

Asher stares at me. "Have dinner with us."

"What?"

"Dinner." His eyes gleam with amusement. "You've heard of the concept? There's a meal involved, usually some wine, good conversation?"

"I know what dinner is," I respond. An evening with Hudson and Asher. Is this what Cinderella felt like when the prince picked her to dance with at the ball? My heart is racing; my mouth is dry. "With *both* of you?"

"Ah." Asher takes a half-step closer. "From the emphasis you placed on the word *both*, I take it you've heard stories."

He's direct; I'll give him that. "You like sharing women." It feels so naughty to say those words aloud.

They nod. "You're not running away screaming," Hudson notes. "Are you intrigued?" His finger traces soft circles on my skin.

I swallow. A devil-may-care urge grips me. My father died today. I've been trying not to think about it, but the news plays about at the edge of my consciousness, trying to sneak into my thoughts when I'm not paying attention.

I could use a distraction. *Two distractions.* "Dinner sounds lovely."

"How about tomorrow night?" Asher pulls a business card out of his wallet and hands it to me. "Call me, and we'll work out the details."

"Tomorrow?" My voice comes out in a squeak. "That soon?"

"Why wait?" Hudson asks.

I can barely breathe. I argue cases for a living, but words have deserted me. I'm afraid I'm staring at them with my mouth open, like a drooling idiot. Before I embarrass myself further, I nod hastily and make my escape.

In the cab home, I finger the crisp edges of the business card Asher gave me, and close my eyes. I can't believe I've agreed to a dinner date with them. Is this what I want? Though Bailey, Piper, and Gabby are in ménage relationships, I've never seriously contemplated a threesome.

Until now.

Click to keep reading The Wager.

ABOUT TARA CRESCENT

Get a free story from Tara when you sign up to Tara's mailing list.

Tara Crescent writes steamy contemporary romances for readers who like hot, dominant heroes and strong, sassy heroines.

When she's not writing, she can be found curled up on a couch with a good book, often with a cat on her lap.

She lives in Toronto.

Tara also writes sci-fi romance as Lili Zander. Check her books out at http://www.lilizander.com

Find Tara on:
www.taracrescent.com
taracrescent@gmail.com

ALSO BY TARA CRESCENT

MÉNAGE ROMANCE

Club Ménage

Claiming Fifi

Taming Avery

Keeping Kiera - *coming soon*

Ménage in Manhattan

The Bet

The Heat

The Wager

The Hack

The Dirty Series

Dirty Therapy

Dirty Talk

Dirty Games

Dirty Words

The Cocky Series

Her Cocky Doctors

Her Cocky Firemen

Standalone Books

Dirty X6

CONTEMPORARY ROMANCE

The Drake Family Series

Temporary Wife (A Billionaire Fake Marriage Romance)

Fake Fiance (A Billionaire Second Chance Romance)

Standalone Books

Hard Wood

MAX: A Friends to Lovers Romance

A Touch of Blackmail

A Very Paisley Christmas

Boyfriend by the Hour

BDSM ROMANCE

Assassin's Revenge

Nights in Venice

Mr. Banks (A British Billionaire Romance)

Teaching Maya

The House of Pain

The Professor's Pet

The Audition

The Watcher

Doctor Dom

Dominant - *A Boxed Set containing The House of Pain, The Professor's Pet, The Audition and The Watcher*

Made in the USA
Columbia, SC
26 March 2019